Not Far From the
TREE

A Novel

Not Far From the
TREE

A Novel

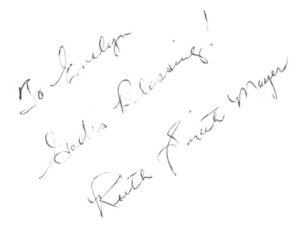

To Evelyn
God's Blessing!
Ruth Smith Meyer

Ruth Smith Meyer

NOT FAR FROM THE TREE
Copyright © 2008 Ruth Smith Meyer

ISBN-13: 978-1-897373-59-0
ISBN-10: 1-897373-59-7

This book is a work of fiction. Names, characters, places, and incidents are the product of the author's imagination or are used fictitiously. Any resemblance to actual events, locales, or persons, living or dead, is coincidental.

All scripture quotations, unless otherwise indicated, are taken from the King James Version.

WORD ALIVE PRESS

Published by Word Alive Press
131 Cordite Road, Winnipeg, MB R3W 1S1
www.wordalivepress.ca

Printed in Canada.

Dedication

This book is dedicated to all who at times are tempted to think the grass may be greener on the other side of the fence, but who stick in there, finding new ways to communicate, support and adapt to each other as spouses, finding in the end that home pastures yield lush growth and rich rewards.

Acknowledgements

I OWE A GREAT DEBT OF GRATITUDE to the delightful members of the Litt family who gave me their time and the pleasure of their company as I prepared to write this book. They reminisced about their parents, grandparents and family memories from their growing-up years and graciously tolerated my questions, patiently clarifying details that gave me a real sense of the family spirit. My life was truly enriched. It was infinitely rewarding to see the faith and spirit of their mother living on, not only in the children but the grandchildren of Freda Litt, the woman I had come to love as a 90+-year-old. They truly are a wonderful family made strong by the hard times over which they triumphed.

I want to make clear that although much of the book comes from their experience, not all the details are true, nor did I include all they talked about. My greatest wish is that the family will find enough truth to make it "their" book, yet others will find themselves in its pages too. I pray all may find healing, hope and courage to face their own challenges in life.

I want to say thank you also to The Ready Writers of London, who have been invaluable to me in honing my writing skills and keeping the story focused.

Chapter 1

THE SCREEN DOOR SLAMMED SHUT behind Rina as she manoeuvred her new-fangled walker toward the porch bench. The basket in the front was loaded with her bag and the letters she wanted to post when she got to her senior's group. Putting the brakes on her "Cadillac," as she called it, she held on to the hand-rests until she lowered her creaking body to the rustic seat.

She still retained her height, if not the weight, she had carried for some years. The long legs that had served her faithfully and endowed her with a willowy look most of her life now made the distance to the bench further. A sigh of relief whuffed through her lips as her posterior made connection with the security of a solid surface.

"Touch down! We have touch down," she announced through an imaginary PA system to no one in particular. She smirked as she shifted her shoulders to find a comfortable position.

She had almost an hour to wait before she could expect her driver, but the beauty and warmth of the morning lured her to wait out in the open air. Even on what she thought of as the north side of the house—thanks to the angle of the roads in this part of the country it was more north-east than north—the spring's morning sunlight bathed the covered veranda in liquid light. The latest daffodils and tulips were still brightening up the front flowerbed, but it was the lilacs wafting their scent that caught her attention.

She sniffed in delight. Ah-hh! After a pneumonia-plagued winter, it was delightful to take pleasure in each new harbinger of spring. Each smell, each sight, took shape in her mind. She pictured them as little heralds sounding a horn, proclaiming to the world in a melodious fanfare a message of anticipation and renewal to mortals.

Her eyes lit up with an impish grin. *I'm so glad to be part of the race . . . human, that is!* She joked to herself. *Ah-hh Rina—you are probably funnier in your own mind than anyone else's. But at least you keep yourself amused!*

Last fall she had not expected to see another spring, so the fresh breezes, laden with the vibrant smell of new growth, enchanted her mind and soul with the tantalizing aroma of hope— hope that she would live to see and enjoy another summer and perhaps one more gathering of the Litz tribe. God kept surprising her with goodness.

By the end of summer there is promise of three more great- greats to add to the list of our offspring. Her eyes smiled as the corner of her mouth curved into a mischievous grin. *Just look what David and I started!*

Rina leaned back, her face still alight with thoughts of her David. My, how she missed him! In spite of the unconventional start to their relationship and the ups and downs of their years together, their ever-deepening love and the light-hearted banter through much of it left her with a satisfying glow. Their shared sense of humour was a saving grace in many instances through the hard times. Their later years, after retirement, released them from the worries that had plagued much of their life and they were free to enjoy each other again. Ahh-hh! She missed his teasing and her chance for a good come-back.

You have already missed out on the birth of our eight great- great grandchildren, my dear David. It's getting harder and harder to remember all the names—especially of the greats and great- greats—and who belongs to who. That lapse, of course, couldn't be due to my age; it must be the vast number that is mine to remember!

Rina chuckled. At ninety-nine, she could legitimately be excused for forgetting a few things, but she wasn't the sort to give in to memory loss willingly, no matter what age!

Marlene came to the door. "Mama, are you all right?"

"Sure, I'm all right!" Rina replied.

"Are you sure you're warm enough? Do you need a warmer jacket?"

"No, Marlene, I'm just fine! It's a beautiful spring day and the sun is warm this morning. I may not even need my light jacket by the time I come home. Don't worry about me so much, girl."

"Mama, I won't worry, but we want to do everything we can to keep you healthy."

"Yes, yes, Marlene! You and James are very good to me!" she assured her daughter. "But I really am quite comfortable right now. You can keep on with your work; I'll call if I need anything."

"The inside door is open, so if you do need anything, I can hear if you call."

"All right, Marlene."

Rina tried to be patient, but she realized that this youngest daughter of hers was just not facing up to the fact that, at ninety-nine, she could not last forever.

Young people! They look at us older folk as fragile things that need to be coddled and protected and kept from dying—as though that wasn't a natural end to life. I guess we are frail on the outside, but if only they would realize how little change there is in the age of our inner selves! Why, inside I feel as though I could still skip out the lane like I used to do along the Malden sidewalks as a child!

Like the changing scene in a movie, she was transported back to the time when her mother worked a few days a week at the hotel down the street, leaving her in the care of her brother, George. Twelve years the elder, he ably looked after his four year-old sister. Usually he was responsible, but sometimes it seemed he couldn't help letting loose his penchant for experimenting with things that presented a challenge, even if they looked impossible. She could see one incident clearly in her mind.

SIXTEEN YEAR-OLD GEORGE sat on the top step of the back veranda. Rina, on her knees behind him, encircled his neck with her arms. She loved this big brother with all the devotion of a four year-old heart.

"George, why can squirrels jump such a long way from one branch to another or to the top porch and back? Why can't we do that?"

"Now, Rina-kins, what makes you think I can't do that?"

"Oh George! You can't!"

"You wanna bet? Stay here, Rina. I'm going up to the top veranda, and I'll jump over to that big branch and come down the tree! I'll show you those old squirrels aren't any smarter than me!"

The door slammed shut and she heard George running up the back stairs. It seemed no time at all until she saw George crouched on top of the railing, sizing up his jump to the tree.

Her eyes were wide in amazement. In her mind, George could do just about anything. Now she was to observe another one of his heroic feats.

"Here goes!"

George shoved off the railing, arms spread in front of him to grab on to the branch.

"Ya-aah!" he yelled as he soared through the air.

Rina held her breath as George's one hand made contact. The other missed, and with a frightened cry he zoomed earthward, his body hitting the ground with a thud, his leg twisted underneath him.

"Owww! Oh, ouch! Oh-hh!"

After a moment, George tried to move. "Oww!"

"Rina," George gasped. "Rina, do you think you can go to the hotel and get Mama? Look both ways when you cross the street and then go down the sidewalk to the hotel. Tell her to hurry!"

"All by myself?"

"Rina, you have to! I think I'll need a doctor too, but get Mama, quick. It's just one block, Rina. You can do it!"

This time there was no time for skipping. Rina hurried to the front of the house, dutifully looked both ways before crossing the street, then she ran—as fast as her little legs would go.

At the main street, she felt a pang of fear. Never before had she come so far on her own. She turned the corner and gasped in dismay! How was she to open that big heavy door?

George's pained face flashed across her mind and she knew she had to try. She walked up to the door, pulled the big latch down and then, with all her might, shoved her little body against the door. At first it wouldn't budge, but it finally opened a small a crack. She gave another mighty shove and squeezed through the opening into the front lobby. Alas! No one was there and she couldn't even see over the front desk.

"Please, please!" her voice almost broke as she frantically tried to think what to do next. "Mama!" she cried out in desperation.

It wasn't a moment until Mr. Mayer's head appeared above the tall desk.

"Why, it's Rina! Are you by yourself? What are you doing here?"

His voice sounded so strict and disapproving. Tears filled her eyes and trickled down her cheek. She wiped them with the back of her hand.

"Oh Mr. Mayer, it's George. He fell out of the tree and he is hurting real bad and he says we need Mama and maybe the doctor. Please, Mr. Mayer, where is Mama?"

"Are you sure he is hurt that bad?"

"Oh yes! His leg is all crooked and, and, and . . . Yes! He is hurt real bad."

"Just a moment, then."

Mr. Mayer opened the small door in the partition between the desk area and the main lobby. He moved to the bottom of the stairway and called out, "Mrs. Kurtz!"

"Yes, sir?" The answer sounded from one of the far rooms.

"Your little girl is here. You are apparently needed at home."

Rina heard the hurried footsteps coming down the hall and descending the stairs. When Mama appeared, Rina burst into tears and ran to her. One look at Rina's face and Mama's arms were around her.

"What is it, Rina? What is the matter? Did you come all by yourself? Where is George?"

"Oh Mama! George was going to jump like a squirrel, and he did, but he didn't hang on like the squirrels and he fell and Mama, he yelled 'Oww!' He is almost crying, his leg is crooked and he is hurt so bad!"

Ellie glanced at her boss.

"I am sorry, Mr. Mayer, but I am going to have to go and see how bad this is. The work is almost finished, so I can either come back later or finish up in the morning."

"Don't worry, Mrs. Kurtz. These things happen in families. We'll manage until morning. Let us know how things are once you have seen for yourself."

If the trip to the hotel was quick, so was the return! Rina had to run to keep up with her mother.

GEORGE'S LEG was broken. Rina was sent to the neighbour's while the doctor did the painful job of setting the bone before he put it in splints and bandaged it well. George was cautioned to take care not to put any weight on it until he was given permission if he wanted to be able to use his leg for the rest of his life.

Chapter 2

RINA LEANED forward as she caught sight of a robin picking at a piece of string and flying off with it, probably to build a nest.

All of nature is that way, she thought—*parents trying to make nests or safe abodes for the young. In spite of their best efforts, not all tragedy and hurts can be avoided—especially if the young are so determined to show their independence by doing stupid things!* A wry smile creased Rina's face. *I did my own share of stupid things!*

ALTHOUGH they lived in town, the shortcut to the school lay across a field, broken by a small stream just a little distance from the schoolyard. Rina had been cautioned never to cross the stream in the spring when it was swollen beyond its normal boundaries. Usually, she heeded that advice and stayed on the sidewalks while the water was high—even though it meant walking home with five of the most obnoxious grades six and seven boys!

For four weeks now, they had been teasing her all way home—trying to make her drop her books, pulling the long braids that hung past her waist and calling her the baby of the family. They could probably see her cheeks get red with anger. There wasn't much ten-year-old Rina hated more than to be called a baby! That big Bart Fields was the worst! He seemed to know what got under her skin! He was in grade eight, so was even more intimidating than the younger ones.

"What are you going to do—tell Mama and Papa that their darling little girl can't stand the boys?" they taunted her. That probably bothered her the most. She was just as good as any boy!

Today they had been whispering to each other while looking at her with mischievous glances, often whispering "Rina" and "on the way home" just loud enough for her to hear. As dismissal neared, dread filled her heart. Instead of studying her spelling words, she mentally planned her escape. The water in the little creek had subsided to almost normal levels and she had often jumped across in the summer. She was sure if she took a running leap, she could get across. Long legs did have an advantage sometimes. When the teacher dismissed them, instead of lingering to talk with her friends and leaving by the front walk to the street as she usually did, she would immediately scoot around the school to the back of the yard, slip through the fence and run across the fields to home. She would be home before the boys knew where she went. She might even watch at the window and make a face at them as they passed her house. She watched the clock, anticipating the moment she could leave.

Miss Stewart rose from her desk. "Put your books away. We will sing our closing song and say our prayer."

Rina held her breath. She had already arranged her books so that the ones she had to take for homework would be on top, ready to grab as she made her get-away.

The *Amen* was said and Miss Stewart declared them dismissed. Calmly, Rina took her books in hand and was out the door before the rest had even got their things together. She made a dash for the back of the school. She managed to get through the fence without catching her dress, then raced across the field toward the narrowest place in the creek. She took a run and, just as she began her leap, she heard the voices of the children coming out of the school. Whether that was what broke her concentration or not, she landed just short of the other side—right in about six inches of water. Her foot slipped off a stone and a pain shot through her ankle. Her books went flying and her shoes filled with cold water. She reached to fish her geography book out of the creek. Thankfully, the rest were on the muddy bank—not good, but better than the creek.

"Fiddlesticks!" she muttered as she scrambled to dry ground and paused to evaluate her predicament. If she was to get home before the boys, she would just have to run, squishy shoes or not!

"Ouch!" Her ankle really hurt. She remembered George and wondered if she had broken something too. What was she to do? She would hate to call out for help. Wouldn't that be great fodder for the boys' teasing?

Determined not to stoop to that, she tried again. She couldn't exactly run, but she would make it home by limping and hopping. If the boys were passing her place before she got there, she would just have to hide behind one of the shrubs in the field across from their house before she reached the street.

The boys must have been side-tracked, because they were still not around the corner to their street when she got there. Moving as quickly as her ankle allowed, she mounted the steps to the veranda, opened the door and sat on the carpet inside. Thankfully, Mama was not home like she usually preferred to be. Thinking better of it, she got up again and hopped through the house. She took off her shoes and emptied the water out the back door.

Peeling off her stockings, she wrung those out too. She grabbed the slop rag from the cellar way and wiped the tracks she had made from front to back door. Her shoes were a mess! What would Mama and Papa say? She was always disappointing Mama with her "escapades," as she called them. Her older sisters, Maria and Marta, had apparently always been ladies, so Mama hadn't been prepared for things like she did. She tried to wipe her shoes as clean as she could. Where could she hide them? Her ankle throbbed with pain as she limped to the stairs and crawled upstairs to her room, slid the shoes under her bed and put her slippers on. She took off her wet, muddy dress and put on a clean one. Her ankle looked red and swollen and it was really hurting. Where should she put her dirty dress and wet stockings?

"Rina! Are you home?" she heard her mother calling.

"Yes, Mama. I'm upstairs." She held her breath, wondering what to do next.

"Rina! What did you do with your books?"

Uh-oh! She had forgotten to put her books out of sight. Now what? Part of her wanted to just disappear, but oh, how nice it would be to let Mama know about her ankle and see what could be done about it. What if it was broken?

"Rina! I think you had better come down here and explain yourself." Her mother's insistent tone left no alternative.

Choosing to sit rather than put weight on her ankle, Rina slid from step to step as she descended the stairs, and then limped to the kitchen, dreading her mother's look of despair. How often had she been told to remember she's a lady! Deep in her heart, she was convinced her tomboy ways were a disappointment to her mother. Now she'd done it again.

Her mother was holding the muddy schoolbooks when Rina reached the kitchen. Her geography book lay on a towel.

"All right, Katherina—start explaining!"

"Mama, you just don't know how awful those boys have been to me!" Rina implored.

"And just what do the boys have to do with the condition of your books? Rina, where are your shoes? Is your foot swollen?"

"Mama, let me explain!"

"Well I think you have a lot of that to do, young lady, so get going!"

"Oh Mama, the boys have been so mean to me for so long. They tease and pester me all the way home every day! I would just like to punch them! But you told me I had to act like a lady! Mama, it's not fair! If I was a boy, I could do it!"

"Rina, even if you were a boy, I wouldn't want you to be going around punching people—even other boys. Now get on with your explaining!"

"Today they kept whispering to each other and laughing. I heard them say my name quite often and something about 'on the way home.' I didn't know what they were planning, so I started figuring out what I could do. The creek isn't very high any more, so I thought I could jump across." She went on to explain her own plans to circumvent the boys' plans. "Just when I was jumping across the creek, I heard the rest of the children coming out of the school and I guess it scared me a bit. I didn't quite make it. My foot landed on a stone in the water and I went over on my ankle. I tried to throw the books on the ground so they wouldn't go in the creek, but my geography book fell in."

Rina paused and dared to look into her mother's eyes. She saw resignation but also concern.

"But I did get home before the boys came up the street!"

"Let me have a look at that ankle." Gently, her mother examined her foot. "Can you bend your toes down?"

"Yes! It hurts a bit that way, but it hurts more if I try to bend it toward the side."

"I think we'd better put a cool, wet towel around your foot for a while to try to keep the swelling down."

Ellie went to get the necessary items. Spreading one towel on a footstool, she gently lifted Rina's foot and wrapped a wet one around her swollen ankle.

"Where are your shoes?"

Rina grimaced and, in a soft voice full of shame, replied, "Under my bed, upstairs."

"Why would you take wet shoes upstairs?"

"Because . . . I didn't . . . want you to see them!"

"Rina, it's never right to try to hide it when we've done wrong. If we leave those leather shoes to dry out by themselves, they will be ruined. Not only would Papa and I find out in the end, you would have to live with misshapen shoes until you got new ones— and that could be painful. Come to think of it, that is a good example of what sin and wrong-doing can do to our lives. We may think we're hiding it, but our lives get skewed and misshapen by those thoughts and actions. Soon they begin to cause discomfort and pain in many parts of our lives."

"I'm sorry, Mama! I just seem to keep doing things that make you feel bad! Maria and Marta must have been real ladies, but I think I should have been a boy."

Ellie laughed. "Oh Rina! You don't have to be like Maria and Marta, but I do want you to remember to be a lady, even if you like to do different or more boyish things than they did. I think I'd better go and get your shoes. We'll dry them out as much as possible and then stuff them with newspaper to try to keep them in shape as best we can."

"Maybe you'd better get my dress and stockings too, Mama. I got them wet and dirty as well."

Mama was still upstairs when Rina heard Papa come in the door.

"How's my favourite daughter?" he asked before he saw what she was doing. "Hey, what is going on here? What did you do to yourself now, you little scallywag?"

"Oh Papa! I took the shortcut through the fields from school to get away from those boys. When I jumped the creek I didn't quite make it. I landed on a stone that was under the water and turned my ankle."

Jake bent to look at her ankle. "Looks as though you sprained it. That'll be sore for a while!" Jake wrapped her ankle again. "Just what have those boys been doing?"

"Oh, they pull my braids, knock my books out of my arms and call me names and tease me about being the baby of the family. I could punch them out, like I did Mike that time, but Mama says I am supposed to be a lady. Oh Papa, it isn't fair! If I was a boy, I could teach those hooligans a lesson! All day today, they kept whispering to each other and looking at me. I could hear they were talking about me and I heard them saying 'on the way home' and I just knew they were planning something even worse."

Rina's eyes flashed with indignation, the colour rising in her cheeks as she clenched her hands into fists. Jake laughed at her ire and sat on the chair in front of her.

"Settle down, little girl! Boys will be boys, but it sounds as though they have been having some fun at your expense. Why don't we think of some ways to overcome your predicament without those fists?" Jake took her hands and looked straight into her eyes. "I want you to really consider this—why do you suppose it's so much fun to tease you? What do you think they expect you to do that would make it amusing for them?"

Rina didn't hesitate. She snapped out her answer: "They just want to make me mad—stupid boys!"

"Aha! Good answer! Now what you can do about it? What can you do that will take the fun out of it?"

"I don't know!" Rina retorted.

"Oh, I think you do! If you can't come up with the answer now, it often helps to sleep on it. You're a smart young lady. I have no doubt that if you think long enough you'll come up with an answer." Jake moved toward his favourite chair with the newspaper. "Uh-oh! Was your geography text another victim of your frantic efforts to avoid the boys?"

Rina heaved a big sigh. "Ye—es! I might have to get a new one. Do I have to pay for it?"

"Your mother and I will discuss that and let you know, but I think you may as well plan on it."

"RINA, COME ON! Breakfast is ready and it's just about time for you to get off to school. What is taking you so long?"

"Coming, Mama!" Rina called back. She took one last look in the mirror. She swallowed hard, not sure Papa would approve of the solution she had devised to overcome at least one of her problems with the boys.

Too late now, she thought, leaving her room to go downstairs. As she slid into her chair, her mother turned from the stove to the table.

"RINA!" she shrieked in utter shock, "What have you done? And WHY? Oh Rina!" Coming to her daughter's side, Ellie's hands stroked Rina's now shoulder length hair. "Why would you cut your hair off?"

Rina's shoulders rose in defense.

"Papa said to sleep on it and come up with an answer—some way to take the fun out of the boys' teasing. If I have short hair, they can't pull my braids."

"Oh Rina! That is a bit drastic. It may have been wise to talk it over with us first." She sighed. "Now that it's done, we'll just have to make the best of it. But Rina, I do wish you would think things through a bit more before making such rash decisions."

Chapter 3 🍂

RINA SMILED AT THE REMEMBRANCE. Papa had been forewarned before he saw the results of his admonition. However, he also tried to impress on her that although it was good to come up with her own solutions, it was advisable to talk them over with her parents before putting them into action.

Even now, Rina suspected that, although her mother felt some grief at the loss of her long locks, her papa was secretly proud of her audacity and courage. For herself, that one courageous act had given her the sense of power and confidence to care less about what the boys said. Just as her father had said, her sense of confidence took a lot of the fun out of their teasing. From that time on she had more fun with the boys rather than providing entertainment for them by being the brunt of their teasing.

Her children and grandchildren sometimes rolled their eyes at her admonition to "let the Lord look after that." However, life had taught her that if we do what we can to get along with people and it still doesn't work, by letting go, trusting the Lord and ceasing to fret, situations often dissipate on their own or are solved in ways too intricate for us to figure out.

"If there's nothing we can do—then it's not ours to do," she said out loud. By letting go and leaving it in God's hands, probably more is changed in our selves than in others. It frees us to see things in a different light and opens the channels of communication that were closed by our own fears or resentment.

In fact, those boys became great friends and allies after that childhood incident.

> *I guess because I so admired George and there were more boys than girls in the neighbourhood it was easier for me to do boy things. Poor Mama despaired at having a known tomboy for a daughter.*
>
> *Once the initial cut was made, I kept trimming my hair shorter and shorter until finally Mama sent me to the barber to get it evened out. I was probably the first female in Malden to have bobbed hair—and to wear pants in public! There were so many things I liked doing that could be done better with pants than a dress. I borrowed a pair of George's that he left behind. At first I tried to keep it from Mama, but eventually Mama just looked the other way and bore the snide remarks made by her church and community friends. I put her through a lot.*

Rina smiled as she remembered another bit of her rebellion. As a young teenager, winter skating on the outdoor rink was one of her great pleasures. Mama and Papa thought a few nights a week were enough.

> *One night I was expected to stay home, but the urge was just too strong. Early in the evening, I made sure the cellar door was unlocked and my coat, hat and skates were up in my bedroom. I went upstairs at my usual time, like a good girl, and waited until all was quiet. I put on my coat, hat and mitts, threw my skates out the window and shinnied down the back porch post. I was at the rink within ten minutes.*

That was the night that Bart first took notice. In recent months she had become aware that he was turning into a handsome young man. The teasing she used to endure had undergone a metamorphosis into enjoyable banter and competitive wordplay between them. They were always seeing who could make the perfect comeback.

"RINA! I thought this was one of your off nights!"

"It is, but I snuck out of the house after Mama and Papa were asleep! You'd better keep your mouth shut about it though!"

"Uh-oh! The little girl is making threats! What are you going to do if I do tell?"

Rina shot a look at him that was a feisty challenge mixed with a bit of a flirt.

"You just try it and find out! But you might not like the results. I am warning you."

She finished fastening her skates and took off. Bart sped after her, catching up and taking her arm.

"Oohh! I lak da fire in dem eyes!" He gave her arm a squeeze and Rina responded with a laugh.

"You ain't seen nothin' yet!" she retorted.

They made a good pair as they circled the rink in perfect rhythm. The frosty air nipped at their noses as their singing blades went gliding over the frigid ice, round after round. Finally Rina begged to stop a bit, so they sat together on the make-shift bench of a plank set on two barrels at the side of the rink.

"You're a good skater!" Bart commented.

"You're surprised?"

"Guess I shouldn't be! You can keep up with the best of us, but I guess I just never noticed—never tried to skate with you before. Usually I've just chased you," he laughed.

"See? If you'd stop pestering the girls, you might notice they're good for something besides being the objects of your harassment!"

"Aw! A guy has to have some fun!"

"And skating with a girl isn't fun? I thought you enjoyed it just now! Sorry for the mistake."

"Now who's doing the harassing?" He poked her with his elbow but then left it resting against her arm. "Actually, Rina, it was quite enjoyable. Would you be ready for another round or two?"

"Sure, but I can't stay too long. I don't want to get caught!"

"How're you going to get in the house without your parents waking up?"

"I left the cellar door open. I'll go in there and go up the back stairs. Their bedroom is at the front of the house so they won't hear me coming in—I hope!"

That was the first of many stolen nights and the beginning of a special friendship between Bart and me. We still did most things with our group of friends and with the church youth group, but it was usually Bart who walked me home. Eventually he began calling for me at the door and people began to think of us as a couple.

One evening when we came home, I saw the curtains parted at the Winklers' house across the street. I looked at the Schwartz's house. Yes, they, too, were watching.

"HEY BART! Don't make it obvious, but look at the neighbours across the way. We're being watched. They pretty well keep an eye on everything I do! I saw them when we left. They probably stayed up just to see when I got home."

"Maybe they would like to see me give you an ardent goodnight kiss too!"

"Oh, I'm sure they would, and I'm also sure they would tell my parents tomorrow morning if you did!"

Whereupon Bart took her hand and made a display of shaking her hand in an exaggerated formality. "Now let them report to your parents what an impeccable gentleman I am!"

"Oh wow! I am sure you have made an impression above reproach." Rina gave a little curtsey with her "Good-night, kind sir!" and laughed as she went in the door.

On their next night out, as they left, Rina checked the neighbours again.

"See? Both the Winkler and Schwartz guardians are on duty! I've got plans for our Trafalgar Street neighbours tonight!"

"Now what are you up to, you scheming woman?"

"Tonight we'll come down Waterloo Street behind us, and then slip through the neighbour's yard to the back of the house and in the back door. We'll see how long they wait up to know what time I come home."

"Oh, you wicked woman—taking advantage of your neighbours' honest concern about your welfare!" Bart chuckled. "But it should be fun! If we do it a few times, we'll see how long it is before they talk to your parents."

Accordingly, Bart and Rina made their way to the rear of the house that evening. When Rina got upstairs, she quietly went to the front hall window and crouched on the floor there. Across the way, every five minutes or so, the curtains would part and she could see a shadowy figure peering up and down the street. After half an hour, she left them to keep looking while she went to bed.

It was two weeks later that Ellie casually asked Rina if the young people's activities were running later than usual the last while.

"No, Mama. Why do you ask?"

"Oh, I was just wondering. I don't always hear you coming in any more. But you do have a curfew, you know. We don't like you being out later than ten-thirty as a rule."

"I know, Mama. I always try to be here by then. A few times I might have been five or six minutes late, but that is all."

"Are you sure, Rina?" Ellie's voice was full of doubt and questioning.

"Why would you doubt me?" Rina tried to keep a straight face.

"Rina! What is going on here? I see that twinkle in your eyes. What are you up to?"

"Oh Mama! I bet the neighbours have been talking to you, haven't they?"

Now it was Ellie who looked caught!

"We—ell! Yes, I must admit it. Mrs. Winkler was over and said she and Mrs. Schwartz wondered if we knew what hours you were keeping. She thought it was their responsibility to at least ask if we knew."

"Did she say what time I came home?"

"No. She said they didn't actually see you but it was way after midnight."

Rina grinned. "Well, they are wrong, Mama." She lowered her eyes and had the grace to look a little ashamed. "Maybe we weren't very nice, but Bart and I saw them watching when we left and watching when we came home every time we went out. We decided to give them something to talk about. We left with them watching and then came home from Waterloo Street, across the neighbour's lawn and in the back door. So, I was in bed, snoring, long before they even got to sleep."

Ellie shook her head but her eyes were already twinkling so her words of rebuke were weakened.

"Rina, Rina! Why do you always find a way to flout authority or cause worry? The Winklers and Schwartzes have been good neighbours ever since we moved here. They rejoiced when you were born and watched you grow and have loved you ever since. Why would you want them to worry about you?"

"Aw-w Mama! I don't necessarily want them to worry, but they're so nosy! Why should they have to know every move I make? Anyway, I thought it was some harmless fun!"

Chapter 4

OUR FUN didn't last that long, though. The big war came along and Bart was of an age to go. When he first talked about signing up, I could hardly stand it. I was so afraid for him. We were way too young to be thinking about marriage—I was only bit past sixteen—but when you are being parted for something like war, it pushes you into adulthood in a hurry. I did love him and Bart put a lot of pressure on me those last few nights!

IT WAS A LATE spring night with a nearly full moon. Bart and Rina walked slowly home from church, hand in hand. He was on one last leave before he would be shipped out. They had talked all weekend; it seemed as though there was so much left to say but no words to say it all. Bart slipped his arm around her and held her close.

"Rina, I know we're young—you especially—but please! It would mean so much to me over there to know I have your promise. It would be something to look forward to and to keep me going if things get rough. Please accept my ring. It isn't the engagement ring I'd like to give you, but let it at least be a promise ring and wear it until I get home and give you a better one."

He had asked her more than once that weekend. She did love him, but she didn't know if she was ready to make such a serious commitment. She slid her arm around his waist, leaned her head on his shoulder and kept walking.

"Dear, Rina. I love you and I want to have that sense of belonging to you before I go. I'd love to marry you and make you truly mine, but I know your parents wouldn't go for that—unless you want to sneak out on them again!"

"That wouldn't work, Bart! At my age, I need their permission."

"I know, I know, but a promise ring would be alright, wouldn't it?" Bart stopped walking, pulled her behind a lilac bush and turned to face her. Putting his hand under her chin, he tipped her face so he could see it clearly in the moonlight. She knew he saw not only the love but the hesitancy in her eyes. "Please, my love . . . my Rina! We have only a few more hours before I have to go. Who knows if we will ever see each other again? It would mean so much to me."

Rina saw his eyes held unshed tears and her heart capitulated. "Oh Bart! When you put it that way, how can I say no? I love you too, Bart, and I sure hope you come home!"

"Oh thank you, thank you, Rina, my Rina!" Bart held her close and kissed her like she had never been kissed before and as though it might really be the last time. It almost took her breath away! He nuzzled her neck and stroked her hair. "My dear Rina! You've made me so happy!"

He reached into his pocket and once more drew out the ring he had offered her before. This time he placed it on her finger, held her hand and kissed it.

"May this ring be a promise of better things and better times to come."

He kissed her again before they resumed their walk home. There wasn't much time left when they got there, so Bart went to say good-bye to Jake and Ellie too. Another lingering kiss and he was gone.

I went to my room that night and wondered what in the world I had done! I remember twisting the ring on my finger and wondering if I really loved Bart. Oh, we had a lot of fun together and I loved dating him and being his special girl, but wearing his ring was to do with the rest of my life! It seemed so permanent and more grown-up than I felt. But I had that stubborn streak in me then already. I gave it my best and tried to be a faithful girlfriend by writing lots of letters and doing what I could.

As time went on, Rina started working—first in the Woolen Mills, then in the furniture factory in Stafford—and there had the opportunity to meet other young people.

I don't know if Bart ever found that I went out on an occasional date with other young men while he was gone— nothing serious, but just for the fun. I was, after all, so young. Ah-hh to be so young again!

RINA BECAME AWARE of a car approaching from the north. Ah! There comes Mack's car. Rina's eyes shone. *My, if I was twenty years younger and he was available, I could fall in love all over again!*

Mack Whiting had been her driver ever since she had started going to the Senior's Centre. He was such a gentle man and a gentleman to boot! He gallantly took care of her, helping her to the car and making sure she had everything she needed—fastening her seat belt and tucking a blanket around her in cold weather—he made her feel so special. He even put up with her mild flirting.

Well, maybe it isn't always so mild, but we both know it is harmless. Where can it go with a seventy something man that is very happily married and a ninety-nine-going-on-one-hundred-year-old who definitely is on her last legs! Talk about a spring and autumn relationship! This would be early autumn and the dead of winter!

She chuckled to herself as Mack got out of the car. She could get up by herself, but why deny him—or herself—the opportunity to help her get up from the bench!

"Marlene!" she called out at the direction of the door, "Mack is here, so I'll be on my way."

Sometimes Mack's wife Lena was along, but usually just in the afternoon. Sometimes she brought Rina home if Mack was busy, but he was alone this morning. Lena knew that Rina found Mack attractive and they got along well together, but she didn't mind. In fact, Lena was a good partner for Mack, and Rina enjoyed seeing the love between the two of them. What a matched pair they were.

Marlene came to the door. "Good morning, Mack! Have a good day, Mama."

"Oh, I will, no doubt about it! Let's go, Mack."

Mack helped her to the car, fastened her seat belt and stowed her "Cadillac" in the trunk.

After some initial small talk, Rina turned to Mack.

"While I was waiting for you this morning I got to thinking about my first beau. You were involved in the second world war, weren't you?"

"Yes, I was."

"I was just about sixteen-and-a-half when my boyfriend left for the First World War. We were essentially engaged just before he left." She cast a look in Mack's direction. "It sure does something to a fella to be in the middle of such carnage, doesn't it? You know, I did everything I could to keep his spirits up. I wrote letters and sent him warm socks and goodies. I helped here at home all I could, but I wasn't in the middle of it. Why do you suppose that some come back and go on with their lives with a semblance of normality and some come back with a monkey on their backs that they just can't shake?"

"That is a big question, Rina. I think it has to do with a lot of things. First of all, the personality of the man makes a big difference. Then, too, although most people in combat see things they would rather not—and no one forgets what they saw—some see especially gruesome or heartbreaking events or find themselves doing deeds they never dreamt they'd be asked to do or would be capable of doing. Things like that haunt a person for the rest of their lives. Did it change your boyfriend?"

"It sure did! He was such a fun-loving person, always finding the humorous side to anything. When he came back, though, that had all disappeared. The jokes he did make were so crass I could hardly stand it. He had also gotten into drinking, and as often as he promised to give it up, it just didn't happen. It seemed he was an entirely different person."

"Was he ever able to get over it?"

"I'm afraid not. He married someone else, had a whole bunch of children and left his poor wife a widow at a young age. He literally drank himself to death."

"That is sad, but I'm afraid it isn't an isolated case. It happened in too many situations—I think especially in the first war, when there was so much face-to-face combat. It must have taken some courage to break it off with him."

"Oh, I can't take the credit for that. I was too much of a wimp to do it the way I should have. It was David, my husband, who helped me out with that. One weekend we happened to ride home together on the train from Stafford, where we were both working. We had such a good visit, in fact, that very next week, he asked me to marry him! I laughed at him and told him I was already engaged. He told me that Bart wasn't the man I should marry and he and I would make a better pair." Rina laughed. "The next week, he wouldn't get off the train until I said yes. When I didn't, he stayed on until my stop and got off with me. He had five miles to walk home from my place, which he eventually did, but he threatened to sit on my doorstep until I said yes. What was a girl to do?"

Mack laughed. "You actually did? Just like that?"

"Well, maybe it wasn't 'just like that.' He said he and another young man and a few girls were going west on an excursion and he suggested I could go along and think it through while we were gone. My brother, who lived in Vancouver, was filling in for a barber in Calgary, so I thought I could go to see him." Rina paused. "I actually knew I should reconsider marriage to Bart. My parents were really worried that I would go through with it and suffer a life of misery. I am rather ashamed of it now, but although I told Bart I was going to go to visit my brother for the summer, I didn't have the courage to tell him I wanted to break off our relationship. I'm sure, down deep, he suspected it, and that probably didn't help his drinking any. But you can't go back and live your life over again. I was young and irresponsible. I was only nineteen-and-a-half."

It was almost a mile further down the road that Mack finally answered. "I guess making mistakes is part of our growing up and becoming mature adults. I know I made my share of mistakes too.

The main thing is to learn from them and not make the same mistake twice. Did you stay with your brother out west?"

"Actually, I didn't. By the time we got there, he had gone back to BC. It happened that at the farm where David was assigned they also needed household help, so we spent our time away in the same place. We actually ended up getting married in Alberta before we returned home."

"You didn't even wait for your parents' permission?"

Even now, Rina's heart felt a stab of pain. She was quiet for a moment, but they were turning in the drive to the Senior's Centre and Mack deserved an answer to his question.

"No, we didn't. That is another part of my life I'm rather ashamed of. David actually lied about my age to get our marriage license!"

Mack, ever sensitive to her needs, let it go at that. "Come on, let's get you into the Centre and get you settled for the day."

RINA ENJOYED the day at the Centre with all her new friends, and now she sat in her recliner letting it all percolate until bedtime. There had been lots of chatter around their coffee when they arrived at the Centre in the morning. At lunchtime there was a decorated cake with the names of all the May birthdays and, as always on those days, the honourees were fully celebrated and made to feel special. The afternoon was their regular monthly hymn sing with Jessica. She always enjoyed that. Nothing like the good old hymns to feed your soul.

The coordinators of the program had become her good friends. Betsy's bubbling cheer and upbeat personality and Rachel, with her quieter interest and care, were a perfect complement to each other. Although she thoroughly enjoyed people from all generations, there was a certain comfort in being with people in her own stage of life. *Goodness knows, even there I am ten and even twenty years older than some of them!*

The trip home with Mack and Lena had been pleasant too. They really were a nice couple. The morning's conversation with Mack stuck in her mind. Even with all the day's activity, she had been thinking of it off and on throughout the day.

THE TRIP WEST WAS A LONG ONE, but the banter among the travelers turned every mile into a comedy routine. It was surprising how even the long miles and unique scenery across the prairie provided fuel for their laughter and fun. For much of the way, David engineered the seating plan so that he and Rina sat side by side.

> *Sly fox! He was not above giving me a playful pinch or squeezing my hand when the others weren't looking. He often made some remark, quite innocuously, about something that held special meaning to the two of us, but the others never caught on.*
>
> *I could barely keep a straight face the time we saw the distance between train stations on the prairie and he innocently remarked, with a wink at me, "That would be a very long walk in the dead of night if a fellow missed his station, wouldn't it?" That time I think the others wondered what we knew that they didn't.*

By the time they arrived in Calgary, they found out that George was no longer there, so Rina didn't know what to do. Her parents had allowed her to come mostly because she could stay with her brother. Now that wasn't a possibility.

"Come on, Rina, don't fret!" David appealed. "We'll just go to the agency where we get our postings and see if there's a job for you close to where I'll be. The other girls are looking for housework too, so there'll be something for you."

"Why not? Papa and Mama won't find out until they get my first letter, and by that time I should be settled in—and making money, to boot!"

When there was an opening for both of them on the same farm, they thought it the perfect solution.

Chapter 5

THE REIBLINGS WERE A NICE FAMILY with five young children. David was just one of six young men hired to help with the harvest. The men slept in a bunk house between the house and the barn, but Rina was given a room of her own in the house. Helen was easy to work with. She let Rina know in the morning what the day's work would be and trusted her to keep at it.

Rina took time to listen to the children and told them stories while she worked. They were soon following her around and asking for more. The conversation with them lightened the work. It fascinated her to hear the children's answers to her questions and the thoughts they would share about the stories she told. She found herself dreaming of the day she would have little ones of her own.

The main work each day seemed to be the making of meals for the big crew of hungry harvesters. What mounds of food they consumed! She sometimes wondered if they just inhaled it! Dishes would be passed around the long table, plates would be piled high and it seemed that in one enormous "Schlu—uck!" it would be gone; the men would rise and be out the door, ready for the next round in the fields.

She and David passed some furtive glances at each other and he always managed a wink or two during the meal before he left, but there certainly wasn't time for a lot of interaction.

Each Sunday, though, work was halted and they went to church in Stavely. For that one day, David and Rina were able to be together a little more. They went on long walks, enjoying not only a break from the hard work but just getting to know each other better. The other girls who came with them from Ontario were company the first few Sundays, but they found the work just too hard and within a month were on the train bound for home. Nate, who had also come with them from Ontario, worked on a farm some distance from them and occasionally he, too, would come to Stavely and they would spend the rest of the day together. But most of the time, David and Rina were left to find their social life with each other. Not that they minded. They found themselves more deeply in love with each other all the time, so time alone seemed good. In fact, David kept reminding her that any time she wanted to take him up on his offer of marriage he would be absolutely delighted. He was ready to take her to the nearest minister to make it official.

THEY WERE STANDING on the edge of a bluff one Sunday in late autumn. David shook her arm. "What makes you so quiet tonight, Rina, my love? Where were you just now? I asked you a question twice and you haven't answered."

"Oh David, I have something to tell you, and I don't know how."

He tipped up her chin so he could see her face.

"Come on, it can't be that bad! Unless you don't love me anymore! If it's anything other than that, we can find a way around." He paused, and when she still didn't speak, he asked, "Are you homesick? Do you want to go back to Ontario?"

"I don't know where I want to be, David." She lowered her eyes, rested her head against his shoulder, and with arms around his waist, pulled her slim frame close to his burly chest, mumbling into his heavy jacket. "I'm ready."

"What did you say?"

Still with lowered eyes, she moved far enough away to speak clearly. "I'm ready to take you up on your offer!"

"Oh, my love—my dear one!" He took a deep breath through his open mouth. "You had me worried!" He playfully shook her as her eyes sparkled with love. "Are you sure? I mean—I am more than ready, but you are sure you don't mind not having your parents present?"

"I really would like to have them here, but there will only be the two of us going back to Ontario, so it would look better if we were married. Besides, and I didn't really want to tell you this, but Garth, one of those new farm hands, has been pestering me lately. If he knew I was married, he would leave me alone."

"Garth? That monster! I'll take care of him!" David's eyes blazed in indignation.

"You'd rather fight him than marry me? Well, if that is the way you feel . . ."

"Not on your life! I will go get a marriage license tomorrow. We're not quite as busy on the farm; I will just tell Mr. Reibling that I have some business in town."

David went down on one knee. "So, my beloved princess . . . my Rina . . . will you do me the honour of marrying me? Please say Yes and make me a happy man till death do us part."

"Oh David! Get up! Of course I will. I will be glad to be your wife!" Rina reached out to take his hand. "I don't know what my parents are going to say about this—or your mother! What is she going to say about it? She wasn't so happy about you taking up with me."

"My mother, bless her, is seldom happy about anything, so don't worry about her. If she had her way, she would probably keep me at home for the rest of her life to do what she wants me to do. Since I am not going to do that, it may as well be you as someone else—and with you, I will be happy!"

They walked in silence for some time. The skies were grey, but the wideness of the rolling hills held a beauty of their own. Somehow the grey wasn't nearly as depressing as it had been when they started out. The clouds couldn't suppress their joy of looking forward to a life together.

"I know your parents would probably like to be at the wedding, but I think they will get used to the idea. If I know them well enough, they will be supportive of you."

"I do have good parents! My older siblings were gone before I was very old, so I was almost like an only child." Rina stopped herself short and laughed a hearty laugh. "Wouldn't Mama be tickled pink? I guess I AM their only child. George is a half-brother, but Maria and Marta are really cousins, even though Mama always insisted we are one family. No "step- anything" was allowed to be talked about. Dad often called me his favourite daughter, which always made me feel so special because I had two older sisters, even if they didn't live at home during my memory. I think it was just a few years ago that I finally figured out I *was* his only daughter!"

David joined in her laughter.

"I can't imagine what it was like for mother to marry her brother-in-law after Aunt Regina died, leaving Maria and Marta. You knew that Mama was engaged to someone else at the time?"

"No! I knew she married Jake's cousin first, but I didn't know that!"

"Yes, her parents insisted on it. It wasn't easy, but Mama said she decided if she had to do it, she was going to give it everything to make it a good marriage. She said they did learn to love each other deeply—then John died when George was just eight years old."

"I guess, compared to what she faced, we are on easy street."

They walked on in silence as they soaked in the closeness that came with this turn of events.

"Rina, I was just thinking, if I can get the license tomorrow, we can get married on Saturday. Do you want to go back to Ontario then?"

"Yes—probably! Let's not tell the Reiblings until after we are married."

"Well then, let's not tell anyone back home either until we get there. Oh Rina, I am a happy man."

David made a trip into town the next day, but he came back without the license because I wasn't of an age to get married without my parents' consent. We waited until the next week, then went into Claresholm with Nate . . . Rina *grinned . . . with me suddenly a year older than I had been the week before! We went first to get the license, then on to the Methodist Church where the Reverend Locke performed the ceremony with Mrs. Locke and Nate as witnesses.*

Nate insisted on taking us out to a hotel for a meal, then he left for his workplace and we stayed for our wedding night!

Then they had to break the news to the Reiblings. They told their employers they would stay on for a bit to finish up the fall work before they packed their bags and got their train tickets to go back to Ontario.

It was when she was trying to figure out how and when to tell her parents that Rina remembered that Bart really didn't know what was going on either. She had written him a few notes after arriving out west, just telling him that George hadn't been there anymore and that she had found work, but she didn't even tell him it was at the same farm where David was working. She hadn't received more than one note from him, so perhaps he had already guessed. But still, in retrospect, she probably should have told him before he found out from others.

They finally settled on sending a telegram to both Rina's parents and David's just before they left, telling them they had been married and would be home by the end of the first week in December.

RINA CLOSED HER EYES. The train was nearing Stafford and her stomach was lurching and swaying right along with the railway car in which they were riding. All the way home, especially mornings, she'd made countless trips to the facilities to deposit the meals she had just eaten.

"Just how do you think I am going to break it to my parents gradually?—Mama and Papa, we have something to tell you—aghh-ahh-oops! There goes my breakfast!" Rina grimaced and put her hand on her stomach and David laughed. Rina sighed, "Oh, I wish it would settle down before we get there!"

"There will be at least half an hour's stop in Stafford before we go on to Malden. Maybe just stopping the motion will give your tummy time to settle down. I'm glad now that we didn't let my parents know when we were coming through Stafford." David put his arm around her shoulders. "Lay your head against me and take little short breaths and try to relax. Try not to worry; that will just make it worse. Your mama is going to be glad to take care of you— not that I am going to shirk my responsibility in that area!" He bent to kiss the top of her head. "My poor, lovely little wife!"

David was right. The stop in Stafford seemed to be just what she needed. They even stepped off the train for fifteen minutes to get some fresh air. Now the train was pulling into the Malden station. She saw her parents come out the door onto the platform.

What mixed emotions raced through her mind and heart as the train slowed to a stop! She had left early in the summer knowing they were not totally in favour of her plans. She had seen the apprehension on their faces and knew they felt a deep level of concern. That concern, she understood, was born of the profound love she had always felt from her parents. Now she was coming back essentially belonging to someone else. They had not had the opportunity to witness her wedding; neither did they know that they were going to become grandparents again.

"Come on, darling! Your parents are waiting to welcome their wandering daughter home! Just hope that welcome will be extended to a new son-in-law!"

"My dear David, they will accept you! I know they will."

"Well, let's go and find out!"

Chapter 6 🍂

DAVID STEPPED OUT FIRST and extended his hand to help Rina down the narrow steps. Jake and Ellie moved quickly, arms extended. Ellie took Rina in her arms and Jake reached with his right hand for David's. His left hand slapped David's shoulder.

"Welcome home and into our family, David. Was your trip good?"

"Yes, sir, it was long, but quite good."

"David! You are part of the family now. You don't need to call me sir! Dad or Jake will be just fine."

"Thank you, Mr. Kurtz—Jake," David smiled as he caught himself and made the change. "I guess it will take a while to get used to it, but I do appreciate your welcome into the family."

Ellie finally let go of Rina and moved to greet David with the same words Jake had used. Jake turned to Rina and she was enfolded in his arms.

"Welcome home, my dear Rina. How is my favourite daughter?"

Rina let herself be held close as she hugged her papa in return. Oh, it felt so good to be in his arms. Finally, Jake backed off a bit, lifted Rina's chin with one hand and looked into her face. "No words from my little chatter-box? What did the West do to you?"

"Oh Papa, it is just so good to be home again. I did miss you!"

"You had time to miss your old Papa when you were being courted and wooed right into a marriage without letting your Papa give you away?" Did she detect a bit of hurt there in the midst of his banter?

"Dear Papa! I just didn't want you to have to say you were giving me away. That way I will always be your little girl!" Rina's eyes glistened with merriment mingled with love. "And yes! I did miss you!"

"Come! Even though it is warm for December, it would be warmer at home. Since we have a new car, I thought I would let you go home in style! Let's get your baggage, and then we will be off."

Settled in the car, Ellie turned in her seat. "I assume you will be staying with us for a while?"

It was David who replied. "If that won't put you out too much, we'd sure appreciate it. I'll have to find some work, and then, eventually, we'll try to get a place of our own."

"We thought we would move our bedroom down to the first floor so you could have the upstairs to yourselves."

"Mama—are you sure you want to give up your room? We can sleep in my old room."

"Yes, you could, and if it was just for a week or two, that would be alright. But you will probably be with us for longer than that. It is time we moved downstairs anyway. We are getting older and stairs are not the best for aging folk."

THAT NIGHT, as Rina and David snuggled together in her old bed, they talked about the welcome they had received.

"So I was right about them accepting you, wasn't I?"

"Yes, you were, but they still don't know that we've already started our family."

"Even though it took Mama a long time to get pregnant the first time, they do know how it happens, David."

"I know, Rina. They just might think we could have waited until I had a job and we had a place of our own!"

"David, darling, I know! But they will love our little one as much as we already do."

"Yes, you are right about that! When do you think we should tell them, then?"

"We may as well tell them in the morning. That way, if I have to leave the breakfast table, they will know why!"

Even in the darkness, David could hear the smile in her statement. He chuckled. "Good thinking!"

THE NEXT MORNING, Rina came to the kitchen to find Ellie beginning to prepare breakfast.

"Let me set the table for you, Mama."

She reached for the plates from the familiar cupboard and willed her stomach to settle down. "Mama, I am looking forward to my mother's cooking, but we've been travelling for so many days that I'm really not very hungry. I'll just stick to toast for breakfast. David will probably make up for what I don't eat, since I think he is still in hungry harvester mode. You should have seen the piles of food the men ate when they were in the fields!"

Ellie cast a look at Rina but said nothing more than, "If that is what you want."

Rina couldn't believe that Mama would accept her not eating a good breakfast. *Mama already knows! She's just waiting to be told.*

Even Papa didn't question her eating nothing but toast and sipping on a cup of tea! By that time, she was quite sure.

When the men were just finishing their coffee, David gave her a look, and she nodded.

"Rina and I have something we need to tell you." David took a deep breath and reached for Rina's hand. "It's maybe a little sooner than we thought, and I am sure you may feel we should have waited. I want to assure you that I love your daughter and want the very best for her. I am so happy to have her as my wife. Of course we have a great deal of joy and anticipation." He fell suddenly silent.

Jake and Ellie waited patiently. Rina felt quite sure that David realized he was rambling. She squeezed his hand in encouragement and watched to see if he wanted her to continue, but he took another big breath and blurted out—"Mother and Dad Kurtz, I'll just come out and say it. We . . . uh, we are expecting a baby!"

Jake and Ellie looked at each other first, then Ellie answered. "We thought you might be. We sensed something, and then this morning—with Rina wanting only tea and toast for breakfast—that isn't like our Rina!"

"So what are your plans?" Jake moved his chair back a bit from the table and glanced first at Rina, his eyes filled with tenderness and concern, then turned toward David.

"Well, as I told you last night, I will be looking for a job right away. If you have any suggestions, I would be very glad to look into them. Our aim is to save enough to be able to get our own place. Of course, with a baby on the way, we will need to save for those expenses first."

"Jobs are not that plentiful right now, but an ambitious young man should be able to find something. I did hear that they are hiring men to help build the highway between Malden and Stafford. Actually, the address was in this past week's paper. You could probably get on with that crew."

David sighed in relief. "I will look into that first thing Monday morning."

"Meantime, David, you could help me move the furniture downstairs from our bedroom. It looks like you will probably be here until after the baby is born, so we might as well get set up so we can all live comfortably until then. Rina, you can help your mother get the bedding off and the drawers emptied so we can move the furniture more easily."

There were tears in Rina's eyes. "Thank you, Mama and Papa! You are being very kind."

She stood and moved toward her mother. Ellie stood to meet her and gathered her daughter into her arms. "My dear girl!" she patted Rina's back. "You have always pushed the limits, haven't you? You are so young, but you know we love you. With a baby on the way, you need to take care of yourself and prepare for parenting. We will help you as much as we can, but you have started a new family, so you and David need to make the basic decisions on your own."

"Thank you, Mama! If I can be half as good a mama as you have been to me, my children should be blessed!"

David stood and came up to them. He put his arm around Rina and his hand on Ellie's shoulder. His eyes shone full of gratitude. "Ellie, you have no idea how much your words mean to me. Your words of support are moving enough, but your blessing us as a new family—I don't know quite how to say it, but that is an offering that I think must be the hardest, as parents, to make, and the most treasured gift a young couple could receive."

Rina knew what David meant by the remark. She doubted that her parents were aware, but she knew David was quite sure the same would not be forthcoming from his parents—at least not from his mother.

"Now, Rina knows that in this family we do not face anything new without prayer. So let's gather in a circle and pray."

Jake put his arm around Ellie and reached for David's hand. David's arm encircled Rina and Ellie held her hand.

Jake began, "Dear Heavenly Father, this family is at the threshold of a new era in our lives. Our precious daughter has grown up and with David wants to begin a new life, a new family unit. We thank you that they have returned safely home. We acknowledge the challenges they will face and continue to grapple with in the coming months. We pray for Rina as she carries this child and learns to become a mother. We hold before you David as he faces the responsibilities of having and supporting a wife and child. We know that you, Heavenly Father, will provide all he needs as he looks to you for guidance and strength. We also pray for the little one who will join our family. Help us to welcome this new life as a gift from you. Please bless them as a family."

Ellie continued with the prayer. "You know, Lord, the many emotions that a new marriage and the promise of a child bring. Lord, we just ask you to wash them all in your love and to help it to be a time of learning. May the child that is born know only the joy with which we welcome it and the blessing of knowing that he or she is a treasure, the apple of your eye. Bless the love that Rina and David share and may each day, each victory or difficulty, each joy or sorrow they encounter only serve to remind them how much you care for them. May they always walk along the pathway you have chosen for them—and please, Lord, help us as parents to know how best to support them along that way. In Jesus' name we ask for these desires of our hearts, knowing that you are pleased to answer."

"Amen!" Jake added, and Ellie echoed, "Amen!"

Ellie's eyes were a pool of love and concern that surpassed the understanding of her daughter. Rina just knew that in them lay a depth of love and support on which she could depend. Tears trickled down her cheeks.

David stood, his arm still around his young wife, his eyes registering first astonishment and incredulity, then gladness and deep gratitude.

"Jake and Ellie, your prayers touched me deeply." His voice threatened to break. "Rina and I are lucky to have you."

"Thank you, David. I hope we can always be supportive of you." Jake gave Ellie one more squeeze, then moved toward the room that had been Ellie's sewing room. "You and I may as well get started. Ellie and I packed some things that we will take to the attic while the women get the dishes done up. Colin Gilbert said he would come and help if we needed him. I think I will let him know he can come right after noon, and we'll get the furniture moved around. No time like the present."

"You are letting no grass grow under your feet! How did you know we would be staying long enough to make it necessary to move furniture?"

"We've been talking for some time about moving our bedroom downstairs. My knee has been giving me some trouble, so this will just give us the push we needed to get it done. Besides, we figured you would need some place to live for a bit and we hoped it would be here."

RINA FELT Marlene's touch on her shoulder.

"Mama! You are sleeping in your chair. Why don't you let me help you get into your bed. You'll be more comfortable there."

"I haven't really been sleeping, Marlene. I was just living in the past!"

Marlene released the mechanism on the recliner to bring her to an upright position and Rina reached for her walker and grunted with the effort of rising to her feet.

"I believe my joints are of the opinion that ninety-nine years of service are enough. Every time I get up, I am forced to apologize to them for making them do it one more time. It's no joke when so many body parts threaten to go on strike." She gave a low chuckle. "It's only my mind that thinks its young—and maybe that's because it lives in the past half the time!"

"Oh Mama! Your sense of humour keeps you—and the rest of us—young." Marlene laughed. "You just tell those joints to hang in there for a while yet!"

James looked up from his paper. "Good-night, Maw! Have a good sleep."

"Thanks, James. I have had a long day, so I think I will."

When she had undressed and got into her nightgown, Marlene turned back the blankets and fluffed her pillow. Rina sat down, then lowered herself on her back as Marlene helped swing her feet in. A deep, satisfied sigh wafted through her lips.

"That does feel good! You are a good daughter, Marlene! Thank you so much for your care. A lot of people my age don't have the luxury and comfort of living with family. I am especially aware of that when I see the people at the nursing home next to the Senior's Centre."

"Mama, James and I are just so glad we can have you with us. You are giving us so much more than we can give you. Your being here and the memories we will be left with are such a gift to us."

"I know, Marlene. You mean what you say and I am truly grateful. Nevertheless, I am aware that not all children look at it like you do, and I don't take it for granted."

Marlene leaned over the bed to pull up the blankets and kiss her mother. "You have a good night's rest now, Mama!"

Her daughter gave her one last look of love as she put out the light and shut the door. Rina was tired, but her mind didn't stop. Her face relaxed in a faint smile. History was repeating itself. Her daughter and son-in-law took her in when she needed them just as her parents did so long ago.

Chapter 7

EVEN THOUGH HER PARENTS WELCOMED them with open arms, the coming months presented some difficulty for the young couple. David's pay was barely enough to cover all the costs. His pride dictated that he needed to pay board, and they needed to save enough for the doctor's bills. The layette for the baby was sparse, mostly because Rina's dignity did not allow for accepting too much from her mother either. As a newly married woman, her desire for independence made it difficult to reconcile her new status with still living under her mother's roof and authority. Not that Ellie exerted her power. In fact, she perhaps tried too hard to give consideration to Rina. It seemed they were walking a tight rope in their desire to accommodate each other and still be mother and daughter. The adjustment was not easy.

The nights, upstairs in their own bedroom when they were away from the prying eyes of parents and friends, were a haven where their love could be expressed. Rina's hunger for acceptance and pardon as well as her desires for independence and freedom, suppressed during the forced routine and acquiescence of the day, turned into fiery passion when she got into David's arms at night. Rina smiled as she bathed awhile in those memories of long ago. It had always been good between them in that way.

It doesn't seem so very long ago, in a way. My, how I miss you, David! The adjustment to living without you didn't even have the relief of nights together like we had back then. My bed felt so empty—still does after all these years, believe it or not.

Christmas that year was rather tense, for there was nothing with which to buy gifts for their parents, much less each other. Rina's discomfort with the extended family had caused her to announce that she and David would not go to the larger family gatherings. She was especially fearful of going to see David's parents.

I think Mrs. Litz always thought of me as the woman who spoiled her handsome son's chances of success. I tried my best with her, but she was always sharp and brusque with me. It seemed I could never do anything right or nothing was ever enough. Oh well, David always assured me that Mom was like that long before she knew me. I guess I just prefer to be liked! She smiled. *I guess that in itself doesn't make me odd.*

Her memory took a quick trip to just after Jessie Ellen was born that May—and Jessie sure was a good thing! The birth, for a first child, Dr. Foster had said, went very quickly. The hardships of the past months were wiped out, as if by a giant eraser clearing a whole blackboard in one swipe, the moment she held their little daughter in her arms. She was a mother! She remembered how David approached the bed his eyes full of awe and amazement.

"OUR DAUGHTER—a part of you and me!" David's eyes glistened with tears as he bent over and gave Rina a kiss.

"Can I hold her?"

"Sure! She's just as much yours as mine, even if I did carry her for nine months. Just make sure you support her head."

David returned her smile as he reached out for his daughter. "But you just finished a grand effort in the delivery, my love, and for that I am grateful because I couldn't do much to help in that department."

Gingerly, he lifted the baby from Rina's arms. His big right hand supported not only her head but most of her body. He moved his left arm underneath his right to make the circle complete and safe.

She watched David's expression move from nervousness to joy, to fascination, then pure passionate love. Was there anything as poignant or as heart-warming as a man with his newborn in his arms? At that moment, Rina could not think of anything more moving. She had thought her heart was completely filled with love for her new daughter, but suddenly it was expanded to include an overwhelming love for her husband as father of her child.

Amazing—but David was like that with every one of our children as they made their appearance! I never tired of seeing him take the newborn baby in his arms and watching as those same expressions washed over his face—well, maybe the nervousness disappeared as he got more familiar with little ones, but the rest of the expressions were the same. So were mine. Each baby is a new experience—a new little person of their own—a new miracle. I never lost my awe of a new baby either. Probably a lot of people wondered why we had as many as we did. I guess sometimes I did too, but every one of them was and is precious.

WITH JESSIE ELLEN'S ARRIVAL, the atmosphere changed. Rina's attention was focused on caring for the baby. A grandchild in the house, while claiming a great deal of attention from the grandparents, also established the solidarity of David and Rina as a family unit. David worked long hours on the highway and came home in the evenings tired and dirty, but he always took time to cuddle little Jessie. Ellie was willing and eager to help when needed, but she was careful not to interfere with the decisions they made and the way they chose to care for the baby.

There was one notable exception, though, when David came home with a new motorcycle and a sidecar and we took off for Stafford in it when Jessie was only four weeks old. That time, Mama did speak her mind. She implored us to reconsider. She was petrified when we didn't take her advice and left, merrily waving at her. It probably wasn't the sanest thing we ever did, but we got there safely.

ALL SUMMER, David had steady work on the road. As the fall days progressed and the daylight hours became shorter, David began to think ahead to winter, trying to find some work that would carry him through the cold weather. It was only late evenings and weekends that he had opportunity to ask around, for his days were long and filled with back-breaking labour. He couldn't find any steady work, but he lined up jobs with several farmers to cut wood, clean out box stalls, trim apple trees and other odd jobs.

Rina had noticed, even out west, no matter what he turned his hand to, David seemed to always be able to do it well. With his inventive mind he was always looking for a new way or something he could create or formulate to make the job easier or do the work better. On the road construction job he had already suggested improvements that impressed his boss and earned him a great deal of respect.

It was the following year, after another summer on the construction crew, that Rina knew there was another blip in their plans for a place of their own. At first, she was hesitant to tell David there was another child on the way, but she should have known better. David received the news with joy and they began to plan where Jessie's crib could be moved to make room for a second one.

When she told her mother, all Ellie said was, "Another baby will make this a busy household. We will probably need to make the bedroom next to yours a place for the children."

It wasn't long, though, before Ellie began to go through her stashes of fabric, asking Rina how this fabric end would suit for baby clothes or what kind of a quilt she should piece for the new baby. Rina had never been big on sewing, but seeing her mother's enthusiasm and ideas, she caught the bug. Soon she was thinking of new curtains for the children's room and thinking of inexpensive ways to make the room suitable for children.

One evening after Rina had put Jessie to sleep, she came downstairs to see what David was doing. Her parents had already retired. David sat at the table, a large piece of brown paper in front of him, drawing out plans of some kind.

"What are you drawing, my love?" Rina studied the lines. "Doesn't look like a house to me!"

"No—not a house. I just got an idea for a machine that would make a better road surface. I don't know if it will go anywhere, but I wanted to put it on paper before I forgot what I had going through my mind. I will keep thinking about it. Perhaps when I get it perfected, I will see if anyone is interested. Maybe I could even get a patent for it. With more and more cars, the roads will have to be improved, so maybe I can make a fortune and treat you to the kind of life I would like to provide for you."

Rina put a hand on his shoulder and kneaded the taut muscle she felt there.

"David, although I really hope we can have a place of our own, what I most need to be happy is *you*. Jessie has already been such a joy to us and I know this new one will be too. So if you make a fortune, I am sure we will find ways to use it, but if you don't, we will find ways to manage and be content."

David looked up from his drawing. By the twinkle in his wife's eyes, he knew there was more coming.

"Meanwhile, it is rather nice to live with my parents and have my mother make sure we have meals to eat and help with the laundry!"

"That's my Rina! Always finding a bright side to whatever comes her way!" He stood, stretching his arms. Lowering them, he took her into his embrace. "You never know what you can get for the price of one ticket. Who would guess mine from Stafford to Dubbin would also acquire the most perfect woman I could ask for in a wife? Quite a bargain, I should say!"

Rina caressed the sides of his face. "Your package deal must have contained some yeast! It just keeps growing. Already it has grown one complete human being, with another beginning to make itself evident."

David turned to put his hand on her stomach. "Ah-hh! Another little bun in the oven making my lovely wife bloom with lush fertility!"

"You make me sound like a jungle forest! I'm not that big . . . yet!"

"Come on—let's get to bed while Jessie is asleep!" Whereupon, David took his wife's hand and led her upstairs to their bedroom.

RINA TOOK another deep breath as she lay in the dark room in her daughter's home.

> *That was still at the very early stages of our marriage, even though at the time I felt like an experienced, married woman. After all, our second child was on the way! I thought I was quite a veteran. Oh how wise youth are—or think they are! After a while they learn how much they don't know!*

Rina stretched and yawned.

> *Guess I dropped off to sleep quite quickly last night. Sun's up already. I wonder if that was James taking off somewhere early this morning. Maybe it was just a noisy truck along the road that woke me up, but it looks like another nice spring day. It's too early to get up yet.*
>
> *Age has its advantages. Oh, what I wouldn't have given, in the days when the children were young, to wake and have the luxury of just laying there for a bit before having to get up and get going.* She smirked at the very thought. *Probably in those days if I woke up without one of the children waking me up to be fed or something, I would have jumped at the chance to get a head start on my day without someone underfoot. It wasn't that way yet when we lived in Malden with Mama and Papa in the first years.*

Rina's thoughts returned to last night's musings.

Chapter 8

THE CHRISTMAS JESSIE WAS a year-and-a-half old was special. She was old enough to catch a bit of the excitement. Her blond ringlets bounced and her bright blue eyes sparkled with delight in all the excitement. Rina made a rag doll for her and Ellie knit the doll and Jessie matching sweaters. Jessie mothered that little doll as though she knew she needed the practice for what was coming. She often brought her to her daddy and asked him to play a tune on the fiddle for her baby. David humoured her with great delight, playing some of Jessie's favourites. It became an evening ritual whenever he was home early enough.

They were present at the gatherings that Christmas and even had a good time at David's family get-together in spite of the undercurrent of resentment that David's mother continued to display. It amused Rina to see her mother-in-law wanting to fuss over the baby, yet rejecting the full inclusion of the baby's mother.

I still think Mother Litz would have been happier if David could have conceived and borne the babies all by himself. That way she could have had grandchildren without having to share David with his wife!

DAVID SPENT many nights that winter toiling over the sketches for the grader he had been visualizing. Rina, while encouraging him, sometimes wished he would let it go and just relax.

"Rina!" he came bursting though the door late one afternoon in March. "You can't guess what happened!"

"What are you so excited about, my love?"

"I showed my grader design to Carl Madison today. He works for a manufacturer out near the lake. He really liked what he saw and said he would take it to his company and see if they would be interested. If I could sell the plans or get a patent on it, it could change life for us!"

"That is great news, David!" Her face flushed with pleasure. "Meet my husband—the famous inventor!" She bowed low as if he were coming through the door onto a stage. "A little drum roll, please! Ta-da-de-da!"

David grabbed her hand, hooked it through his arm, made a bow of his own and announced, "And accompanying him, his lovely wife—the inspiration of his life!"

Ellie came through the back door with the mail in her hand. "My goodness! What is this all about?"

Rina hurried to tell her the good news and Ellie listened with rapt attention.

"That sounds very hopeful. I don't think I would spend the money just yet, though. And perhaps it would be best to just practice all those fine airs in private for the time being." The twinkle in her eyes kept their hearts merry even as she brought reality into focus.

DAVID HAD JUST FINISHED a day of hauling manure for a farmer that spring and was planning to start on the road again the following week. He'd come home weary, had a bath and went to bed earlier than usual. When Rina had settled Jessie and readied for bed herself, she felt a twinge as she fit her bulging form in beside David's sleeping body.

"Uh-oh, my love," she whispered, "you'd better sleep fast if that is what I think it is." She sighed. "I'm more than ready to carry this baby in my arms instead of inside, but I know David had a hard day."

It seemed to be only moments until she woke with a contraction that let her know this was it. She waited through a few more, but they were coming quite regularly and fairly close to each other. She reached out to David's shoulder, giving it a little shake.

"David, sorry to wake you up, but I think you had better go for the doctor."

"What? What time is it?"

"I would say it is around two o'clock, but your next offspring is anxious to arrive. You'd better go for Dr. Foster unless you want to deliver the baby yourself!"

David was already scrambling for his clothes. "No way! I like them when they get here, but I have no great compulsion to play doctor! On the way out, I'll let your mom know where I am going and then I will be back as soon as I can!"

He came to give her a quick kiss, and left. She heard him almost running down the steps. It wasn't long until she heard her mother's footsteps coming up those same stairs. There was a soft knock on her door.

"Rina? Are you all right?"

Rina was up, folding back the quilts on the bed.

"Yes, but I don't think I will be in labour as long as I was with Jessie. I hope Dr. Foster is available right away. He might not be in time if he isn't."

"Don't worry, my dear. He will probably be here within minutes. That's one advantage of living in town. Let me help you get the bed ready before your next contraction."

"All right, but the main thing we want you to do is make sure you listen for Jessie if she should wake up."

"That I will do when I have you settled again."

It wasn't long until David came back. Dr. Foster and Nurse Dunkerly were close behind. Jessie was carried to a cot downstairs and Ellie settled down on the couch beside her.

It was about five-thirty when a beaming David came down the stairs to tell Ellie that she had another granddaughter.

"Wonderful! Jessie slept right through. It's an early birthday present for her—your first two daughters—with birthdays only three days apart!" Ellie commented as she rose from the couch where she had been resting. "Is Grandma allowed to come and see now?"

"I'll be glad to introduce you to Mary Evelyn Litz! I'm sure her mother will be anxious to see you too!

Mama did come upstairs then. She marvelled at the ease with which I had children. She'd had so many miscarriages it seemed miraculous for me to have the second child without any problems. Little did she know then what was to come!

JESSIE HAD BEEN ASLEEP for over an hour, the baby was fed and settled and Rina hoped she would have six or eight hours to sleep. She snuggled up to David.

"David, love, do you think if you get a job on the road again this summer we could rent our own place?"

"The road to Stafford is done, Rina, so I don't think I will be working with that crew unless you want me to be away for a week at a time. But if I can find a comparable job, I think we can do it."

"I haven't minded all that much living here once I got used to it, but with two children I think it is a little wearing on Mama and Papa. They aren't young any more. If we had our own space it would be different, but during the day we're all together."

"I know, Rina. It is time we found another place."

"Thanks, David."

Rina sighed in contentment as she closed her eyes. Already she could see herself in a house of their own. She pictured herself hanging curtains, choosing where to put the furniture, using her own dishes, hanging pictures on the walls—making it their own cozy nest.

Much as David tried to find work for the summer, he was just not able to find anything in the Malden area. He started looking further afield. One day he went to Stafford and came home late in the evening. When he came through the door, Rina saw a look of apprehension on his face. She juggled Evelyn into her left arm and went to greet him.

"What is it, David?"

He gave her and his little Evvy a kiss.

"What do you mean, love?"

"You look as though there is bad news. Is there?"

"Not really!" He bent to give her another hug, whispering in her ear, "Let's wait until we are alone."

Rina returned his hug and said no more. She gave him a reassuring look and he went to wash up.

"Did you have supper?'

"No—not supper, but I did have a snack before leaving my parents'. If you would like to fix me a sandwich, that will be enough."

When the children were settled and David and Rina were in their bedroom, Rina turned to her husband. She put her hands on his shoulders, looking him straight in the eyes.

"All right. Now, what is it?"

David's eyes rolled toward the ceiling. Almost reluctantly, he looked at her again.

"Rina, I hardly know how to tell you this. I hardly know if it is something I even want to consider."

"David, just tell me! The suspense is killing me! Is it something so bad?"

"I don't know, Rina. It is something I never thought I would want to do, and certainly something I didn't think I would ever ask you to do. But I have looked for so long and I do think it would be a good opportunity and it may not have to be for long!"

"David, please! Just tell me—then we can discuss it and decide together."

"All right, Rina, here it is. Today I found a man in Stafford who is looking to train someone in mechanics. With more and more cars all the time, it is the coming thing. However, he can't hire full time, and there would be a period, when I am learning, that he couldn't pay all that much. Dad said he could give me work to offset the shortfall and they would make room for us in their house, which would save on rent. In the end, it would give me opportunity for a business of my own." He reached out to take her in his arms again. "We would have our separate living space, but—you know how Mom is! I know it could put quite a strain on you, and that worries me."

Rina felt her heart thud so hard she wondered if it hit the floor. She stayed close to him, her head on his shoulder so he couldn't see her face. She hoped he couldn't feel her despair.

"Rina, if you don't think you can endure living in the same house as my mother, I will understand. I'll keep looking. I hardly know if I can myself."

Rina felt as though there was a war going on in her heart and mind. David had already looked for work most of the winter. He was right—mechanics was a wave of the future that held the promise of steady work. He was also right that it could put a real strain on her—on them and their relationship—to live under his mother's constant disapproval and criticism. She was four months pregnant with their third child. What would it be like having a baby and two toddlers in someone else's house when that someone didn't think much of her to start with? In the end, what was good for David would also be good for her and for their children. Reaching for strength from deep within, she cried *Help me, Lord!* and lifted her eyes to find David searching her face, his eyes full of concern and anxiety.

"David, I married you for better or for worse. If this is a little 'worse' patch we have to go through to make a better life for us and for our children, then far be it from me to keep you from it. We will find a way to make it work."

"Oh Rina, my darling! Are you sure? It could get tough! I do think it is a real opportunity, but I will only do it if you promise me one thing."

"What is that?"

"That if you can't stand it anymore, you'll tell me—promise?"

"All right, I can do that. Maybe if we are there all the time, your mother will see I'm not so bad after all. Maybe we can establish a better relationship."

"That would be nice, but don't hold your breath, love."

IT WAS HARD for Jake and Ellie to see them go. Through the years with them, they had learned to accommodate each other and life had settled into a routine. Rina's parents were aware of the difficulty with David's mother and voiced their apprehension; however, they supported them in the prospect of a new career for David. They helped in the packing and preparation for the move.

When all was loaded and ready to go, they sat for one last meal together. Jake, at the head of the table, was ready to ask a blessing on the food.

"Can we hold hands around the table and make this a blessing for you as a family as well as the food?"

"You welcomed us into your home with a prayer. It would be a true gift to have your blessing as we leave." David's eyes reflected his appreciation.

"Gracious Father, how good it is to come to you with our thanksgivings and our concerns. Our hearts are full of gratitude for the love of family—especially this daughter and son-in-law and our precious granddaughters. It has been such a privilege to share their lives and the growth of this family.

"Now, as they start on this new venture, we pray your Spirit will go with them. They will face challenges and tests for which they may need more strength than they think they have. Lord, we pray that, at those times, they may draw on your unlimited strength and plenteous aid. We pray you will also grant them joy and satisfaction to balance the difficult times.

"Help them grow in their faith and trust in the days ahead. Bless David as he begins a new trade and learns new skills. Bless Rina and give her patience, tolerance and a serenity that will overcome any obstacles that would hinder growing relationships. Bless Jessie and Evelyn too, as well as the new little one who will soon join the family.

"Above all, help them remember whose they are and in whose strength they live.

"Bless, now, this food and the strength it gives, that we may bring you joy and blessing always because of what you have done for us. Amen."

They didn't have time for lingering over the meal, but that blessing remained like a warm cloak around them as they said their goodbyes and left. Rina was trying to be optimistic, but she had a hunch she would need those prayers.

Chapter 9

MOVING TO STAFFORD WAS AN ADVENTURE into the unknown, but living in the same house with David's parents and two younger sisters soon soured any hopes for a new life or, in particular, a new relationship with her mother-in-law. Even though it had been arranged so they had separate living quarters, David's mother found ways to make life miserable, especially during the day when David was at work. Rina was criticized for just about every move she made: the children were too noisy; did Rina have to go up and down the steps that often? Why did she clean on Friday instead of Saturday? Did she not know how to dress her children?—anyone could see they were not warm enough. Why did she not let the children play outside more? Why did she leave the children outside so long?

Rina struggled to be patient. She found herself trying to guess what her mother-in-law's reaction to just about anything would be so she could act accordingly. Usually, though, she didn't get it right. She wondered if it would be best just not to care, but it was hard to keep from at least seeking to please her.

What bothered her most was that no matter what time they went to bed, it seemed Fanny Litz knew exactly when they were settling into some private time.

Invariably, she would call up the stairs, "David. Daa-aavid! Can you come downstairs? I need your help!"

David would scowl, get up, pull on his trousers and obediently go do his mother's bidding. By the time he came upstairs, Rina, no matter how she tried to stay awake, was often asleep or one of the children were aroused by their grandmother's loud call. Sometimes Rina felt guilty about her thoughts, for David had it hard too. He worked long days, liked to play a bit with the girls before their bedtime and he also really needed a good night's rest. Instead, he scarcely had any time with his wife and the nights were often shortened considerably by the late-night needs of his mother.

As Rina's pregnancy advanced, the summer weather made the upstairs progressively hotter and the steps more difficult. The large trees were a saving grace, but even they couldn't keep up with the heat if it lasted more than three days. They kept the windows open during the night and closed during the days, but still the hotter days were uncomfortable. Occasionally, she asked her sister Marta's daughter, Clair, to come and stay with the girls while she went for a little break. Clair was going to stay with the girls when it was time for her to give birth, so it was good for the children to get used to her. David's youngest sister was eleven and she could help watch the girls too, but Rina was never sure if she would be allowed to do it when she needed her.

On the hottest days, Rina liked to sit in the backyard to do what work she could out there while watching the girls at play. Jessie was already a little mother hen with Evelyn. She watched her little sister carefully and tried to keep her out of the dirt, and she picked up the playthings Evelyn dropped when she was finished playing with them. Rina smiled to think of the difference between the two. Jessie always had everything organized and neat, even at a very young age. Her little sister seemed the exact opposite and didn't seem satisfied until any neat pile or boxful was spread around the room or across the yard. Sometimes Fanny would join them out of doors, but she brought with her a constant stream of criticism and condemnation and whining about what David could have done with his life—with a definite emphasis on the "could."

"David was always such a smart boy. He did so well in school and was always first in his class. He could have been a great inventor or even a professor! Oh, if only!"

"If only what, Mother Litz?"

Fanny Litz shot her a look that could have cut her heart out if Rina had been inclined to let it.

"As if you shouldn't know!" she spit out. "Getting married so young and three children within five years! That pretty well keeps his nose to the grindstone, wouldn't you say?" The added "Humph!" was probably meant to drive the dagger to the hilt.

"Hmm-mm! One could really be persuaded to feel sorry for the poor man if only he weren't so happy to be the father of those children." Rina could scarcely keep the humour and sarcasm out of her voice.

"Young people! They are so short-sighted. They don't even know what is good for them in the long run! They seem to be determined to throw away their parents' dreams for them."

Rina sat still for a moment, enjoying a fresh breeze that passed through the yard to bring a bit of relief from the late August heat. When Fanny drew a breath for another comment, she interjected a question of her own.

"How old were you and Dad Litz when you started your family?"

Fanny's mouth opened and closed, but not a sound escaped her lips. She rose, picked up her chair and started stomping toward the house.

"Well, I declare! Such impudence—from a young woman who is entirely dependent on the goodness of well-meaning people!" She sputtered until she disappeared through the back door.

For two whole days, Rina saw nothing of her mother-in-law. Instead of waiting until bedtime to call David, he was caught as he came home from work to be asked for some favours. The second day he was offered, but refused, supper with his parents, upon which he was given a long list of tasks that "really needed to be done."

"Mother, I've had a long day's work, Rina has supper waiting for me and I want to see the children. These tasks can wait until the weekend."

"Daa-avid," his mother wailed. "I didn't think you would turn out to care so little for your mother that you'd deny her help or a bit of company for supper. Why can't you stay with us for just one night?"

"Oh Mother! Stop whining! If you want to be with me so bad, perhaps you could make supper for the whole family sometime. Rina is at her due date and she could use a break!"

"Well, David!" she stomped her foot in frustration and rage, "I'll be! If that's the way you feel, you'd better go upstairs!"

David turned and went out the door. As he closed it, he heard Fanny's cry of irritation and disappointment.

"Rina, what is going on with Mother? Did something happen to upset her?"

"Why do you ask?"

"The last two nights she has called me in when I got home from work and wanted me to do some little jobs. Tonight she wanted me to stay for supper—just me!"

"You've had supper?"

"Of course not! I was sure you would have supper ready as you usually do. But I did tell her if she wants me to stay for supper she can fix a meal for the whole family."

"Oh dear! How did that go over?"

"Not so well. I think I made her angry—or angrier! I have the feeling she's been angry for a few days."

"Guess I'd better 'fess up!"

"So you do know what it's all about?"

Rina told him about the conversation they'd had in the yard, including her simple question.

"Ah-ha! I bet she didn't tell you that she was younger than you were when she got married and that her parents were dead set against their marriage—that I was born soon after and that she and Grandma still hardly talk to each other?"

"No, she didn't bother to mention that. Maybe that's why I have seen neither hide nor hair of her since then. Maybe she's afraid I will ask her about that. I probably hit a sore spot that she hasn't even come to terms with."

"Until I was nineteen—or at least I thought I was—I had been told I was born a year later than my actual birth date. I really was already twenty. So you are probably right. She still would rather not admit it."

In subsequent days, somehow that little bit of understanding took some of the barbs out of Fanny's complaining and criticism. Rina was more able to let it roll off her back and extend sympathy to her mother-in-law instead of taking her comments as a personal attack.

IT WAS ONLY two nights later that David called the doctor and went to get Clair. In the wee hours of the night, Bernadette Marie joined the Litz family. She was welcomed with love and not a little pride as David proclaimed the news that they now had a ladies' trio.

Bernie was a good baby, much loved by her older sisters. It was a mercy to not have a crying, fussy infant that would further disturb Grandma downstairs. Four-year-old Jessie liked to amuse the baby and was quite adept at rocking her to sleep. That helped on the busy days. Rina often complimented her on being "Mama's special helper."

That next year was hard—three children underfoot, Mother Litz watching every move and constantly complaining and passing judgment on everything from the way I kept house, the way I raised the children, the noise we made, the smells of my cooking—well, just everything!

That summer, I borrowed Marta's old baby carriage and, with the baby and Evelyn both in the carriage and Jennie with a harness to keep her safe, I walked the sidewalks for miles every day I could—just to get away from the constant censure and negativism.

That was enough—then I was pregnant again when Bernie was only six months old! I remember well the night I broke that news to David! We had just settled into bed and into each other's arms. I cuddled up to him and whispered. . .

"David, guess what?"

"Daa-aavid, DAVID! Come quickly! I need you!"

"Mother! What is it? Can't it wait until morning?"

"David! Can't you even come and help your own mother when she needs it? Have you forgotten all I have done for you? You should be ashamed. Please come at once."

"All right, Mother. I'll be there in a minute." David turned again to Rina. "What were you going to tell me?"

"Daa-aavid! Are you coming?"

"You may as well go, David. I'll try to stay awake until you come back and we'll hope that the children stay asleep through all the noise."

David buttoned his shirt and opened the door. "Please wait for me, darling. I'll try to make it as quick as I can."

Why must she come up with some flimsy excuse every night? Rina wondered. Last night she had suddenly not been able to stand having a cobweb in the back entrance. As though that couldn't have waited until morning—it had probably been hanging there for weeks! Or why couldn't it have been done when David came home?

Finally, after a good half hour, Rina heard David's footsteps coming up the stairs.

"What did she want this time?"

"Oh, it was really, really important this time!" David sighed. "She thought she might have heard a mouse in the cellar way tonight and she needed to have a trap set! I don't know what she did when I wasn't here. Dad would have done it for her. This has to stop; she finds some excuse every single night!"

With a sigh, David hung his robe on the chair and climbed wearily back into bed. Propping his head on his elbow, he leaned toward Rina. "Now, what was it you were going to whisper in my ear before I left?"

"Oh David, I don't know if now is the time to tell you."

"Come on, darling. Please tell me."

"Well then, David. I will tell you. Our family is going to expand again."

"Oh Rina! Really? You're not joking, are you?"

"No, my dear David! I do think there is another little one on the way. I know we had hoped to have a place of our own before another one, but—we'll manage somehow. By the time this one arrives, you should be finished with your training period and perhaps you can either be hired on at better pay or find somewhere you can have full-time work."

"Ah-hh, Rina! I am happy to have another child, but I had hoped to provide a bit better for you, my love."

"We're together, David. That is what is important. Just hold me close, David."

David accepted the news, but his mother was another story. We decided not to tell her until we had to, because we figured she would have plenty to say! I wore looser clothing and sweaters or large shirts a lot that spring and kept "complaining" that I was gaining weight. Eventually, I could hide it no longer. One warm day in late August, I was out hanging up clothes and I just had to take my extra shirt off. I thought Mom Litz was busy inside the house, so I didn't see her coming.

"Rina Litz! I don't believe it!" Fanny spat out the words, her eyes blazing.

"What don't you believe, Mother Litz?"

"You . . . you . . . you . . . how could you do this to my son?"

"What did I do to your son now?"

"You know very well! You are in the family way again, aren't you? All that talk about gaining weight! That is as good as lying. How could you do it?"

"Mother Litz, I hope this won't come as too great a shock, but since you don't seem to understand, I will tell you that I didn't DO this all by myself. Your son had a bit of a hand in it as well."

"Don't you make fun of me, you, you hussy! David is working himself to the bone to support all the children you do have. We are making great sacrifices to help him get started as a mechanic and letting you live in our house for next to nothing. Now you put this extra burden on him—a burden he doesn't need right now. He would have been better off without you."

That time it was hard to let it roll off my back. She said some nasty words and, much as I didn't believe them, they really hurt because I knew how hard David was working. Looking back, it seems that I could have let that go too, but at the moment it seemed like the last straw. Poor David—it was hard to wait until he came home that night. He knew the minute he came in the door that I was bursting with frustration, but I made him wait until the girls were in bed. I didn't trust myself to say it in front of them.

"All right, my love—now it's time to get the load off your chest. Shall I hold you tight so you don't splatter all over the walls when you explode?" David reached out for her. Rina chuckled a bit, then began laughing hysterically. Finally her tears turned to crying. After a few moments, she wiped her eyes and gave him a weak smile.

"I guess I needed that bit of humour, David. It did help take the edge off." She kissed him on the lips and looked into his eyes. "Remember the night you told me about the opportunity here in Stafford and the promise you asked me to make?"

"Yes, I do." His eyebrows raised in question marks.

"Well, David, I think the time has come. Today your mother asked how I could do this to you—burden you with another child. I think I've had it!"

"*You* did it to *me*?"

"I told her that I hoped it wouldn't shock her too much to find out I hadn't done it all by myself, that you had a hand in it too!"

"Oh my! What did she say to that?"

"That is when she called me a hussy and told me you would have been better off without me."

"What?" David almost shouted, his face getting red with anger. "How can she do that to you?"

"David! Whoa! I think it's my turn to hold you tight now!"

Little puffs of air escaped through David's clenched teeth. "Okay, okay! But I quite agree with you that the time has come. I'll look for work and another place for us to live—the sooner the better."

He didn't lose any time. We found another house to rent just over a few streets. Although it hardly seemed far enough away from David's mother after all that had happened, it was a place of our own. We moved within a week.

One would have thought the years living with his parents had been the best experience of his mother's life the way she cried and carried on about "losing my precious son and his family and the audacity of you leaving when you should be staying to help as we get older." But nothing deterred David from his intentions of leaving as soon as possible. The night they had their first meal in their own place was a celebration indeed, even if their stew held nothing but hamburger and the few vegetables Rina could scrounge out of the bit of garden they'd planted. Despite the way she had grown up, that night was the first time they prayed together more than grace before a meal.

"David, could we pray—I mean more than grace—since it is a real celebration and a new step in our lives?"

"Sure! Do you want to go ahead? I'm not that good at praying out loud."

"Yes, I can, but David, it's just talking to God like you would talk to me."

"Maybe I can another time, but you pray tonight." He reached out and clasped her hand.

"Dear God, it's so good to be in a home of our own tonight. Thank you for giving me such a good husband in David and for how hard he works at providing for us. Lord, thank you also for Jessie, Evvy and Bernie. They are so precious to us, and now we are looking forward to another one. Thank you for providing a place for us to call home. Bless not only this home but also bless us as a family that we may be able to learn to love each other and show the world by how we live that we love you too. Bless each of our friends and all who will come through these doors that they may find you a real part of our family and meet you, too, when they come. We trust in you to provide all we need. May David find the work he needs to provide our living, and help me to be the kind of wife and mother that will keep this a happy home. In Jesus' name, Amen."

"And thank you for such a dear wife and good mother for our children," added David, squeezing her hand.

"You had the privilege of growing up hearing your parents pray. You learned well. Thank you, my dear."

Chapter 10

DAVID KEPT LOOKING for work and doing odd jobs—mechanics when he could, and horse training when nothing else was available. He was good at that too, but a full-time job seemed to be impossible to find. I had to cut all the corners I could to make ends meet, but we managed. It was a lot better than what we'd had for a while.

It was a great pleasure for me to fix up a space for the new baby in this house of our own, even if I didn't have a lot of money to spend on it. Everyone kept telling me that it would be a boy because I was carrying this baby so much differently than the first two, but I didn't know whether to let myself believe it. Wowser! It was something to see David's face when Murray Alden was born—his first son. He was so proud! It still made her smile to think of that moment.

DAVID, WITH HIS SON cradled in his arms, leaned over Rina to give her a kiss. "Our young man didn't keep the doctor waiting very long, did he? As usual, you were a real trouper! Thank you, Rina, my love, for this son! You've made me a proud daddy again!"

Rina's eyes twinkled. "You're a little like your mother, David darling: you're forgetting that I didn't do this by myself. In fact, I think he has the Litz chin and feet too, by the looks of it, so you must have had quite a bit to do with the creation of this little man."

"Ah-hh Rina! That is what is so special. He is a bit of both of us, yet the good Lord made him a person all his own. I am just so thankful that you are his mother, and I realize that you had everything to do with the carrying and birthing of our babies. That's what I am thanking you for. You've had a hard night's work."

Jessie had already started school that September and Murray was just 16 months old when David heard of an opportunity to drive bus in Windsor. He went down for a job interview and found a house for us.

Windsor was hours away from all our family and friends. I wasn't sure about moving that far, but he needed a job, so Mama and Marta came and helped us pack up and move out of the house that had so recently become our first little nest. I hated leaving it—not because it was a luxury home, but because it was our first. We hadn't had much time to enjoy it. I made curtains and did a bit of painting, but I had dreams of fixing it up to make it really nice. It felt as though I was killing my dreams as I packed.

We still didn't have a lot of furniture when we moved into the Windsor house. The older children slept on mattresses on the floor. Jessie's school was quite a distance from the house, so I had to pack up the three younger ones and walk her to school. At the end of the second week, one of the girls in the school yard told me she lived on Albert Street too. She said she knew the people that used to live in our house, but she didn't know who had moved in. She said she would be glad to let Jessie walk home with her. I was quite relieved!

Rina turned over on her side. She heard noises in the kitchen. She should be getting up soon, she supposed. In spite of that thought, she returned to her memories.

IT WAS NICE to be able to let Murray sleep a little longer now that she didn't have to go walk Jessie home. Bernie was still asleep too, and Evvy was amusing herself with her doll. Jessie should be home any time now.

Finally, Rina went to look out the door and up the street. No sight of her yet. She returned to her ironing for a few minutes, then, feeling uncertain, she put her sweater on and went down the steps to get a better look. A few adults were in sight, but no children. Where could Jessie and her friend be? Was it Shirley or Sally? She hadn't asked exactly where it was that she lived.

"Some mother I am! But she seemed to know where our house was—how silly of me!" She went back into the house even more unsure of what she should do. Maybe she had better go look for her, but that wasn't the easiest when she had three other little ones to tow. Oh dear! It wasn't much fun living in a city where she didn't have any friends or family to call on. In either Stafford or Malden she would have had a choice of family or neighbours she could trust to stay with her little ones while she went looking. She went into the bedroom and bent over Bernie's mattress.

"Come on, Bernie, can you wake up? We're going to go for a walk."

Sweet little thing! As usual, she woke up smiling. Quickly, she got her dressed and into a warm jacket. She was just getting Murray out of his crib when the telephone rang. Impatient, she grabbed the phone.

"Hello?"

"Mrs. Litz?"

"Yes, it is!" Who was this calling, anyway?

"I think I have your little girl here."

Rina gasped. "Where have you got her? Who are you?"

"Don't worry, Mrs. Litz. I am a bus driver. I believe your husband is my co-worker. As I was coming to one of the bus stops, I noticed Jessie walking along Albert Street crying, so I asked her what the matter was. She said she couldn't find her house. She couldn't tell me her address, but she remembered her telephone number. If you tell me where you live, I can perhaps drop her off at home."

"We live at 140 Albert Street. Where are you?"

"I just stopped at 20 Albert Street, but I am coming that way. Poor Jessie must have turned the wrong way!"

"Thank you so much, Mr. . . . ?"

"Bellingham."

"Thank you, Mr. Bellingham. I am greatly relieved that she is safe. I will be waiting at the street for her."

Rina's heart pounded as all the possibilities raced through her mind. How stupid of her to have trusted a young girl without making sure she knew where they lived.

As she tucked Murray into the baby buggy and urged the girls out the door, she prayed, "Lord, thank you for taking care of our little girl better than I did."

"Come, darlin's, we are going to wait here on the sidewalk for Jessie to come home. She is going to be coming in a big bus like Papa drives."

She hadn't thought about the stops the bus would be making on the way. Because of her anxiety it seemed to take forever, but eventually she spotted it coming down the street.

"See, Evvy? Here comes the bus."

One more stop at the corner and then the bus was in front of them and the door opened. Jessie's face was still tear-streaked, but she was smiling.

"Mama! I got lost! I didn't know where our house was."

"Thanks again, Mr. Bellingham! I had been walking her back and forth from school, but today one of her friends said Jessie could walk home with her because she lived on Albert Street too. She seemed to know where our house is—I don't know what happened, but thanks again."

Mr. Bellingham nodded with a smile and the bus pulled away. Rina bent down to be on eye level with Jessie.

"Now Jessie, can you tell me what happened? Where did your friend get to?"

"We walked from the school until we got to Albert Street. She pointed and said #40 is just five houses down that way and that I could find that easy. She lived a few houses the other way. But I looked and looked and I couldn't find our house. When I looked back to tell Shirley I couldn't find our house, she wasn't there either, so I kept walking. I didn't know if I would ever find our house or you and Papa again." Her lips trembled and tears began to retrace their streaks down her face.

Rina gathered her into her arms. "There, there, my dear, precious girl, you are safe at home now. Mama is so sorry that you got lost. I thought Shirley knew where we lived, but we live at #140, not #40. Come, let's go into the house and we'll see if we can find a glass of milk and a cookie."

Silly, stupid city! If only we were back in Stafford this wouldn't have happened, Rina muttered to herself. Why couldn't David have found a job closer to our family and friends? Why did she have to cope with long days and four small children and a school too far away for a little girl to safely go by herself?

She took off the children's jackets, got out milk and cookies and settled them at the table with comforting words, all the while chafing at the circumstances that led to this frightening event.

Face it, Rina! It isn't the city's fault! You just weren't careful enough, and it could have led to the loss of your firstborn!

Rina continued to berate herself. That felt even worse than finding fault with the city or David! Tears threatened to fill her eyes, but she didn't want the children to see her crying. Jessie had been through enough without seeing her mother fall apart. Oh, if only she could talk to Mama. What would she have done in similar circumstances?

Rina knew very well what her mother would have done.

While the children were happy with their milk and cookies, Rina went to get potatoes to peel for supper. As she peeled, she did as her mother would have done. She prayed.

"Heavenly Father, you know how alone I feel here in this strange city with no family, no friends and neighbours that haven't been all that friendly. You have given us these children, and I am so thankful for them, but they do keep me busy and sometimes I long for other adults that I can talk to. We haven't even found a church nearby where we can find the fellowship we need to sustain our souls. And now there's today's mix-up and I don't know how I can forgive myself for putting Jessie into such jeopardy! She could have been completely lost or kidnapped or killed. My precious baby! And it would have been my fault. Lord, how could I have been so stupid?"

Tears sprung to her eyes again. She blinked hard and shook her head.

"Lord, how am I going to tell David? What will he think of me? Please, Lord, can you forgive me for being so careless with one of your good gifts? Please, Lord?"

If we confess our sins, he is faithful and just to forgive us our sins.

"Ah, yes, Lord! Thank you for reminding me of that! Thank you for your forgiveness. Just help me to forgive myself, and please let David forgive me too!"

For as the heaven is high above the earth, so great is his mercy toward them that fear him. As far as the east is from the west, so far hath he removed our transgressions from us.

"All right, Lord. I guess that is far enough! If David can see it that way, I promise I will learn from this and not be so careless again!" Tears came into her eyes and this time trickled down her cheeks, but now they were tears of relief. She finished the potatoes and then wiped her tears with the back of her hand.

When David came through the door, Rina greeted him with a hug.

"Hi honey! How was your day?"

"A usual kind of day. Why?"

"Did you happen to talk to one of the other drivers—a Mr. Bellingham?"

"No, I didn't. He just pulled into the depot as I was leaving. Why? How do you know him?" His eyes registered his perplexity.

"Your day may have been usual, but ours wasn't. Come on, sit down for supper. I'll tell you all about it as we eat."

"Now you've got me really curious. But I'll get washed up. I am hungry and supper smells wonderful!"

Once they were seated and had prayed, David waited until the children were served before he looked at Rina.

"All right now, spill it, my love."

"Well, you know how I always walk Jessie to school and go for her again? It is quite a long way for Evvy to walk, especially when the weather isn't nice, but we manage. In the afternoon Bernie and Murray's naps are shortened, although Murray often sleeps on in the buggy."

"I know, Rina. I know it takes a lot of your time in the day, but it was the closest house I could find. What happened today?"

"This morning when we got to the school yard, we caught up to some other girls. A little girl, Shirley, a few years older than Jessie, asked where we live and why I was bringing Jessie to school. I told her where we live and that it was too far for Jessie to walk by herself. She said she had played with Jessie before and that she lived on Albert as well, and Jessie could walk home with her so I didn't need to come back this afternoon. She said she knew, because our house was just down the street from her and she hadn't known who moved in there until I told her."

"That was very nice of her!"

"That's what I thought." Rina paused. She told David what had happened, the misunderstanding about house numbers and how the telephone call had startled her.

"At first I thought someone had nabbed Jessie! I just about panicked. I was so relieved when I knew she was safe, but I could hardly wait until the bus stopped and I could see her. Poor little girl!"

David looked at Jessie, who was busy eating her supper. "Was it scary for you, Jessie?"

"Yes it was! I didn't know if I would ever see you and Mama again. But Mr. Bellingham made me feel safe. He even gave me a candy when I got on the bus."

"I guess it is a bit of a coincidence that both #40 and #140 had new tenants, and it is understandable that Shirley misunderstood, but I blame myself for not making sure! You can bet on it that I will be doing the walking from now on."

David took his wife's hand. "Rina, it was an understandable mistake. You wouldn't have intentionally put our daughter at risk. Don't beat yourself about it!"

"Thank you, David. I needed that."

The problem was solved the following week when David's boss arranged to let Jessie ride to school on the city bus. It warmed Rina's heart to know that in this big city someone cared.

Chapter 11

Life for the Litz clan can't seem to stay on an even keel for any length of time, Rina thought.

WHEN THEY HAD been in Windsor for only eight weeks, Jessie came home from school with a sore throat. The doctor diagnosed it as diphtheria and quarantined their house. If Rina had thought she felt alone before, she felt truly isolated now. Because David had not really been exposed to Jessie, he was boarding out until the quarantine lifted. That way he could continue work. He brought their groceries, medication and other needs and left them on the porch. Twenty-four hours a day, she was cooped up in the house with a sick child and three other lively youngsters. Now Evelyn's throat was sore!

"Mama! It hurts!"

"Yes, my love, I know it hurts. Here, let Mama rock you a bit."

Rina picked Evvy up and cuddled her close. Her hot cheeks burned through Rina's sleeves. How many nights had it been since she had been able to sleep through the night? She was nervous to let herself sleep in case Jessie would stop breathing. She had hoped that perhaps she was over the worst of it, but now Evvy was sick and Murray was being fussy today. He hadn't wanted to eat his dinner. She hoped he wasn't getting it too—he was so little yet! It was entirely too possible for little ones to die of diphtheria. Jessie was just now beginning to take a bit of broth or Jell-O.

If David could at least be here to help . . . but she was the only one their little ones had to care for their needs. Thankfully, so far Bernie continued to be her sweet little self.

By the next night, there was no doubt in her mind. Murray's little voice became croupy and hoarse. He was thirsty, but when she tried to give him a drink he would whimper and turn his head away. His body was hot. Rina bathed him with cool water in an effort to keep the fever manageable. When David came to the porch with groceries for them, she told him through the barely open door that she now had three very sick children.

"Maybe I should just come home, Rina. It's almost too much for you."

"Oh David, I'd really like to have you here—God knows how much I'd like to have you here—but we need the money and I'd hate to have you get it too."

"I know, my dear, but I dislike seeing you carry the whole load. It's hard enough when they're all well, or even sick one at a time. But with three of them feeling so ill, it must be really hard for you."

"I guess I'll manage, my love. It helps even to talk a bit through a crack in the door. It will be nice to feel those arms of yours around me again."

"I can echo that sentiment! Wow! It feels like a long time, and I suppose it will be a while yet. I'd better leave before I just open that door and come right in where my heart is!"

Rina threw him a kiss through the window of the door. "I'm afraid that is all you're going to get right now, but know that I love you!"

"I love you too! I'll be back on your veranda again tomorrow. I hope you have a bit of sleep tonight. I hear Murray crying, so I'd better let you go . . . 'Love you, darling!"

She picked Murray up to comfort him and was shocked at the intensity of his fever. It was only a few hours since she had bathed him, but she'd better do it again. She went to get more water in the basin.

"Mama, Mama, I am thirsty. My throat hurts."

"I know, Evvy. Just a minute. I will give you a little apple juice, but I have to bathe Murray too. When I am done I will try to hold you both for a bit. If I sit on the couch, I think I can handle both of you at once."

Rina laid a towel on the table and quickly stripped Murray of his clothes. Wringing the water from the washcloth, she wiped down his face and then his entire body, wetting the cloth frequently. Murray just lay there, whimpering hoarsely. Her heart twisted to see him so lethargic. At least he was still breathing. The doctor had said to watch for drooling, which could indicate that his airways were becoming blocked. It was difficult for her not to panic even thinking about how she would feel if that happened.

Finally, he felt cooler to the touch, so she dressed him again. Jessie had gone to sleep, so she gave Evvy a drink, then Bernie a bowl of potatoes and left-over vegetables, and took both Murray and Evvy to the couch to hold them as she sang little ditties to comfort them.

Later in the evening, Rina put Bernie to bed. She felt so tired she wondered how she was going to make it through the night. She needed to wake frequently to check on both the little ones to make sure they were breathing all right. Finally, she propped Evvy up on some pillows on the big bed, lay down beside her and held Murray on her own propped-up body. It wasn't long until all three slept, although she slept fitfully, aware that she needed to check Murray often.

For three long nights that is how they slept. On the fifth night, Evvy was good enough, she thought, to sleep on her own mattress. Murray, though, was still very feverish and often through the night, Rina woke to his croupy cough or his hoarse cry. He was losing weight and getting very weak and his face actually looked bluish. Finally, David sent the doctor in again to check on them. The doctor gave Rina a few more suggestions and another medication in an effort to soothe Murray's throat.

That night was the worst. There was very little sleep for either of them. His fever went up again, and Rina bathed him twice through the night, fearful that he would take convulsions. By the wee hours of the morning Rina felt almost dead on her feet. She settled down on the rocking chair, with Murray in her arms, around five to try to get him to sleep. She started humming a little tune.

"Oh, dear God! Please, no! I can't be getting it too!" Her throat felt scratchy. She swallowed again. Yes, it did hurt. "Dear God, what do you expect me to do now? Please, Lord, don't let it get bad."

Morning came. She fed the girls what they could eat, had a little Jell-O herself and, when they were settled, lay back on the couch and prayed in earnest.

"I know it will cost more than I should spend, but I am going to call Mama. I need to speak with someone and David will be at work already."

At Ellie's "Hello?" Rina's voice almost broke in relief.

"Mama, it's me, Rina."

"Rina! What is the matter? Your voice sounds funny."

"We've been coping with diphtheria, Mama. Jessie got it first. She is getting better, but when Evvy came down with it she was worse than Jessie. Murray got it too. He has been really sick."

"Oh Rina! I am so sorry! Is David helping you?"

"No. The doctor said David had better leave right away. He hadn't really had much exposure to Jessie, so he went to a boarding house because we are under quarantine. He hasn't had any symptoms, so I think he will be all right. He comes with groceries and any medications we need and leaves them on the porch. Sometimes I open the door just enough so we can talk a bit, but I've had to do it by myself."

"Oh Rina. I had better come to help you."

"No, no, Mama! We wouldn't want you to get it. I just needed to talk to someone this morning. I think I may be starting with it too."

"Rina! You can't manage four little children if you are sick!"

"We'll see how it goes. The doctor may have some ideas."

"Well, Rina, I just feel so helpless if I can't even be there to help you. We will be praying for you anyway. I'll see if I can think of something else to do for you."

"Thanks, Mama. It's been good just to talk to you. I shouldn't make this long because it costs too much, but you have no idea how good it is just to hear your voice and know that you and Papa will be praying for us."

"That we will do! Rina, we love you and all your family. Say hello to David and the children for us too."

"I will, Mama. Thank you. But I had better go. Goodbye."

"Goodbye."

When David came to the veranda that night, he could see, even through the window in the door, that Rina wasn't feeling well.

"Rina! What is the matter with you?"

"I probably shouldn't stand in the draft for very long, David. I guess I am getting it too. I don't have much fever yet, but my throat is really scratchy and sore."

"I'd better take some time off work and come home!"

"No, David, not yet. If I get too bad, maybe you will have to, but let's see how it goes. Murray's fever is still high. Last night was pretty bad. He has lost a lot of weight and is quite weak. Maybe we should ask the doctor to come again just to check him out. So far, Bernie is still all right. She must have a strong constitution."

"Oh Rina, it almost kills me to see you having to bear such a burden."

"I know, David. But we will have to pay rent at the end of the month, we still need groceries and we've needed medicine, so the best thing we can do is keep you well. If I should get really sick, we may have to change plans, but I pray that I won't. I called Mama and Papa, and they are praying too."

"If anything should do it, that would be it. Rina, I love you so. You are such a trouper!"

Rina gave a weak grin and a salute. "Trouper Litz, at your service!"

"Rest all you can, Rina. I'll call the doctor and ask him to come, then I'll stop by in the morning to see how you are feeling. Call me at the boarding house if you need me through the night."

"Thanks, David." She threw him another kiss and closed the door.

When the doctor came and examined Murray, his brow gathered into deep furrows of concern.

"I think we had better arrange to have a nurse come in. I would recommend the hospital, but they are so busy I'm afraid he wouldn't get the attention he needs. He needs twenty-four hour care."

"Are you sure we can't care for him?" Dollar signs flashed before Rina's eyes—dollars they didn't have.

"Mrs. Litz, you are sick yourself and need to take care so you don't get worse. Murray needs professional care. I will call Miss Garnet and Miss Harrington. Between the two of them they should be able to give Murray the care he needs."

Before Dr. Murphy left, Miss Garnet appeared, took her orders, and then, when the doctor departed, began giving some of her own.

"Now, Mrs. Litz, you take Jessie to bed with you. Since Bernie and Evvy are already asleep, I'll keep an eye on them and look after Murray. You try to get a good night's rest."

"You know, that does sound very good!" Rina sighed in relief as she led Jessie to her bedroom. She got her daughter settled, then prepared for bed herself. For the first night in many, she actually got undressed, expecting to be able to stay in bed for the night. She turned back the covers, lay her head on the pillow and pulled the blankets up to her chin. She took a few deep breaths. It took some time for her tired muscles and taxed mind to unleash the tension and strain of the last weeks and feel the sweet emancipation of knowing that someone else was in charge—she could rest.

A few times during the night she roused, conscious of her burning throat. But she was so tired that she was soon unconscious once more. It was almost eight a.m. when she awoke. *Oh dear, David usually stops in around 7:30. I probably missed him.*

Jessie was still asleep, so she quietly got dressed and went to the kitchen where Miss Garnet sat on the rocker with Murray in her arms.

"How is he? Did he have a good night?"

"He is still a very sick little boy! I had to bathe him a few times to get his fever down. How are you? Did you sleep well?"

"It was wonderful to get a full night's sleep—the first in some time! I woke a few times because my throat is quite sore, but I think I was making up for all those nights I hardly slept. Thank you for helping us out."

"It's my job. Make sure you get enough to drink. If it is hard to swallow, just take sips at a time, but keep at it. Miss Harrington should be here momentarily to take over for the day and I will be back again tonight."

"Did David stop by this morning?"

"Yes, he did, but I told him you were still sleeping. He said he would stop by this evening again."

Miss Harrington was just as efficient as her counterpart. Rina was relegated to the couch when she wasn't in bed. Bernie was quite content to play close by her mother. The older girls were still resting much of the time too.

About five o'clock there was a knock at the door. Rina thought it would be David, but when she roused herself, she was shocked to see her mother standing there.

"Mama! You can't come in here!" Rina shouted through the door.

"But I came to help you out. You can't do it all on your own. Let me in."

"Mama, I won't let you expose yourself to danger. Besides, we have a nurse here looking after Murray now. You have to go back!"

"I'm here now, so I may as well come in."

"No, Mama! I can't let you do that. Look—here comes David."

She saw the alarm on David's face when he spied her mother. A heated argument began. She couldn't hear it all, but she could see there was a battle of wills. Finally, Mama came closer to the door again.

"David says he won't let me come in. I just thought about my second cousin who lives in the city. I will see if she will take me for the night and let me make some soup and a few things for you before I go back to Malden. If it is alright with her, I'll stay for at least a few days and do some cooking for you."

"Oh Mama! Thank you, but you really shouldn't have come. I have to go and lay down again, but take care and don't overdo it. Who is staying with Papa?"

"He will be all right for a few days, but Maria's Herbert is living in Malden now and he said he would spend the nights with him until I return. You go and lay down now and take care of yourself. I will bring some soup tomorrow if my plans work out. Otherwise, I will call you."

What a mother! Rina could hardly believe that Mama would come down on the train all by herself just to look after her. Much as she thought she shouldn't have, it was nice to know she cared that much! Especially feeling like she did right now, it warmed her heart. As she snuggled down on the couch, her mother's love enveloped her just as tangibly as the knitted afghan that covered her.

No matter how old you get, a mother's love is still a real comfort, she thought.

Chapter 12 🍂

IT HAD BEEN A HARD NIGHT. Rina's throat felt so sore she was afraid it would crack, and breathing became hard at one point. She alternated between being hot and cold. She wrapped a quilt around herself and went to the couch to try to sleep sitting up for a while, but that made her whole body ache. The nurse was busy with Murray. She worried about him too, but was glad she didn't have to care for him. She wasn't sure she could have done it, feeling this way.

This night seems to have no end. I guess things always look worse in the dark of night. What a comfort it would be to have David here—or Mama. But I can't expose either of them to such danger if at all possible. At least we have a nurse.

"Dear Lord," she prayed quietly, so as not to hurt her throat, "please keep me from getting too much sicker. You know I have four little ones depending on me. Please take care of Murray so it stays at that number. Thank you for sending Miss Garnet and Miss Harrington with their expertise to look after him. Thank you that both David and Mama are concerned and would like to help, but I don't want either of them to get sick too. You are the only one that can keep that from happening. I feel tired and weak right now, so I'm just going to give the whole messy situation to you and trust you to take care of it."

For five days, her mother delivered meals to the door. Each of those days, the girls were unbelievably good, and for four more days after that, the nurses were there day and night to look after

Murray. Rina was thankful that her fever didn't get too high. She had a lighter case of it. The food that was delivered to the door took the burden of cooking off her shoulders. Mama and a few neighbours who had found out about their situation seemed to know appropriate foods to fix so she could spend her time resting and only needed to do the few tasks that remained. One of the neighbours even offered to do the laundry for them. By that time, Rina felt a little better and Murray was well enough that she could take over the day care, although the doctor recommended keeping the nurse on night shift for a little longer. On the sixth morning after her mother's arrival she got a call.

"Rina, I just got a call from Herbert." She could hear the worry in Mama's voice.

"What is it, Mama?"

"It seems that Papa has had a small stroke. I think I had better leave for home right away."

"Oh Mama, is it bad?"

"They don't think so, but they are watching him closely in case he has another one and I think I had better be there."

"Of course, Mama, you need to be with him. I wish I could come with you, but I can't. I do hope he is all right."

"I hope so too, Rina. I'm not finished with him yet."

"Mama, thanks for coming. It did feel good to have your care, even if you couldn't be in the house with us."

"Rina, before I go, I want to suggest something—and I have talked to David about it already. You will need to take care for a while, even after the quarantine is lifted. You don't want any complications to develop. Jessie, too, had it quite bad and Murray was so sick that it will take him a long time to recuperate. Plus, David has such long days on the bus. I think he should just keep his room in the boarding house and you should come to Malden with us—just until David can find a job closer to home."

Rina was silent for a moment. "Mama, that does sound good. I haven't enjoyed living here so far away from family and friends. Jessie doesn't like the school here either. I guess with time we would make some friends and get used to it, but it hasn't happened yet. To be honest, I don't know if I really want it to happen. I'd like it better being closer to family, but it has to be David's decision in the end. I will stick with what he wants."

"Fair enough, Rina. Just give it some thought. We'll be ready for you if and when you come."

"All right, Mama. You go home and tell Papa we need him to get better. We'll be praying for both of you."

"I will, Rina, and you take care of yourself. You know diphtheria is nothing to fool around with. You need to take it easy until you are well over it. 'Bye for now."

"Goodbye, Mama."

David ended up agreeing with her mother and plans were made to go back to Malden as soon as Rina and the family were well enough to go.

A SOFT KNOCK sounded on Rina's door, bringing her back to the present.

"Mama, are you all right?"

"Come in, Marlene. I guess I have been lazy this morning. I've been awake for a while just remembering our time in Windsor. The doctor was worried that the diphtheria would be hard on my heart, but I guess if he would have known how old I would get to be, he wouldn't have needed to worry about it."

"I guess not! Look at how many years and all the hard work you've done since! It's all right if you want to stay here. I just wanted to make sure there was nothing wrong when you slept longer than usual. You don't want to get too far off track with your meals or your blood sugar will go up."

Rina threw back the covers. "If you are here now, you may as well give me a hand to sit up. I can do it, but it's nice to have help." She grinned up at her daughter, her eyes twinkling with merriment. "I need to keep you feeling useful, you know!"

It wasn't long until Rina sat at the table eating a bowl of oatmeal porridge while Marlene washed dishes.

"You weren't born yet when we were in Windsor. We weren't there long either! Usually it was your father's jobs that made us move, but that time, moving back to Malden, it was because of me.

I just didn't like Windsor, although I'm sure having the diphtheria didn't help. It left me tired and weak, with headaches, for quite a while. Your papa had long hours and that left me with four little ones at home—none of us except Bernie feeling well. My mama's suggestion that we come home to Malden just looked too good. Even then, I wouldn't have if Daddy had really wanted to stay, but he felt bad that he couldn't help more when I wasn't feeling well. He thought Mama's suggestion was a good one. So we packed up what little we had and left."

"How long did Daddy stay in Windsor after you came to Grandpa Kurtz's?"

"Oh, I can't quite remember, but I think it was almost two months."

"Did he come to Grandpa's too?"

"Yes, he did. I was expecting Doris by then. He got a job at a garage." Rina finished her oatmeal and started sipping her coffee. "There I was, back home again! Seems I just kept doing that."

"How did you feel about that?"

"'Guess my feelings were sort of mixed. I wasn't feeling well, then I was pregnant again, so in a way it was good to have Mama look after me a bit. But with four little ones and Papa just having had a stroke and finding it hard to get around, I knew it was too much for them. I felt I was just making the burden greater. We found a house to rent a few months after your father joined us, so that was better."

"Grandma must have been much like you. Is that where you learned to take everything in stride as things came along—like taking people in when they were in need and just accepting it as though it was yours to do? You never seemed to get flustered or resentful; you just welcomed people in as part of the family or as though it was what everyone did."

"That's the way it seemed to you?"

"Yes! You never complained when Daddy invited people home for supper. Remember that time when the man Daddy worked with—I think it was Mr. Graham—came for supper?" Marlene laughed. "He was really struggling with depression and Daddy told him what he needed was to have supper with a family." Her shoulders began to shake as she first chuckled, then abandoned all control to let herself dissolve into a full-blown giggling fit. She sat on the chair at the end of the table and laughed until the tears ran down her cheeks. She attempted to catch her breath. "When . . . when . . . when he got to our place, he saw the table set for the whole family. He apologized and said Daddy had told him to come, but he hadn't realized we were having company!"

Rina joined in with gales of laughter as Marlene related the story. "When you told him that it was just our family and that we always had room for one more, he didn't really believe you until you yelled 'Supper!' and we children came running from every direction!"

Rina took her glasses off and wiped the tears from her eyes. "I thought his eyes were going to pop right out of his head as I introduced him to each of you. If he ever got to see a 'Ma and Pa Kettle' movie after that, he probably thought he had seen it all before!"

Mother and daughter joined in waves of merriment as they recalled the utter astonishment and uncertainty Mr. Graham revealed in his expression.

Marlene wiped her eyes. She could scarcely speak for laughing. "His eyes just got bigger and bigger and he almost looked as though he thought he had landed in an insane asylum. I think we had a few more manners than the Kettle bunch, but it's probably an understatement to say we overwhelmed him."

"Once he resigned himself to the reality of such a big family, he did enjoy himself, though, and told your father that it was better than a whole bottle of medicine!" Rina gave her eyes a final wipe and put her glasses back on. "He came a few more times after that—I guess he got over the shock."

"Whenever anyone dropped in, Daddy would always welcome them and go put the kettle on. I am sure many thought 'Wow! What a man, that he should be so hospitable.' Then when the kettle boiled, he would say, 'Rina—make them some tea and give them something to eat,' as though he thought he had done the lion's share!"

"A real fifty-fifty deal, eh? Ah, well, I usually didn't mind, but there were a few times I resented it a tad, like when someone came just at the time I'd sat down for a minute's rest after a hard day's work. But that's the way it is in a marriage. Everyone has to give a bit! Your dad worked hard to make a living for us all. You know I still miss him! I'd be glad to make a cup of tea for him or his company anytime if he was still here."

"I'm sure you would, Mama. When we were small we hardly got to know Daddy because he was off to work before we were up, and if he did get home before we went to bed he often had a rest and then ate after we were sleeping.'"

"That was because of his stomach. He had to be relaxed when he ate. He was often too tired to eat when he first came home. It would have been nice if we'd known a whole lot sooner that it was a hiatus hernia that was bothering him for much of his life. "

"I know—he always seemed to have a bad stomach. I am awfully glad we got to know him better in his retirement years, and especially when both of you lived here for a bit before he had to go into the nursing home. It was so good to see that side of him on a daily basis." Marlene started giggling again.

"Remember the time he tied Rip to the lawn mower to keep him out of his way? A dog ran past on the road by our place and Rip took off after him—lawn mower and all. There was the little beagle running for his life, a big Doberman hot on his heels, a lawn mower in tow and an old man shouting and running as fast as he could after the whole lot!"

Rina laughed. "Now don't get us started again! I can still see it! Your dad didn't really like Rip to start with, but he didn't want James's lawnmower to get damaged!" Another laugh erupted from deep within her chest. Off came Rina's glasses as she once more laughed until the tears ran down her cheeks. "That was funny! It was just good that no cars were coming right then."

"That old lawn mower was bouncing and weaving like crazy! I don't know what would have happened if that little beagle would have gone through the fence! Poor old Rip, coming to a sudden stop, would have got whacked in the behind by a lawn mower before Daddy had a chance to do it himself!"

Marlene chuckled again as she rose to her feet, wiping her own eyes. "If we all need a good belly laugh each day to stay healthy, you and I should have it made today! I should take advantage of it and get doing the newsletter that is due the end of the week. Do you want to sit on your recliner, or what do you want to do?"

"Would you mind getting my pictures out? I want to mark a few more of them so if I'm gone you will know who and what they are. Maybe that's why the good Lord hasn't taken me home—I should have had them done years ago. Since I'm still kicking around, I might as well make myself useful."

Marlene brought the big box and set it on the chair beside her mother.

"Do you need anything else?"

"I don't think so. I think I stuck a pencil in beside the soap boxes here."

The big box held six laundry soap boxes she had long ago cut down as file holders. Each box held large envelopes salvaged from the mail and relabelled to indicate which year the pictures were taken. She had got that far but had neglected the marking and getting them into albums.

I doubt whether I will ever get them into albums, but at least if I write on the back who is in the pictures, they will be less apt to be thrown out when I am gone. Then they can be given to the families of those photographed, since they would probably appreciate that pictorial bit of their history— at least I hope so, anyway.

Hmm-mm! Since I have been living in 1928, I may as well start there. We couldn't afford to have many pictures taken then. Here's one of the Windsor house. I almost forgot we had a picture of that! It didn't really hold many happy memories, but it was the place where we learned how important family and friends are to us. Here we are on the front steps of the house before we got sick.

Ah-hh, this one is after we got back to Mama's house.

IT WAS NICE to be at Mama's, but oh, how she missed David. He came a few weekends to look for work and finally found a job with one of the garages in Stafford. Rina called around to see if there were any houses available to rent, but they still lived with her parents for another two months before she finally found a place. They moved in time for Doris' birth in November, but Rina went back to Mama's house to have the baby.

Each new baby changes the framework of a family, and so did Doris. Murray was still recuperating from his illness, but suddenly he was no longer the baby of the family. When Rina got back home, she couldn't believe how big he was. Jessie just took another one under her wing—such a little nurturer! Evelyn, from that time on, found her niche with her Aunt Marta and Uncle Stuart. David, of course, was just as proud of Doris as each of the others.

Here's Evvy at Marta and Stuart's house.

They really took the responsibility of being Evvy's godparents seriously. Marta often helped out whenever Rina got bogged down in her responsibilities.

Many times Rina found herself uttering a "Thank goodness for Marta and Steve! Evvy almost lived with them during that time in Strafford—in fact Rina thought she liked it better there than at home. There she was the center of attention without competition from the rest of her siblings. Rina conceded that you really couldn't blame her for that.

They even made a little cart to take her back and forth from our place to theirs and she would ride in it like a little princess.

The little stinker! Once, when she was about five and a half, I remanded her for something and she made quite a statement:

"YOU SHOULDN'T TALK to a visitor like that! My home is at Aunt Marta's and I just came here for a visit and then I got the measles—that is why I had to stay!"

"Just a minute there, missy! You are *my* daughter, not Aunt Marta's, and you will listen to me or you might just find yourself in bed without supper!" whereupon, Evvy got a little swat on her bottom.

"Mama!"

"Mary Evelyn! That is enough!"

Evvy's lower lip protruded into an exaggerated pout. She watched out of the corner of her eye to see if that would make her mother reconsider her attitude. When her best effort didn't have any visible effect, she opted for lifting her head in regal snobbery and walking proudly out of the room. Rina figured Evvy knew better than to push the limits any further, so she let her go.

Chapter 13

RINA PUT THE LAST of the 1927–28 pictures back in their envelope. Then she pulled out the 1930 envelope and scattered the contents on the table.

Here is our Dubbin residence! What a palace! Rina's wry grin belied the truth of that statement.

LIFE IN STRATFORD became quite comfortable. They had lived there a bit over a year and a half since their time in Windsor. It seemed almost too good to be true.

I guess it was! Rina grimaced at the memory.

One night at the end of August, David came home from a training session with a horse after his regular work.

"Rina, what would you say to another move?"

Rina was glad she had her back turned to him. *This husband of mine—always coming up with a new idea to make better money— and I'm sure that's what this will be about. If only it wouldn't usually mean another move! I think we should have all our furniture on wheels!*

"Where would we be moving this time, David?"

"Aw, Rina, don't say it like that!"

"I'm sorry, David, but you know number six is on the way, and this time we have a decent house where Marta can help out when I need it."

"I know, Rina, but this would be a chance to start a business of my own. We'd have the garage downstairs with living quarters above. That way my work would be close to home."

"Where is it, David?"

"It's in Dubbin, which is just about five or six miles from Malden, so we would be quite close to your parents. I really would like to give it a try—I would be working for myself, and what money I get will be ours. Instead of running from one job to the other to make ends meet, I could take as much work as I need to all in one place and not far away from the family."

"That sounds as though it could be good," Rina relented and turned toward her husband. She stroked the side of his face. "I want you to be happy in what you do, and you have been working so hard."

"So I can say 'Yes' to Mr. Rundle?"

"Mr. Rundle? Who is he?"

"He is the man who owns the place. It's an old blacksmith shop that was made over into a garage. There are living quarters above it with an outside stairway and entrance."

"I hate the thought of moving again, but I guess if that is what you want . . ."

"I do think it is a real opportunity for me—well for us, really! Did you want to have a look at it before we move?"

"How soon do you want to start?"

"Mr. Rundle said the sooner the better. The man who was running it found another place in Seaforth, so in order to keep the customers happy and before they find another place to take their business, it would be good to get going right away."

"I guess I trusted you when we moved to Windsor, so I can trust you again."

"The Dubbin place isn't as good as the house in Windsor, but you are good at fixing things up to make it look homey, so I think you can make this place into a decent home."

"I'll start packing again."

"I'll get my brothers to bring their wagons to load the furniture. Would this weekend be too soon?"

"If we are going to move, it would be good to do it now so the girls can get started at the school when it begins rather than later."

RINA'S FIRST SIGHT of their new living quarters almost daunted her willing spirit. The front of the property was strewn with car parts and odds and ends of metal and steel. She could see by the little two-by-four building out behind the garage that the bathroom facilities were housed there, and her spirits sagged at the implications. How many trips up and down the stairs would that require? The worn and not-too-sturdy stairs to the living quarters were at the back of the building. Seven months pregnant as she was, those steps didn't look particularly inviting.

As she ascended on her first trip up, she wondered what she would find. At the landing, she took a deep breath, turned the knob and opened the door. The first thing that greeted her eyes was the large tear in the worn linoleum that covered the kitchen floor. A dry sink stood against the wall under the window to the left of the door. One door of that piece of furniture, with a hinge missing, leaned out at a crazy angle and an open drawer revealed a filthy oilcloth lining. The walls had been papered in the long-ago past with a light pattern of tiny orange flowers and tea pots, but it was faded and streaked with tell-tale signs of water stains.

From the ceiling a single bulb hung from an electrical cord. At least there was electricity! There was room on the other side of the door for a table, but with seven people, it would be crowded. An old kitchen stove stood opposite the dry sink. She hoped it worked well. Firewood or coal would need to be carried up the steps.

Almost dreading to go further, she moved toward what appeared to be a hallway off of the kitchen. To the left was a room that she assumed would be a living room or at least a sitting room. The bare floorboards had been painted, but they were quite worn in the centre of the room and toward the door at the far end. In this room, too, the walls had antiquated brown-toned wallpaper with darker brown roses surrounded by gold and dark brown leaves. Slowly, she moved through the room toward the open door.

There she found a small bedroom, barely big enough for a double bed and a bit of room to move around it. Back in the hall, she found two more bedrooms on the other side, one not much bigger than the first and the second not as big. The last three rooms had only rough board walls. She sighed deeply. It would take every ounce of her creativity to make this place liveable!

She and David would take the biggest room so there would be enough space for the new baby's cradle. The three older girls could have the next biggest, but would have to sleep three to a bed. The smallest room could probably hold two cribs for Murray and Doris. There wasn't room for dressers in the children's rooms, so she would get some orange crates from the grocery store and cover them with old sheets. Decorated with a bit of patterned fabric, they would do.

She heard the men coming up the steps, so she scurried out to the kitchen to direct them to the right places. She was glad the children were with her mother for the day so they could get things set up with less interruption.

When David appeared on the bottom side of the bedsprings, she asked, "Where do I get water so I can wash things up a bit before we put dishes away?"

"Oh, I forgot to tell you. We will have to carry water from the neighbour's pump across the road. I'll get you a pailful as soon as we set this in the bedroom."

Rina gulped in stunned surprise. "We have to carry all the water we need from across the road?"

"Don't worry, Rina. I will do it. I know you can't—right now, especially. I'll make sure you have all you need. That's one advantage of having my work right downstairs."

"I would like to wash the bedroom floors before we set up the furniture. So if you want to unload your tools and things first, I will do that as quickly as I can."

David did go right away to get her a pailful. Using the rag mop, she quickly washed the floors—except for the kitchen.

"David, could you get me another pail of water?'

"Already? What did you do with it all?"

"The floors were quite dirty, David. As it is, I will need to wash the living room floor again, but the bedrooms should be alright."

With the next pail of water, she put in a bit of vinegar and washed the kitchen windows first. Then she added more disinfectant before she washed the inside of the cupboard. Inside, she found some screws that she surmised came from the offending hinge. She looked in the warming oven of the range and found a small box of matches. She lit a few and immediately blew them out. From the pail of tools and supplies she had brought with her she got a small bottle of glue. With the matchsticks well covered with glue, she stuck them into the holes from which the screws had worn loose and broke them flush with the edge. When the glue was dry, she would fasten the hinge once more.

Just washing the sink inside and out made the water filthy. She would need another pail of water to finish and make it presentable before she would feel comfortable to put their things into it. Thank goodness they had their own kitchen cabinet for their dishes!

Her niece, Clair, arrived to help with the second load. "This isn't the nicest place you have ever lived," was her only comment before she went to work. It kept both the women busy putting things away. By the time they had the furniture in place and the beds made up, Rina was exhausted.

Clair came from the bedroom to the kitchen. Rina wearily turned from the cupboard where she was putting the last dishes in place. "Herbert is coming down the road with the children. I'll go and show them the way in."

"Oh, thank you! Those stairs look formidable to me right now." Rina pulled a chair from the table and sat down with an exhausted sigh.

"This is where we're going to live?" Jessie's incredulous voice floated up the stairs and through the open door. Jessie, Evelyn and Bernie came through the door first and, soon after, Clair, with twenty-two-month-old Doris in her arm and four-year-old Murray held firmly by the hand.

"Hi darlin's! Did you have a good day at Grandma's?"

"We have to live here?" Evelyn asked.

"We *get* to live here!" Rina corrected with a forced cheerfulness.

"Can't I go home with Clair and live with Aunt Marta and Uncle Stuart?"

"No, Miss Prissy! We would miss you too much, so you get to stay here with the rest of us."

"Where are we going to sleep?"

"Yes, Mama, where are we going to sleep?" Jessie wanted to know.

"Come, I will show you the bedroom. All three of you are going to sleep in the same bed! Won't that be fun?"

"But Mama," Evelyn objected, "Bernie moves around so much. She sometimes kicks me."

"No I don't, Evvy!" chided Bernie.

"Now girls, you will get used to it. See, this room doesn't look bad. I put your curtains from our other house up here, and I will fix up an orange crate for your clothes. It will look pretty."

"Anybody home?" Herbert came through the living room. "Your mom sent some supper along in case you might be hungry. She thought you might not be set up to make a meal yet and maybe would be too tired anyway."

Rina sighed with relief. "Oh good! That's just like Mama! We probably would have dined on bread and jam tonight if it was up to me. Come, children, let's see what Grandma sent for us. Jessie, will you go downstairs and tell your daddy that supper is ready?"

Before long, the family was gathered around the table, dining on potato salad, coleslaw and sliced beef. Apple pie was a tasty dessert.

THE THIRD WEEK in September there was a hard frost and a few days with a cold wind. Those days did more than herald autumn weather—they revealed an alarming lack of insulation in their living quarters. With both a new baby and winter in sight, Rina knew she had to do something to make it warmer. She asked any of the neighbours who got a daily paper to save them for her. She did the same at the corner store and asked if they would also save any cardboard cartons. By a week before her due date, the outside wall of their bedrooms and the north and west walls of the kitchen were covered with layer upon overlapped layer of newspapers stapled on, then topped off with neatly cut squares of cardboard firmly tacked on to keep everything in place. She had even fashioned a leaf stencil and made a decorated border by using crayons to colour them. The rest of the rooms would have to wait until after the baby was born.

Chapter 14

ON OCTOBER TWENTY-SECOND, 1930, the children were taken to their grandparents, and by early morning of the twenty-third, Rae Bartholomew had arrived—another son that pleased his daddy and made him determined to give his family a good start.

I think Rae was born with a spark of mischief in his eyes, looking around to see where he could start using it! Rina chuckled. *Poor little tyke! We could barely keep him warm enough some days that winter. Even with the walls thickly covered with paper and cardboard, the window frames weren't the tightest and the snow sometimes drifted in through the gaps. We wore more clothes in that house than anywhere else we lived. The fuel all had to be carried upstairs too, and the oven was always full of bricks ready to wrap for warming beds or feet or whatever was in jeopardy of getting frost-bitten.*

Oh, here is a picture of Doris with Trixie in front of the garage. I didn't like them to be out there much because there was so much old machinery there. I was afraid they would get hurt. But of course, that is where they wanted most to be. They liked climbing up on things and pretending they were on a car or tractor or something. If Rae would've been older when we were there, he would have more scars than he already has!

"How ARE YOU getting along, Mama?"

"Oh, you know how it goes—or maybe you're not old enough for that. I get looking at the pictures and remembering, and then I forget what I am supposed to be doing. I have written on the backs of any that needed it from '27 and '28. I'm on 1930 now and remembering the old garage at Dubbin. Rae was born there and just about froze in his cradle sometimes. It was so cold up there.

"My papa died just about a month after Rae was born. It was so hard! He had been coming along so well after the first stroke. He just took another massive stroke and was gone! For so long I felt like a part of the larger family, but when I finally figured out I was Papa's only child, I realized why we always had a closer relationship. He was a special man and he always made me feel so special too! Mama was grief-stricken and hated living alone. After Christmas she decided to come and help me with the work. She felt so sorry for me living up there in that drafty barn of a place. Did I ever tell you that water had to be carried over from the neighbour's pump? Daddy usually did it, but sometimes I had to, with all that washing by hand for eight people—including a toddler and a baby in diapers. It was a big job."

"Didn't you say that Grandma caught a cold there because it was so chilly?'

"Well, she had actually caught the cold before she came, but then she got pneumonia. The doctor came to see her and ordered her back home. "

"I thought it was something like that." Marlene finished her glass of water and moved toward her office. "A lot of memories in those pictures, aren't there? I would like to join you, but if I am going to get that newsletter done I'd better get back to my computer."

I was so embarrassed when the doctor came. It was a really cold day and most of the children had their coats on to stay warm—as did Mama.

DR. PERCY, after examining Mama, was placing his equipment back in his bag when he paused, looking up at Rina with a puzzled look bordering on disgust.

"Mrs. Litz, your mother needs to get back to her house where she can stay warmer. In fact, why would you and your children be living in a place like this when your mother has a solid, warm house that is big enough for all of you? This is really not fit for habitation. Your husband should know that."

She wished she could just fade through the walls or sink through the floor. She felt such a mixture of shame and defence she didn't know which to express first.

"Dr. Percy, I know it's not the best place to have our home, but David is trying hard to make a living for us. We hope this can be a temporary place until he gets a little ahead." She paused and hung her head. "It isn't always this cold." Her voice diminished in strength. "Besides, when he is trying so hard, a wife has to stick by her man."

"That's an admirable sentiment, Mrs. Litz, but perhaps a bit misplaced. You have to think about your own health and that of the children. Perhaps you could at least move back with your mother to nurse her back to health and stay for the rest of the winter anyway."

He put on his hat and went to the door. "Try to find someone with a car to take your mother back to Malden so she can stay warm, then get the medicine I have prescribed at the drug store. I will visit her there tomorrow."

When he left, Rina shut the door and leaned against it. "Oh Lord, what have I done now? Papa is gone and now am I going to be the cause of Mama going too? Poor David is working so hard and I wanted to stick by him and show him my support. Wasn't that the right thing to do? We've been apart too much already. Please help us know what is best. Please, Lord?"

It seemed like only moments until David came through the door.

"Clint Bentley said he would take you all back to Malden in his car. What all will you need to take along? I can bring more in few days; just take what you need right now."

Rina reached out and put her hand on David's shoulder. "Dr. Percy must have talked to you. What did he say? And are you sure this is alright?"

David pulled her into his arms. "He gave me quite a talking to! He told me I should know better than to keep my family in such poor quarters, that your mother was way too sick to be in such a cold house and that I had better get you all to Malden as soon as possible if I want to keep you alive." He looked like a hurt puppy. "I am so sorry, Rina. I know it isn't the kind of house you deserve, but I thought this would be a start for us in our own business. I meant well, and yet, I'm not treating you the way I thought I would or the way I would like. I just can't seem to succeed in anything I try."

"Oh David! I know you are trying. I told Dr. Percy that I understood that and I wanted to stick by you. I wish he wouldn't have been so hard on you."

"Oh, I deserve it, Rina. I shouldn't have asked you to move in here, especially with the baby and winter coming on. But right now, Dr. Percy said we have to get your mother out of here and she needs to have someone to care for her. You may as well take the children and go with her. It will be easier for you there. I will come for the nights whenever I can."

"Oh David, I don't like when we have to live apart."

"I know, honey-babe! I'll probably be there most nights. But you need to look after your mom. I would feel awful if we were the cause of something from which she didn't recover."

"She did have a cold before she came."

"Yes, but she shouldn't have come here when we can't keep it warm enough. You get together the diapers and clothes you need for you and the children. Clint will be here in about half an hour. I'll look after the children until you are ready."

By evening, Rina had her mother in her own bed and the children settled in the rooms upstairs. She decided to spend the night on the couch with Rae in a makeshift bed beside her. That way she could hear if her mother needed her through the night. She had to admit it was nice not having to wear coats in the house.

Most nights, David did make it to Malden. He was quieter and often didn't want much to eat. From that time on, he seemed to have a stomach-ache most of the time. It took Ellie several weeks to be up and about very much. Rina tried to make tempting food to get both David and her mother eating again.

"Come on, Mama, you always liked potato soup with onions. Try to eat a little more. You have to get eating again to get your strength back."

"Rina, it is good soup, but I just don't have much appetite. With your papa gone, I just don't seem to care much whether I live or die. I miss him so much.'

Rina reached over and took her mama's hand in her own. "I know, Mama. I miss him too, but we still need you, so please try to get better."

"I think you would manage without me, Rina. I can't stay around forever."

"I know that, but you are only sixty-seven and we would like to keep you around for a bit yet."

"Life just isn't the same without Papa."

"Aw-ww Mama! I know, but give yourself some time. You will learn to get along. It's not like you to give up."

"I know, Rina. Maybe it's just that I still don't have my strength back and I got sick so soon after Papa died. It just makes me feel that it isn't worth it to go on. I don't want to worry you, though. You have enough on your plate."

"Mama, I am glad to be able to look after you, but let's hope that soon you will be looking after yourself again and enjoying life."

By the end of January, Ellie was noticeably weaker. She spent most of her days on the rocking chair or couch, reading to the children or snoozing when they were playing or sleeping. Rina glanced over to where Ellie sat, her head against the back of the rocking chair. Her face was wan, her eyes half shut.

You are going to die on me, aren't you, Mama? The thought seared itself in blazing colour on the inner sanctum of her brain. Her reaction was immediate. *No, Mama, no! I need you yet! Please, Lord, let her stay with us for a while yet.*

That little moment of clarity also brought into sharp focus what a great influence her mother had in her life—how precious their relationship was and how much she treasured the gift of independence and trust she had received from both her parents. She knew very well that her actions, her adventures, her "escapades" were not always in line with her mother's highest wishes, yet she had always felt Mama's patience and steadfast belief that, in the end, her daughter would do the right thing. What a blessing to have the freedom to try things on her own and in her own way and yet be certain of her parents' support! She had made mistakes—lots of them, and she probably would still make some, but she liked to think that she learned from her mistakes and was becoming more skilled and mature at thinking things through before dashing headlong into the first idea that came to her.

What a blessing to have had parents like that! Not everyone was so fortunate. To think that she might not have a long time left with her mother brought a literal physical pain to her chest. She determined to make whatever time she had left count by giving her mother all the care and appreciation she could.

In the days following, Rina often brought up incidents from the past for them to remember together, then would tell Ellie what she had learned from the experience and how much she appreciated the belief and trust that helped her mature and become confident in her ability to make right decisions.

"Remember, Mama, when I cut my hair because the boys kept pulling it?"

"Yes, I do! I always liked your lovely long hair, and all of a sudden it was gone!"

"You could have really scolded me, but you didn't! Now I know that it may not have been such a good solution to the teasing I had endured, but your acceptance of my attempt to do something to stop it gave me confidence to take action instead of accepting that I couldn't be anything except the butt of someone's teasing. Thank you for being that kind of mother!"

"Oh Rina, that wasn't such a big thing!"

"Oh, but it was, Mama. Then I just kept cutting a bit more and a bit more off. Finally, you just gave me some money and told me to go to the barber and let him even it off for me. I think I was the first girl in Malden to have a bob cut. You probably got some grief from your friends and the church people about that, but you never told me or made me feel as though I had brought shame to you."

"Rina, it really doesn't matter what other people think if you are doing the right thing." Ellie's shoulders shook as she chuckled. "Not that I think that cutting your hair was an undeniable necessity! But to me, it wasn't that important either way. If that is what you had to do to gain some self-esteem and show your individuality, I could accept that. You could have done far worse!"

One day at noon, Rina asked her mother to ask the blessing. As usual, she was touched by her mother's honest conversation with God. When Ellie was finished eating and had gone back to her rocker, Rina tucked the little ones in for their nap and settled down on a chair near her mother with a pile of mending.

"Mama, did I ever thank you for your prayers? The one thing other than your love that envelopes my memories of growing up is the way that everything was surrounded with prayer. There may have been a few times when it irked me because I knew that praying about it was going to impress on me the error of my ways, but usually it was such a comfort because the relationship between you and God was so real. Your prayers always brought God into the situation and there was such security in the knowledge that we were not alone. That helps me even now. Sometimes I forget, but because of the way you always looked to God, it is apt to be the first place I turn when I am in trouble."

"Rina, I don't think I could have made it through the early days of my marriage to John if it hadn't been for prayer. I was still in love with my first beau even though I had gone through the break-up with him and was married to John as my parents wanted. I struggled a lot between that lingering affection and knowing that, if my life was to hold any happiness, I needed to leave love for Gerhard behind and begin to love John."

Ellie closed her eyes and rocked in silence for a moment.

"God was good, though. I think my love started with pity for John when he started sharing more of his feelings of grief with me. I had asked him to do that. It was hard for him and I began to ache for him, but somehow that grew into love. I still remember the night after he and your dad had been working in the bush. As they worked, he realized it was the anniversary of the day he asked my sister, Regina, to marry him. A wave of grief hit him that day and for the first time he could hardly wait to tell me about it. That night I realized that I really did love him."

The soft squeak of the rocker marked a steady rhythm that drummed on Rina's heart with the wrenching agony that her mother was describing.

"It wasn't the deep love that came later, but it was a reassuring touch that set my heart at rest and let me know that I had done the right thing—well, maybe not so much that as I knew that God was honouring our willingness to give it our best. I knew from that moment on that true love would come."

"Mama, I can't imagine how you could have done what you did. How hard it must have been for you!"

"But Rina, you yourself recognized part of the good that came from it. You just told me that what I learned—to turn everything over to God—helped envelope your childhood in security. So you see, just because we think something is hard doesn't mean that good can't come from it if we are willing to grow through the difficulty. It becomes not just something you learn to live with, but a life of true joy. In fact, what I have seen in your life makes me think that the apple hasn't fallen far from the tree, as they say. You haven't exactly run away from the difficult things in your life! You may not fully know the joy of that faithfulness yet, but it will come."

"But Mama, I never faced anything as hard as that!"

"We see the difficulties of others as a whole, big picture. What we ourselves face comes to us one moment at a time in the daily wear and tear of life. If we ask God into those moments, we receive strength as we need it. Remember that, Rina, and you will face each one of your troubles with a calm acceptance. But remember, too, that you need only take them one moment at a time. If they are too much for you, then it is not your problem. Turn it over to the One who is able. Eventually you look back on life and see how faithful and wise God has been."

"That is good advice, Mama. Thank you for sharing it with me. Having you for a mother is such a blessing."

Rina's heart swelled in agony, knowing the time for her mother's insight might be almost gone. Ellie's health and strength were clearly fading.

Chapter 15

RINA REPLACED THE ENVELOPE in the box and reached for her walker. She had to find an easier chair to sit in. The rest of the pictures could wait until another day.

Funny, but even after all these years, I hate to think about my dear Mama dying!

"Are you alright, Mama?" Rina heard Marlene's chair roll back from her computer desk.

"I've just had enough of sitting on this hard kitchen chair. The pictures will have to wait; I'm headed for the recliner."

"Here, let help you." Marlene moved the chair out of the way.

"You baby me too much! I can surely make it from the kitchen to the recliner on my own."

"It's good for me to have a change in position anyway, Mama."

"I was just remembering the winter that my parents died. Rae was born in October, Papa died in November, the kids and I moved in with Mama in January. Your daddy announced that he had found us a new place to live at the Swinging Gate Inn in Cozy Corners when Grandma was quite sick, so he moved our things from Dubbin while I stayed on until Grandma died in February. It was quite a year!"

"How did you do it all?"

"I guess it was then that I began to take Grandma's advice seriously, and that is how I did it."

"What advice was that, Mama?"

"She told me to take life one moment at a time and reminded me that God would give me strength for each one. She also said if anything was more than I could handle, then it wasn't mine to handle. I could leave those with the Lord."

"Ah-hh! I have heard you say that many times!"

"Well, it is still true!" Rina felt for the arms of the recliner and lowered herself into its welcoming comfort. "That feels better!"

"I'll bring you a drink yet and your morning cookie, then I will get back to my work."

"Thanks, Marlene! You are a good daughter!"

Marlene's kiss landed like a butterfly on her forehead before she disappeared into her office. Rina smiled at the warmth and lightness it brought to her.

FOR THREE DAYS before Ellie died, she scarcely ate a thing. Sipping away at a cup of tea was about all she took for nourishment. She slept a lot, and Rina tried hard to keep the children quiet. Murray and Doris seemed to sense there was a reason that they should play quietly. A sense of sorrow yet hushed expectancy filled the house. Then at mid afternoon on the third day, Ellie called Rina.

"I'm hungry. I'm hungry for oatmeal porridge. Would that be too much trouble?"

"Of course not! It will take me a little while to make, but I'll start right away. Is there anything else you want?"

"No, I don't think so. Are the others in the living room?"

"There are only the three little ones and me right now."

"No, I meant the others."

"Who did you mean?"

"The ones who came for me."

Rina was puzzled. "I will get your porridge, Mama."

When Rina came with a small dish of porridge, Ellie had her eyes closed. She paused, wondering whether to wake her or let her sleep. Ellie moved slightly and opened one eye.

"Help me sit up, Rina."

Rina set the bowl on the bedside table. Tenderly, she lifted Ellie to a sitting position, then sat beside her to give her support and reached for the bowl. Ellie took the spoon and succeeded to get a small mouthful. Three times the spoon travelled between the bowl and her mouth.

"Um-mm! That tastes good!" She took another spoonful.

"That's enough. Thank you." Ellie patted Rina's leg and reached toward her with her lips puckered. Rina leaned closer and was rewarded with a kiss on her cheek. Suddenly, Ellie's hand dropped and she fell backward. Being unprepared for the sudden collapse, all Rina could do was to ease her fall to the bed.

"Mama! Are you alright?" But one look at her mama's face told her that she was gone. "Oh Mama! Dear Mama!"

Gently, Rina picked up Ellie's legs and swung them around, then straightened her torso so she was laying the right way on the bed. She leaned down to place a kiss on her mother's cheek.

"That one's for you, dear Mama!" A sob caught in her throat as she realized that her mother's last effort in life was a kiss for her. "Oh Mama, what am I going to do without you?"

She sank to her knees on the floor beside the bed, caressing her mother's worn hand. Feelings of loss and sadness flooded over her. Admitting her helplessness and inability to cope with the present reality, she turned her face upward.

"Dear Lord, this is one of those times when I truly need to take it one moment at a time and depend on you for strength and comfort. You know what an anchor-post Mama has been for the fence of my life. Now she is gone. Please, Lord, will you take over and keep me from being pulled out of alignment with your will for my life? My parents have been such an unwavering and steady influence in my life. Thank you for blessing me with such good parents. Help me, right now, to know what to do first."

David was at work, but if she telephoned the inn, she should be able to reach him. Maybe she should call the doctor first. She closed the door to Mama's room and went to the telephone. With the doctor notified, she called David.

"Hello?"

"David—" Rina's voice broke.

"Rina? What is the matter?"

"Oh David, it's Mama. She's—she's gone, David."

"She died?" Rina could hear the unbelief in his voice.

"Yes, just so quickly! She said she was hungry for porridge, so I made her some. She ate three or four bites, gave me a kiss and then she—she just collapsed, fell back on the bed, and she was gone."

"She didn't choke on the porridge, did she?"

"No. She smiled and said it tasted good, and then she reached over to give me a kiss. Her arm fell down and she went backward. I couldn't do anything but ease her down on the bed."

"I'll just put a closed sign on the door and come right away."

"Oh, I would like that, David. I did call the doctor. He was out on a call but he will probably come soon."

"I'll be there as soon as I can get there. I love you, Rina."

"I know, David. Hurry, I need you."

Rae woke up, so Rina fed him while she waited, to keep him happy. Murray and Doris roused from their naps too. David got there before the doctor. He hurried in the door and took Rina in his arms.

"Rina, my love, I know how you are going to miss your mama. I will too. She was a good mother to both of us."

They sat awhile, remembering the ways Ellie had been so supportive of them. The doctor had just arrived and was still in the bedroom when Jessie, Evelyn and Bernie came home from school.

"Come here, darlin's." Rina reached out to her daughters. David, with Murray already on one knee, lifted Bernie up onto the other one. Rina put her arms around the older girls.

"You know how Grandma has been sick and hasn't eaten much lately? Today she said she was hungry for oatmeal porridge. I made her some and she ate a little. She asked where those other people were—the ones who came for her. I didn't know who she meant, but I think now that it was the angels, because when she was finished eating she said 'Thank you,' gave me a kiss and then the angels just took her to heaven. The doctor is in her room right now, but it is just her body there. Grandma has gone to heaven."

"Is she going to come back tomorrow?" Murray asked.

"No, Murray, she won't be coming back."

Jessie put her arm around Murray. "You'll miss Grandma, won't you?"

"So will we!" chimed the girls.

There was a knock at the door. David set Murray and Bernie on the floor. Above their heads, he looked at Rina. "It's the under-taker," he mouthed. Aloud he said, "Why don't you take the children to the kitchen for milk and cookies?"

"Come, children. I made cookies this morning. Why don't we all go out to the kitchen and have some? Everyone find a chair and I'll have them on the table in no time at all. Jessie and Evelyn, you help the little ones." Rina closed the door behind them and went to the cupboard for the cookies.

The next three days were busy. Rina sent a telegram to George out in Vancouver. He replied with a telegram and a promise of a letter. She felt sorry for him, for he was not able to come. Maria and Marta and many friends and family dropped by even before the formal visitation began. It was gratifying to hear all the ways her mama had influenced and helped people over the years. Everyone had a story about how they had felt Jake and Ellie's love and concern. It seemed there were even more people at the large funeral than had been at Papa's a few months earlier.

A few family members stayed until the next day, and then everyone was gone. The house felt almost as empty as her life now felt without her mother. David was anxious to get his family settled in Cozy Corners, so Rina was torn between heart-break and healing as she and her sisters packed up her mother's house and she prepared once more to follow her husband on a new venture. It seemed every drawer, every chest, every closet held some precious memories from the past.

Maria and Marta made sure to be there the day they went through the things that remained in the Remembrance Trunk, which still stood in the spare room. What memories the items in the chest evoked!

"Most of the things in here didn't have much connection for me, except for the stories we told around the trunk now and then.

You girls know more about it." Rina squatted down on the floor and opened the lid with care.

"Marta, do you remember the day we put the things in the trunk?" Maria asked.

"Barely! I remember how special it always was when we gathered around the trunk and told stories of our first mama."

"Mama did it one of the first Sundays after she and Dad were married. She chose some things of our mama's to keep for us because she wanted to make sure we remembered her. I still recall when she picked up the pile of Mama's aprons. I thought I could still smell Mama. You know, that was a really nice thing for her to do. It helped us keep alive the memory of our first mama because she and Papa kept telling us stories every time we went through the things."

"I sometimes wondered if I really remembered her or if I just remembered her because of the Remembrance Trunk and the times we spent around it. I guess it kept the faint memories alive. Shall we each take one of the aprons?"

"I think so. I don't think George would want one. Even though he, too, referred to her as 'our first mama,' she really wasn't his mother. And besides, he's never worn an apron yet, to my knowledge!"

Maria pulled out the old woollen vest that her papa had worn. "I will take this if that is alright with you. I think I suggested we put this in here after he died."

"Yes, you did, Maria, so then I will have the ink well and pen that he used to do his books. George already has the little bank that looks like a safe that papa had when he was a boy."

"Remember how Mama found the combs Papa bought for her before he died?"

"What do you mean?" Rina's curiosity raised her eyebrows.

"We decided to put some of Papa's things in on that first Christmas after he died. We asked if we could put that little bank in. When she went to get it out of his drawer, she found a pair of combs he had bought for her and hidden in the bank until Christmas. They were the same ones she had admired when they went to Toronto for their tenth anniversary. She didn't know he had purchased them, so it was almost as if he had given her a present for that first Christmas without him."

"Wow! That sounds a little creepy."

"No, Rina, I don't think so. It was more—well, warm and beautiful."

"I already got Mama's ring, the outfit she knit for me and the silver cup when I got married, and I think you got her birthstone ring, your outfit and the little china dog, didn't you Marta?"

"Yes, I did. We'll each take a quilt and divide the pillowcases and the few things that are left."

"You lost both your parents at a very young age. I guess I should be glad I had mine so long, but I do miss them terribly."

"Oh Rina! Sure you do. And remember, your parents really were ours too, even if we weren't born to either of them. They were the only ones we had for many years, and they were good parents! We miss them too. Mama Ellie was always so careful to assure us that we were all one family even though we were quite a hodgepodge household."

"Maria is right! I barely remember my first mother. I remember more about my Papa, but Jake became a real papa to me too! I think they loved us all as their own."

"Do you want the trunk itself, Rina? I guess I am to get the glass cupboard, but other than that, I have all the furniture I need and I think Marta does too, don't you?"

"Yes, Rina. I was to get the bedroom suite because my parents bought that, and if I can have my mama's rocking chair, you are quite welcome to the trunk and anything else you need."

"Thanks! I could use it. We aren't exactly blessed with furniture." Rina's eyes crinkled with laughter. "Of course, as often as we move, the job is easier that way."

WHEN THE LAST room was emptied, David came to take Rina and the load of furniture that was theirs to move into the living space at the Swinging Gate Inn. The final closing of the door to the only home she had known until she and David moved to Stafford was an emotional experience. She asked David to wait outside while she took one more tour of the house.

"Are you sure you don't want me to come along?"

"I like having you with me most of the time, David, but I think this is something I have to do alone. Do you mind?'

"Of course not. I just wanted to be there if you need me."

"You can keep your arms ready for a big hug when I get back. I might need it then."

"I sure will. Take your time and call if you need me."

She went upstairs and wandered through the rooms: the large front bedroom where her parents had always slept and then, later, she and David had shared in the first years of their marriage; then the room that had been George's until he left for the west at only eighteen years of age, the same room which had housed her firstborn babies; the spare rooms which, in her earlier memories, had been used by her older sisters when they came for weekends or holidays; and finally, her old room where she had read into the night, from which she had escaped to go out with her friends, where she had dreamed dreams of adulthood and adventure. She leaned against the bare wall and smiled. Her life now held a good dose more of reality than the romanticized version of adulthood she had conjured up in those days.

I did marry a man who loved the unconventional and shared my passion for adventure as I had hoped. That trait I so desired has led us on quite a diverse path. Sometimes I wonder, with six children in tow, whether I can maintain enough enthusiasm to keep up with him!

Gently, she closed the door and started down the steps—the same steps her mother had descended to marry her dear Papa.

But I still love my David as much as Mama loved her Jake and I will stay with him for the whole ride!

She moved through the room that was a "sewing-room-turned–bedroom" in the last years. She lingered awhile in the large kitchen/dining room. Memories of family meals, homework and family discussions flooded her mind. As she walked into the front living room, she knew what she still needed to do. From the front door she called, "David, can you come in here for a minute?"

"Coming!"

When he came through the door he already had his arms stretched out to her and she gladly went to him.

"Are you alright, my love?"

"I think so, David. It is hard giving up this house and the place that was home to me for so many years, but I suddenly thought about what Mama and Papa would have done at this milestone."

"Pray? Yes, you are right. They did that at every crucial time of their lives as well as every day, didn't they?" He hugged her close. "Do you want to start?"

"Dear Father it seems right now that I am closing the door to a big part of my life. There are so many memories within these walls, so many things that happened here and helped my life become what it is now. Thank you, Lord, that the building that was done here wasn't so much in brick and mortar as it was in the building of character and spiritual and moral values. Thank you that Mama and Papa gave me the gift of a strong faith and a trust that helped shape my life.

"Lord God, it is also special to me that David and I started our family here. Thank you for the support we felt from my parents, right from the beginning. As I wandered through these rooms, I remembered my youthful desire for a husband who loved adventure and had a hankering for the unconventional. You have fulfilled that desire so beautifully in my dear David.

"Please, dear Lord, help us in our unconventional ways to always put you first. Guide our sense of adventure into the paths that would bring glory and honour to you. Lord, especially help us steer the children you gave us into paths that will bring them to you—the Way, the Truth and the Life—so that we will always walk in the light of your Word."

When Rina did not continue after a long pause, David shifted his weight on his feet, then drawing Rina even closer, he prayed.

"Lord I'm not as good at saying things as nicely as Rina, but I am thankful, too, for the memories this house holds for me and for Rina, the wonderful woman who grew up here and now is my dear wife. I have not been able to provide for her as I wish, and I feel as though I have failed her often, but I do love her so and pray that you will bless us all, for Jesus' sake. Amen"

Rina lifted her eyes to David. They were shining with tears. "David, if those words were half as sweet to God as they were to me, he will be pleased! I hope you know how much I love you too. These are hard times, but if we stick together and keep asking him to help us, we'll make it through."

Chapter 16 🍁

WHEN SHE GOT SETTLED IN at the Swinging Gate Inn at Cozy Corners, Rina was glad for the experience she had in working at the hotels in Malden and Stafford before her marriage. With six children to care for, it was hard to look after the inn rooms as well. She was so glad for the way Jessie took responsibility. For a ten-year old, she was a big help in looking after the little ones. She often felt guilty for putting such a heavy load on her young daughter, but she didn't know how else to manage. Evvy, too, was learning to take responsibility and helped in the little ways she could.

There was a nice fenced area at the back of the inn where the children could safely play in the summer. David hung a tire swing from the limb of the big oak tree and put up a teeter-totter fashioned from a low trestle and a board he sanded smooth. He also built a small sand-box that kept the smaller ones amused for long periods. To the now toddling Doris, Rex, the dog, was a friend, an aide in walking as well as a guard. She even used him as a pillow or mattress when she got tired. If he grew weary of having his fur pulled, his ears inspected or his tail yanked, he would gently roll her off and go to the far corner of the large yard. If she got into danger, Rex would be there to place his body between her and the peril, or to cushion her fall.

Rina sometimes felt as though she would wear a path from the living quarters to the inn's kitchen to the back door to check on the children in the yard. She knew Jessie could be depended on to look after the little ones, and when Evelyn was home she would help—even Bernie was good at playing nicely with Murray!—but even so, Rina still felt the need to at least take a look now and then to make sure everything was going smoothly.

In August, David drove to Stafford to get supplies. When he returned, Rina saw him drive in, but noticed he didn't come in right away. After a while she went to see if there was something wrong. He was sitting in the car with the windows open, and he was gripping the steering wheel and staring straight ahead. His face was red, he was breathing hard and he looked angrier than she ever remembered.

"David! What is the matter?"

"Rina, I don't know if I am safe to talk to right now!"

"All right, David. I'll wait until you are ready. Just remember that whatever it is, we'll face it together. I have to go serve the only customer we have in there, then I will come out again."

David just nodded his head and stayed sitting. As she walked back to the house, she thought if she had looked closely enough she might have seen steam coming from David's ears, he was that angry. She wondered what had upset him so much. She was glad the girls and Murray had gone to the neighbours' to play. Ray was asleep.

Feeling uneasy about the unknown incident that caused such anger, she quietly prayed, "Lord, you know what it is. Please help David work it out. Lord, help him put his trust in you."

She refilled the customer's coffee cup and asked if there was anything more he would like. The moment he paid and left, Rina went to the back door. David was just getting a parcel out of the car, so she waited until he came in with it. She closed the door and looked at him.

"Are you ready to talk about it, David? What is it, my love?"

"You won't believe what I saw on the way home today!"

Rina hardly knew if she wanted the answer to something that made him that angry.

"What was so bad, David?"

"I saw my grader! *My* grader! The one I designed! The township just bought one from the company Carl Madison works for. It was *my* design and they haven't asked my permission to use it, nor have they offered me a single penny for it. Here I am slaving away at any little job I can find and they are making money on my design!" He punched his clenched fist into the other open palm, grunting in anger.

"The driver even had the nerve to tell me it was a new design called the Litz grader! He said it does a much better job than any grader he has ever tried. The nerve of that company!"

"David! Wait! Why don't you get in contact with the company— or at least with Carl Madison?"

It seemed David was suddenly drained of energy. He sat down and put his head in his hands.

"Oh Rina! When Carl took those plans, I was so hopeful that it would be a way to give us a better life. I didn't hear anything back from Carl—I guess I should have hunted him up. I did inquire once, but he had moved from Seaforth and I couldn't find out where." David ran his fingers through his hair and sighed in despair. "Why is it that nothing works for me? Even this place isn't paying us the way I had hoped and you are working yourself to the bone trying to keep both the inn and our family going. I didn't mean for you to work so hard."

"David, don't despair! Call the company and ask if they are aware of where those plans came from. Perhaps they will make some compensation. Even if they don't, I guess you have the satisfaction of knowing your plans work. You've made at least one grader operator happy!"

David's face twisted in a grimace. "That should pay for at least a few months' rent, I'm sure!"

David did make phone calls, wrote letters and went to visit anyone he thought might give him some advice to handle the situation. Finally, he received a letter from the company.

Dear Mr. Litz,

In reference to your letter of August 10, we have no record to prove that you had anything to do with the design of our newest model grader. It is mere coincidence that it is called the Litz grader. Your claim to be the owner and designer has no basis in fact. There are many people by that name.

Please do not contact us again. Any further correspondence should be directed to our lawyers, Furnham and Furnham, at the address below.

Yours truly,
Josiah Beasley

The receipt of that letter threw David into a depression that took the joy out of his life. Rina tried to encourage him by suggesting that he turn his ingenuity to other projects—to learn from this experience. He was told that in the future he should make a copy of the plans, mail it to himself making sure the post office date stamp was clear, and then never open the letter so there would be proof of the date the plans were made. But that didn't help the fact that he had been gypped out of any revenue from his grader plans.

The melancholy David felt about the grader affair was not helped by the fact the inn was not bringing in enough money to support their family. In addition to that, the teacher at the school was inept and the girls were falling behind in their work. His stomach was giving him constant trouble so that he could only eat small meals—and those had to be consumed when he was relaxed. If he ate as soon as he came home from work, or in a hurry, he would be in agony from heartburn or stomach pain. It seemed the only time he felt comfortable to talk to Rina about how he was feeling was at night after they were in bed. Some nights Rina wouldn't be finished with the work until late and then he would wake up and want to talk. Even though she knew he needed to pour out his thoughts and feelings, there were nights she was so tired it was hard to stay awake and fully listen.

"Rina, I feel like such a failure! Nothing I try pans out. Sometimes I think if we could stick it out, some of my ventures would eventually start to pay, but meantime we have to feed and clothe our children—you too. How long is it since you have been able to buy a new dress?"

"David, the whole country is in depression and there are many people who are having hard times. Don't blame it all on yourself. We thought mechanics would give you a life work that would pay well, but no one can afford cars right now or at least get new ones. I wish, too, that we could give our children more, but we will give them lots of love and hope they will grow up to remember that more than the things they didn't have."

"The township afforded a new Litz grader!" David spat out. "If I would have been paid for the plans or something on each grader that is sold, we could relax a bit."

"David, please let go of that. It will eat away at your insides, and those people will hurt you twice—once by being dishonest in their dealings, and once by ruining your mental and perhaps even physical health. Darling, we will find another way."

"It will mean another move if this inn doesn't work out!"

"What must be done we will do, David. Please try to let go of your worries and get some sleep." She gave him a kiss that she hoped was reassuring. Every part of her body ached with weariness. She was glad that David could share his feelings with her, but after her long days of hard work, she really needed her sleep. She was so exhausted and depleted by nightfall that it was hard to listen with full empathy. In the morning, she would be able to listen in a more refreshed state of mind, but David seemed to need the cover of darkness to spill his inner feelings.

Rina gave David another kiss, turned over on her other side and reached for his arm to tuck around her as she lay spooned against him.

"I'm still glad you asked me to marry you!"

"Are you sure of that, after all I put you through?"

"Yes, I am! You just go to sleep and dream about a woman who loves you more than she can put into words."

David kissed her shoulder.

"That's my girl! True blue! I'm amazed at how God blessed me with such a woman. "

Oh Lord! You know how deeply I love David. Sometimes that true blue turns a little green when I see David so discouraged. There's a bit of envy that keeps trying to raise its ugly head when I see others able to manage better than we. Some people seem to get all the breaks and we just get broke! She almost chuckled out loud. *But then there are those who are worse off than we. At least we love each other and David always tries to be good to me and to the children—although the children hardly see him because he works so hard. Anyway, I'm too tired to even talk to you about it tonight, and I can't see what more I can do, so I'm just going to dump the whole thing at your feet and let you take care of it. Good night, Lord!* And she was off to sleep almost before she could finish the sentence.

With winter's approach, business dwindled even further. David began to search elsewhere for work. Finally, he came home late one afternoon with a bit of hope.

"Rina, I think I have found a job. It looks as though it could be a steady one. The pay isn't really high, but decent and if we can be sure it will come every week, that's more than we have right now!"

"What is it?"

"Delivering produce from the depot to the stores around this part of Ontario. It will mean long days and being away from home, but the paycheque will be there every two weeks. "

"That sounds pretty good. But we will probably need to find a place to live in Stafford. Did you look for something?"

"I asked around and got the addresses of a few places for rent. One on Monteith sounds as though it could be a respectable space for a manageable rent. I thought perhaps we could go have a look at it tomorrow. Mrs. Higson won't mind watching over things here while we are gone. At the rate of afternoon business recently, she won't have much to do!"

THE HOUSE HAD three bedrooms upstairs, a dining room, a living room, a pantry and a kitchen large enough for a table for them all. Rina thought the living room could be transformed into a down-stairs bedroom for them and the dining room could be their living room. They visited the landlord, gave him a month's rent to hold the house for them and went home to begin the packing process.

On moving day, David's brothers came with their wagons to load up their worldly possessions. When nearly everything was loaded, David's father came to take her and the children to Stafford, where Marta and Clair were already cleaning their new abode in readiness for their furniture.

"We should be there not much more than a half-hour after you get there." David set the small washstand on the back of the wagon and wiped the perspiration from his brow. "We'll start with the bedroom furniture and bring that in the front door and up the steps. The wagon with the downstairs furniture can be brought to the back door."

"All right! Make sure the loads are tied on tightly. We don't want any more broken furniture on this move—especially having to go up Schlueter's hill."

David snapped a towel at her. "You get going! We've moved a few times, so I think we'll make it."

As they approached the house on Monteith, she saw the windows were open.

Marta will have that house aired out so well there will be no sign or odour of any previous dwellers if I have any idea of what she is up to!

The moment the vehicle stopped, the children were ready to bound into the house to give it their inspection.

"Just a minute, children—shoes come off inside the door, but out of the way. I expect Marta and Clair have the floors washed and you aren't going to dirty them again. Make sure you set them behind the door so when the furniture comes the men don't fall over them. Now go slowly, don't run. The house isn't going anywhere. It will wait until you get inside. "

Rina gathered an armful of curtains from the trunk and proceeded to the back door.

The house did smell clean. The cupboard doors stood open and looked freshly washed.

"Hello?" she called at the bottom of the steps. She could hear the children's excited chatter. "This room is for Evvy and me, Bernie and Doris can sleep over here and Murray and Rae can have this room."

"Why can't Doris and I sleep with you and Evvy?" Bernie wanted to know.

"We don't need to. Because there are enough rooms we only need to have two in each room."

"Can't I sleep with you or Evvy instead?"

"Well, maybe you could sleep with me and Evvy could sleep with Doris."

"I don't want to sleep with Doris! She wakes up too often and I'd have to take care of her—you take her and then Bernie can sleep with me."

"That is alright with me. Would that be all right with you, Bernie? Would you like to sleep with Evvy?"

"Sure! That would be nice."

As she climbed the steps, Rina felt the smile rise from her heart and sneak up to curl her lips even as it brought a glistening drop of moisture to her eyes.

Jessie—always the peacemaker and little mother hen. What a treasure she is to this family! Even though some may think of Evvy as looking out for herself rather than her siblings, there is something in her that I can see will stand her in good stead when she faces the world. She knows what she wants and goes for it. She has a good heart! And Bernie—Bernie is usually complacent and content, finding good in any situation and being happy just to be. What a wonderful variety God brings from two parents!

Chapter 17

"WHO WOULD LIKE TO help me hang some curtains?"

Jessie reached for a curtain.

"Bernie, you take the little ones over to the boys' room and I'll help Mama start hanging curtains here."

"We'll have to hurry, Jessie, because the men will be here with the furniture any minute. I just thought it would be nice to have the curtains up before the beds were set up. That way it will feel homey right away tonight."

They heard the clatter of footsteps coming up the stairs. Marta poked her head in the door.

"Oh, there you are! Clair and I just went to get a few things for lunch. We'll get some sandwiches made so they are ready. Perhaps the men would like to eat before they unload."

"I'm not sure David will go for that! I imagine he will want to get things off the wagons first, but it won't hurt to have them ready. I thought they might be here by now."

The upstairs curtains were hung and they had most of the downstairs ones in place, and yet, the men had not arrived. Rina began to feel a sense of foreboding. They were at least an hour late.

"Where would they have gone?"

Marta went out on the front veranda where David's father sat. "There comes one wagon down the street now."

When the wagon rolled to a stop, David's brother Art hopped off and called out, "Rina and Dad, get in the car. We need to go to the hospital."

Rina's hand went to her throat. "What happened? What's the matter?"

Art reached out to put a hand on her shoulder. "Rina, don't panic, but there was a bit of an accident."

"Art! Tell me quick! What happened?" Her legs felt weak and she began to tremble. "Hurry! Just tell me!"

"Rina, we were coming up Schlueter's hill and the load began to slip. David climbed up to tighten the ropes. We aren't sure whether he just slipped or whether the rope broke, but he fell off. They took him to the hospital."

"Did he have broken bones? What was the matter with him . . . he *is* alive, isn't he?"

Art gently led her to the car. "He was breathing when they left. They said it was head injuries. He had blood coming from his ears, but we don't know how serious it is. I think we had better go. Marta and Clair, you can stay with the children, can't you? Ken is coming with the other load."

"Yes of course, Art. We will stay here and get the furniture in the house. You just go, Rina. You need to be with David."

Numb with fear, Rina allowed herself to be led to the car. She covered her face with her hands. All she could think was how her mama had faced the time her first husband, John, had been gored by a bull and she had been left a widow.

Oh David! Hang in there! I need you. What would happen to me and to our six children if we did not have you? We thought we were in a tough place before, but this would be so much worse.

"Dear God, here's something else I can't handle. It's got to be you that takes care of this one. But if you bring David through this, I promise not to get discouraged no matter what comes, as long as we have each other! Please, Lord, keep him safe and make him well again."

Okay, Rina! Practice what you preach. If this is too big for you, then let go and let God take over. Breathe deep! Come on! Breathe deep and let go. Just let go. God can hold David in his hands better than you can. Breathe!

Slowly, a peace descended and she did let go. Dumb as it was, all she could think then was whether David's feet were clean! She chided herself for being worried over such an insignificant detail. She smoothed her hand over her cotton house-dress and was horrified to realize she still had her apron on. Quick as a wink, she removed it and stuck it in her bag. "Worried about your husband's feet and you're wearing a dirty apron!" she snorted.

Even though it seemed forever, she was glad the hospital was not far away. In a matter of minutes, they were there, standing at the front desk asking for David Litz.

"Yes, I am Mrs. Litz, David's wife. Can I please see him?"

"I believe the doctor is still examining him, but I will talk to the nurse and see if you can go in. Please have a seat for now."

"I think I will just stand here and wait if I'm not in the way."

"All right. I will be right back."

Rina backed up against the wall. "Dear Lord, just clear the way for me to be with David." The whispered prayer brought back the peace that had fled momentarily upon entering the hospital. "I know that you have him—and me too—in your hands. Thank you, Lord."

"You can come in, Mrs. Litz. Just follow me."

Her legs felt so weak she wasn't sure she was going to make it down the long hall. Was she, like her mother, going to be faced with widowhood? How would she manage?

The door to the examination room opened. There lay David, his eyes closed. The right side of his head was swollen and scraped. The doctor raised his head and extended his hand.

"Mrs. Litz? I am Dr. Rosenfeld. I have examined your husband. He has suffered a rather severe concussion. We will do all we can to keep the swelling down, but we will just have to wait and see what, if any, lasting effects this will have on him."

"He will be all right, though, won't he?"

"Depends on what you mean by all right. At the least, he will most certainly experience headaches for some time, but he should recover eventually. He could experience some anxiety or depression for a while, and light and noise could bother him, so it is best if you can keep things as quiet as possible when he comes home. We will be keeping him in the hospital for at least a week to keep a watch on him."

Rina hardly knew whether she could believe it. Because of her mother's experience, she had been prepared for the worst. Suddenly, depression didn't seem such a chasm anymore. Not that David needed further reason for depression, but if he at least was alive and expected to remain so for the time being, she felt only relief.

The doctor stepped away from the bed. "Why don't you speak to him—see if he responds to you?"

Rina stepped to David's side and reached for his hand. She bent to give him a gentle kiss on the lips.

"David! It's Rina. Can you hear me?"

His head moved slightly.

"Darling, it's me, Rina. Can you wake up and talk to me, dearest?"

It seemed to take a great effort, but finally his eyes opened. The effort to focus appeared to be too much and he shut them again.

"Come on, David. At least say my name."

Again, his eyes opened. His forehead furrowed between his eyebrows. He blinked and again opened his eyes. "Rina?" he whispered.

"Good, David. Yes, it's me!"

"What happened? Where am I?"

Rina glanced up at the doctor with question in her eyes. Should she tell him? The doctor nodded.

"You are in the hospital here in Stafford, David. You fell off the wagon full of stuff we were moving."

"We're moving?"

"Yes. Remember? We are moving from Cozy Corners to Stafford. "

David's eyelids fell shut again for a moment, then opened once more.

"I can't remember. My head hurts too much."

"That's alright, David—just rest. We need you to get well. I love you, David."

"Love you too, honey-babe!"

"Glad you remembered that, sweetie!"

"Always!" David whispered before falling asleep once more.

The next four weeks were a long nightmare. She had to balance settling into a new home, caring for her six little ones and spending as much time as she could at the hospital with David in that first week. During that time, in his periods of lucidity, David wanted to plan what Rina should do if he didn't recover. She didn't want to hear it, and implored David just to rest and get better. She could well identify with her mother's struggle in those hours before John died. She wondered how she would manage if David died. She had six little ones.

Up until recently, she was not feeling particularly close to God. Would she let such an experience drive her to the arms of God or would it cause her to feel abandoned by him? She hoped it would be the former, for right now she needed all the help she could get. During the months of David's recuperation, with her mother's quiet encouragement speaking even from beyond the grave, she began in earnest to seek comfort and guidance from above.

She just couldn't imagine what it would have been like for her mother to pick up the pieces and go on. It still didn't seem fair that one person should have had to endure so much. Through her growing up years, her mother had always seemed to be so strong. Only now could Rina begin to appreciate the reality that it was the difficulties that had produced the strength she saw in her.

After eight days in the hospital, David came home. It was nice to have him in the house, but his inability to tolerate noise and his incessant headaches made the days difficult. Six children make a lot of noise even when they are being good. Again, Marta came to the rescue and often took at least two or three of them to her place for part of the day.

Isn't it good, Rina thought, wiping another tear, *that we don't have to face all the difficulty or make all the adjustments at once? One day, one step, one moment at a time—that is the only way to get through our troubles. Mama was wise enough to know that it also helped to take those steps hand in hand with God. I finally began to absorb Mama's example in a very personal, day-to-day dependency on God in those weeks of David's recuperation.*

CLOUDY DAYS made David feel gloomy. Sunny days gave him excruciating headaches. It seemed he spent more time in the darkened bedroom than anywhere else. His mind was used to being active—always figuring out some new invention or an innovative method for doing the usual—but now, even thinking too hard seemed to bring on another headache. He felt useless in all the inactivity. As days turned into weeks, David worried that his job would be gone by the time he was able to work. Since he had only begun to have hope again and because depression was a result of the concussion, it was an easy slip down the road to that deep dark pit once more. Finally, Rina took it into her own hands. When David retreated to their bedroom for an afternoon rest to appease his headache, Rina closed the kitchen door so David wouldn't hear as she called his boss.

"Hello, Mr. Farquarson. This is Rina Litz, David's wife."

"Oh! Good day, Mrs. Litz. How is your husband doing?"

"Thanks for asking. He is still battling headaches, but he is improving some day by day."

"We're glad to hear that! Do you have any idea when he will be able to start the job?"

"That is one reason I am calling. You still are expecting him and wanting him to work for you, then?"

"Most certainly! We understood from the doctor after the accident that it could be a month or two at least before he was able to work, but my brother-in-law is able to fill in until Mr. Litz can handle it."

"Thank you so much, Mr. Farquarson! The doctor said depression often follows concussion and David has been really worried the last few days that you might not hold his job for him, so I am hoping this news will help him overcome that depression. It may even ease his headaches."

"Would it help if I came to visit some evening to reassure him that the job is his as soon as he can manage it?"

"Oh, Mr. Farquarson, I couldn't ask you to do that. You must be a busy man."

"Yes, I am busy, but the welfare of my employees is part of what I look after. Would tonight suit you? I could be there a bit before seven."

"I certainly hadn't expected that, but it would be so kind of you."

"Then we shall see each other around seven tonight! Good-bye."

Chuck Farquarson's visit was better for David than spring tonic. He sat beside David's easy chair and spoke in quiet tones about the job and how confident he felt that David would be a good employee. He talked about the different routes for each day and something about the store managers along the way and the personal traits and idiosyncrasies of each. More often than not, he would chuckle and finish with a kind remark about how that man was working hard at his business and commend him for his zeal.

"I hope you won't think I am a gossip, David, but if you know what each manager is like, you will know how best to handle them and keep them happy. We like satisfied customers. That is one reason why I hired you. You seem to be interested in people and in finding ways to do the job to the best of your ability. Take your time to heal, and let me know a few days before you are ready to start."

The grasp of his hand and the honest visage of his eyes as he said his goodbye authenticated the sincerity of his comments. David let out an audible sigh as the door closed behind his visitor.

"What a relief! I'm glad he came. After visiting with him I'm really anxious to get to work."

Rina felt warmth spreading from her innermost parts upward, upward until it bloomed in a happy smile curving her lips and a sparkle in her eyes. David had no idea that she had called Mr. Farquarson. That would stay a secret inside of his loving wife, but she was glad it had worked its miracle.

"That sounds like my David!"

She sat on his knee, put her arms around his neck, gave him a kiss then looked deep into his eyes with happiness that still bubbled up from her heart. "Welcome back, my love!"

"Ah-hh my honey-bun, have I been such a trial to you?"

"Just a minute here!" She tapped his forehead with her finger. "I think you've got it wrong. It is you going through a trial. You know when we got married I promised to love you for better or worse, through sickness and health, so it's not so much that you are being a trial to me but that we have been going through a trial together. So when I see a glint of anticipation in your eyes and an enthusiasm about your new job, it looks very much like the light at the end of the tunnel. It gladdens my heart to rejoice with you! Now, I'd better get off your lap before I cut off the circulation in your legs! You'll have more than your head aching!" Her merry laugh as she attempted to rise brought relief to the darkened room as surely as raising the shade to let in the sunshine.

David held her tight. "Not so fast, pretty woman—light of my life! There's a bit of a tax on that gift you just gave me!"

"Just how much of a tax, and how am I to pay it?"

"Another kiss will do—for now—my dear."

Rina gave him a long lingering kiss, running her fingers through his hair at the same time and ending with a gentle massage on the back of his neck.

"Will that do as a down payment?" she asked, slipping off his lap and bending down to place another kiss on the top of his head.

David reached up to stroke her face.

"What a loyal, loving and longsuffering woman I married! What would I do without you?"

"I hope you never have to find out, my love. I know after your accident the question of what I'd do without you haunted me for days. I was quite sure I didn't even want to think about it. I hope neither of us ever have to face that reality—at least not until we are very old. I guess the truth is that one of us will sometime, but I pray that God will be pleased to allow us to grow old together."

"And to that, I will say a hearty 'Amen.' I must admit that, since the accident, I have sometimes wondered if I am more of a burden to you than a help, though."

"Oh David! Don't ever think that. I'd rather go through hardship with you than even a life of ease without you. But I can't imagine how life could ever be easy without you—" the twinkle in her eyes made him wonder what was coming next— "especially raising six Litz children, most of whom take after their defiant and insubordinate parents—can you?"

The sense of camaraderie between them felt like old times.

"Now woman, speak for yourself! Don't drag me into your blanket statements!"

"Oh, no dragging necessary! I seem to remember quite clearly a young David Litz staying on the train past his own stop in order to persuade an engaged woman to dump her fiancé in favour of marrying him! If that isn't defiance, tell me what is!"

David stood up and put his arm around her.

"All right—you win! But if I had it to do all over again I wouldn't hesitate for one minute to do it just the same way as I did. Would you?"

"Not a thing, except maybe to say an unqualified 'yes' right away!"

Chapter 18 🍁

MR. FARQUARSON'S VISIT PROVED to be the turning point for David. His headaches came less frequently, and his mood showed a positive change, for he began to sketch out some plans for swings in the backyard and he put up a better clothesline for Rina. Two weeks later, Rina woke one morning with David up on one elbow watching her.

"David! What are you doing?"

"Good morning, honey-bun! You looked so sweet laying there sleeping. It's about time I made myself useful to you. You have been working so hard and taking such good care of me. I am going to go visit Mr. Farquarson this morning and tell him I am ready to go to work."

"Are you sure you are ready, David? What do you think the doctor would say?"

"When I was there on Monday, he said if I felt well enough, I could go whenever I thought I was ready. I think I am."

"That's good news, love!" Rina's eyes shone as she reached up to stroke the side of his face and ran her fingers through his hair. "Just make sure you don't overdo it. I don't want you to have a relapse or anything."

With a steady income, life seemed easier than it had for some time. Rina still took painstaking effort to use every penny wisely so as to cover the rent and the necessary items to feed and clothe their family, but knowing how much was coming and even which day it would be available each month seemed like such a treat.

Most often, it was three or four o'clock when David left each morning in order to get the supplies to stores early in the day. By the time he finished his route and got the truck back to the depot and loaded for the next day, he managed only a quick supper and then headed to bed to get rested for the next day. Whenever Rina began to feel sorry for herself, thinking it was not much different than being a single mother, her mind would go back to the day they moved when she thought that might actually happen! That usually stopped her negativity and she more often than not turned her face upward with a determined grin.

"Thank you, Lord, that at least I have him beside me in bed for part of each night anyway. Most weekends, when he doesn't go out training horses or fixing cars, we have some time to catch up with each other. Thankfully, I don't have to worry about getting the money, I just need to find ways to make it stretch. And we do sometimes have the bonus of some broken boxes or packages that Mr. Farquarson lets us have for nothing. Forgive me for my complaining!"

We lived on Monteith for a little over a year, then we were on the move again! Looking back, that seemed like such a peaceful year after David got better from his accident. There were no other sicknesses or children's accidents. Even my pregnancy, beginning in June of the next year went smoothly—no morning sickness or anything. I still missed Mama and Papa, but we were close to Marta again. David's mother and I steered clear of each other most of the time, but I developed a good relationship with his father during that year. He sometimes came around and did some of the heavier tasks for me when David didn't have the time for them.

Rina grinned thinking about it. He had to do it when David's mom didn't suspect, but he got quite good at that.

SHE REACHED OUT for a glass of water beside her recliner. As the cool water slid down her throat, Rina remembered how refreshing it was to know that at least one of David's parents had some appreciation for her. Theo Litz gave her a lot of affirmation during that year and even apologized in a roundabout way for his wife's hostility.

A few years later, when he was dying of cancer and had to go to Toronto for treatments, who did he want to have accompany him? Not his wife, not even his daughters. He asked for me! Of course, Fanny found it too distasteful to do the things that would be expected of her. So I went and spent the two weeks down there doing what I could and learning how to care for him when he came home. But that was after we were living back in Malden again. I hated leaving Monteith Avenue!

THE LEAVES were ablaze with fall colours when they had Thanksgiving dinner with Marta and Steve. The walk back to their house was a rare time for them—the whole family taking a casual walk through the fall sunshine. Purple-lined clouds dotted the deep blue sky and the leaves fluttering down and crunching beneath their feet lent an air of serenity. Jessie and Evvy walked ahead. Evvy occasionally picked up an exceptionally bright leaf and chattered away about the things she would like to make with her stash of treasures. Bernie and Murray were kicking up the leaves as they walked, just happy to be in the out-of-doors with their siblings and parents. Four-year-old Doris took turns toddling along and riding piggy-back on her dad's back when she got tired. Rae sat in Marta's old carriage, excitedly chattering away at all the activities and sights.

It was later that evening that there was a knock on the door. Rina was surprised to see Uncle Albert, the husband of her father's younger sister, standing at the door.

"Why, come in, Uncle Albert. What a surprise! Is Aunt Lena with you?"

"No, she stayed at Carl's place. We were all there for dinner, but I had something I wanted to run by you, and I thought since we were only a few streets away, I would come and see you in person rather than write a letter or do it by telephone."

"Well, come on in! Take a chair. David is just out playing a bit of catch with the older children. I'll tell him you are here."

She moved quickly to the back door.

"David, can you come in? Uncle Albert just came."

Rina picked up a sweater or two from the chair beside Uncle Albert and sat down just as David came in the door. He walked quickly across the room, hand extended.

"How nice to see you, Uncle Albert! How is your family?"

"They are quite well. We were all at Carl's today. There are twenty of us if we all get together, and we were able to do that today. "

"We were at Marta and Steve's today—just got back about an hour or two ago. Nice day, isn't it?"

"Yes, it is. We've had quite a nice fall." Uncle Albert stroked his beard. "You're probably wondering what brought me here, so I'll tell you." He stroked the beard again. "You know I have several houses in Malden?"

"Yes, we do." Rina answered, not quite able to keep a puzzled look from her face.

"The people that lived just kitty-corner from where you grew up, Rina, just moved out. Mrs. Clemmer actually died of tuberculosis a few months ago."

"Oh, I'm so sorry to hear that."

"The rest of them have moved to Kitchener to be closer to family, so the house is empty right now." As his hand moved to his beard again, Rina wondered what was coming next.

"I know that you have had some difficulties in the past years, and I just wondered if it would be of any help to you to live in the house rent-free for at least a few years. I'd like to do that for you if you would accept it. Of course, it will take a bit of cleaning up, but if you don't mind doing that, I would let you have it for five years and then perhaps, depending how things are going, you could either pay a little rent or make some improvements in your spare time. I know it would mean driving back and forth to work, David, but it still might help you out. "

Rina looked at David. It seemed like a big decision to make in a few minutes. She could almost see the wheels turning in his head, but before he could say anything, Uncle Albert spoke again.

"This is a little sudden for you to give an answer right away, so I will let you think about it and get back to me. I would like to know by the end of the week if possible. Because of the T.B. it should be fumigated and then it will take some washing of walls, ceilings and floors to make it liveable. I have some paint on hand that could do a few rooms if you want. I'm afraid the Clemmers didn't take the best care of it. The yard hasn't been kept up either, but there is lots of room in the back for a garden, which should help you out too. I don't think you are afraid of hard work, and it is a nice little house."

"Uncle Albert, this is very kind of you." Rina reached out to touch her uncle's arm. "We appreciate your thoughtfulness."

"Yes, we do!" David reached out to shake his hand again. "We'll definitely let you know in a few days, and it does sound good. Thank you, though, for giving us a little time to think about it. We hadn't expected anything like this."

Uncle Albert rose. "I may as well get back to Carl's. I know there will be pros and cons to consider, but I would like to help out my niece and her family if I could."

"Thanks, Uncle Albert. Your kindness does mean a lot."

When the door closed behind him, David reached out to put an arm around Rina.

"Wow! What a turn of events! Usually our moves have come because of job changes when we had no alternative. It will mean almost a half-hour trip to and from work since I can't take the train because of my hours. But having a house rent free is nothing to sneeze at."

"There is going to be a lot of work to get it ready to move in and being four months pregnant won't make it any easier. Guess I can ask Marta and Clair to help and maybe there will be a few of the rest of the family that will pitch in again—if they're not tired of helping us out!"

David moved to the couch and pulled Rina down beside him.

"The children will have to change schools again. That is always hard on them, but at least we know the Malden school is a good one."

"I guess the children will have to double up in rooms again, because I don't think there are enough bedrooms for just two per room. I don't know for sure, but I don't think there is a downstairs bedroom, and the upstairs is small enough that I can't believe there would be four upstairs. I was never inside, but judging from the outside, I would think the bedrooms are small."

"Do you think moving into a house where there has been tuberculosis is a good idea, especially with you pregnant?"

"If Uncle Albert gets it fumigated, it should be all right."

"I think if we can get someone else to do the cleaning, it would be best if you didn't take that risk."

"I hate to ask someone else to do it all."

David gave her an extra squeeze and lifted her chin to look in her eyes. "I know, honey-babe. It's usually you doing the hard work, but it won't hurt for you to let someone else do it for once. I can help in the evenings when I get home early enough, but I think some of the nieces and nephews—well maybe all of them—will help. You can concentrate on the packing here."

"So we'll tell Uncle Albert we'll take it?" Rina's eyes reflected a mixture of hope and uncertainty.

"Things have been going better for us than they have for a while, but not having to pay rent could give us a real boost. So, yes, I think we should accept. Do you think you can take another move?"

"If we can get the help we need, I think so. It's hard to think of upsetting the apple cart when things are better than they have been for a while. There are always advantages and disadvantages to every move, but at least we'll be moving into familiar territory. I'll really miss Mama and Papa, being so close to our house and them gone, but a lot of the people I grew up with will be close by. Even the children have some friends in Malden because of the times we've lived there."

"Let's do it, then. We'll give it until tomorrow night, just to make sure, but then I'll call Uncle Albert."

"It's getting dark, so we should call the children in and give them a snack before bedtime. I don't think they will need much after our big meal at Marta's."

David moved to the back door to call the children. Rina went to the cellar to get apples and grapes she had picked from the vine at the back of the property. Her mind churned with a flood of mixed emotions about pulling up stakes from a place that had become comfortable and a plethora of details connected with a move to Malden. She felt herself yanked between the warmth of knowing her uncle really cared, the relief of not having to meet the rental payments each month, tired-to-the-bone despair at having to go through all the work of moving and the grief of being further from Marta and Steve, who were such a support for her when David was away long hours.

As she climbed the stairs, another thought washed over her. Jessie and Evvy had really settled in Stafford in the past year-and-a-half. How would it affect them to pull up roots again and move away from their friends here? Her heart felt heavy at having to break the news to them. Jessie had even been making a little money by helping young mothers in the community. She conscientiously saved most of it and spent only a little on the odd bit that especially appealed to her. Rina sometimes wondered if Jessie was missing her childhood by being so sensible and responsible, but she hardly knew what to do about it because they really needed the help and reliability of their oldest child.

Rina sighed as she got out the cookie jar and began to slice the apples into quarters. The door burst open as five little Litzes tumbled into the kitchen, followed by their father.

"Okay, children," he admonished, "wash your hands and sit at the table. Your mama is getting you something to eat, then it's off to bed."

Rina set a bowl of washed grapes and plates of apple quarters and cookies on the table. Her heart swelled in gratitude for this diverse assortment of individuals that God had entrusted to their care—diverse, but they were all of the same parents. Maybe it was the fulfillment of the dream she often had, growing up as the youngest of her own unusual family. As the "baby," she often felt she had missed out on being in the middle of the family unit. She understood better, as an adult, the reasons for some of those feelings of distinctness. She was her father's only child, and she had not been a part of the other family units represented in the widely spread and unique formation of their family. Even though her parents had been successful in blending their family in many ways, maybe it was because of those underlying dynamics that one of her dreams had been to have a large family that really and truly belonged together. A smile spread across her face. With number seven in the oven, she should feel quite satisfied in having accomplished that goal.

"Eat up, darlin's. It's almost bedtime." She pulled out a chair and joined the rest of them at the table. "You know, it's Thanksgiving and that is a time to think of all we are thankful for. I was just remembering what it was like growing up as the youngest of my family. My older sisters were so much ahead of me that I don't really remember them living at home. Even Uncle George was quite a bit older. Anyway, I am feeling very thankful for our family right here around the table. Each one of you is precious. Isn't it nice to be part of a big family?"

"You don't remember your sisters living at home?" Bernie turned big questioning eyes up to her mother.

"No, I don't. Maria was already in teacher's college when I was born, and by the time I could remember, she was married. Her Harold was just four years younger than me, so he was more like a cousin than a nephew to me. I remember Marta getting married, but I was only a little older than you at that time."

Bernie giggled. "That would be funny if Jessie and Evvy were already married!"

"Bernie!" Jessie and Evvy chorused in objection. Evvy poked Bernie with her elbow and glared at her. "Sometimes I think this family is a little too big!"

"Evvy!" Bernie wailed, "That's not nice!"

"No, that wasn't very nice, Evvy!" their mother agreed. "I think it would be nice for you to tell Bernie you are sorry. She was just trying to imagine what it was like for me."

"Oh, all right, Bernadette-boo; I'll let you sleep with me again tonight."

"We've had a big day, so finish up here and then you need to get to bed. Rae's almost asleep already, so if you older girls help Doris get ready for bed and the rest of you all get ready quick, I'll come and read you a story before you go to sleep."

"We will!"

"We'll hurry!" they all chimed as they scurried up the stairs.

THE HOUSE got fumigated, the troupes rallied and the family made the move at the end of November. The house did have four bedrooms upstairs. One of them was barely big enough for a bed. Because there were only two boys, that is the where they slept. The other smaller rooms each held a bed and two girls while she and David claimed the last room. It was big enough to hold a crib for the first year or so of the new baby's life, and then it would have to move three to a bed either in the boy's room or one of the girls' rooms, depending on its gender.

Chapter 19

THE PERSISTENT RINGING of the telephone brought Rina back to her easy chair. Why was Marlene not answering it? She was about to try to get out of her cozy spot when she heard the back door bang and Marlene taking the kitchen phone off the hook. The conversation didn't last long and Marlene tiptoed into the living room.

"Oh, you are awake?"

"I didn't think I was sleeping!"

"It sure looked like it when I went through here to go get the mail."

"I might have dropped off momentarily," Rina conceded.

"That was Jessie on the phone. Are you up to having three more daughters descend on you?"

"Who's coming?"

"Jessie and Bernie were down to London on some business and are meeting Lenora for lunch. They wondered if all three of them could drop in for a bit. I thought it would be alright."

"Sure is! I'm always glad to see any of my family!"

"I'll make a salad for our lunch so we'll be done when they get here."

Rina leaned back again on her recliner and smiled as she waited for lunch to be ready. What a nice surprise to have the girls drop in for a visit. No matter how glad she was that they had lives of their own, the promise of a visit with her girls was always a delight. As a young woman and busy mother she had never given thought to seeing her own children as grandparents and some of them even great-grandparents! It still amazed her. She almost felt as though she was seeing something that shouldn't be hers to see; and yet, her daughters, in her heart, were always her babies. What a conundrum—the actual physical maturity (the older ones were getting close to *eighty*) and the perceived age and relationship in one's heart and soul, where they were still young and always would be!

"THEY'RE HERE!" Marlene announced from the sink where she was washing up the few dishes from lunch.

"Good, I'll get up to meet them."

"Just stay where you are, Mama. They will come to you."

Rina couldn't see the back door from where she sat, but she was watching the living room door for the first sight of her daughters. She wondered at the quiet greetings at the door. Was her hearing getting that bad? Jessie was the first to come through the door.

"Hi Jessie. It's good to see you."

Bernie came next with Lenora close behind and then—was she seeing things? Rina blinked her eyes and looked again. Realization dawned slowly then jubilation flooded into her heart.

"Evvy! What are you doing here? Come here and let me give you a big hug. When did you get to Ontario?"

Rina struggled to get up. Evvy gave her a hand and then gathered her into her arms and held her close.

"Mama! It is so good to see you." She gave her another hug. "It wasn't too much of a surprise, was it?"

"That kind of surprise is good for the heart, my darling."

Jessie, Bernie, Lenora and Marlene stood there, smiling triumphantly. She gave them each a hug and sat down again.

"Now, you schemers tell me the whole story. When did you arrive, Evvy—and how long did you know about this, Marlene?"

"I've known that Evvy was coming for about two weeks now. I did tell you that Jessie and Bernie were down on business. That business, however, was picking Evvy up at the airport! She arrived from Vancouver just before lunch. Do you think you can stand having her around for a week?"

"Just give me a try! I might not want to let her go! I guess I could say what your dad used to say when his family was all around him. 'I've had a stroke—a stroke of good luck, to have my family around me.' That is just the way I feel right now. Are we going to have the rest come sometime while you're here, Evvy?"

"Yes, Mama," Lenora moved to plant a kiss on Rina's cheek. She stroked the side of her face and smoothed back her hair. "We are planning to have all your kids and in-laws and as many grand and great-grands as can make it on Saturday for a picnic. Is that okay?"

Rina leaned back in ecstasy. "You bet! It will be like old times. Couldn't Peter and Bobby make it this time, Evvy?"

"No, Mama. Bobby had another bout of bronchitis and he doesn't like being away from his workshop too much, so Peter stayed at home with him this time."

"Well, sit down, girls, and let's get caught up. How are all the people at the workshop, Evvy? I sometimes wish I could go back out there and see them all again, but I guess time for that kind of thing is past for me. Starting that sheltered workshop for people like Bobby was the best thing you could have done for him, but the benefit didn't stop at him. Look how many more lives have been helped by having a place to learn and to work! Your church even has more members because of you working there. You shared your faith as well as your love. I used to like to watch you relating to the people there—staff as well as clients. "

"Yes, Mama, but it filled my life with meaning as well—Peter's too. Bobby changed our lives in such a good way." Evvy reached out for her mother's hand and stroked it. "The people at the workshop who were there when you visited often ask about you, Mama. They like looking at the pictures 'Grandma' coloured and things you helped them make. Some of them remember Papa too. Remember how Daddy worked hard trying to devise a method of extracting copper wire from the obsolete hydro meters we had given to us? The boys took the meters apart and separated the metal to sell for scrap from the copper that got a higher price to help with our expenses."

"Daddy got a lot of satisfaction from making something out of nothing—figuring out a way to help," Rina commented.

"You liked figuring out how to make a difference in their lives too. I remember taking you out to a farm to purchase a bushel of beets. Then you came with me to teach the girls how to pickle beets. I'm so glad for the time you spent with us after you retired. I got to know you in a way I hadn't since I left home."

"That wasn't just yesterday?"

"No, it wasn't! I hate to say how long ago it was, but I was only nineteen when I left home and I'm just a *bit* older than that now!"

"Oh yeah!" her sisters chimed in, "just a *wee* bit older!"

"Then Jessie followed you a few months later and the two of you left all of your family responsibilities on my poor young shoulders." Bernie's voice was quiet and sweet, but replete with woe. Her eyes were widened with assumed injury that lasted a full few seconds before the sparkle of humour took over and everyone howled with laughter.

"Oh, don't give me that sorrowful song and dance! By that time you were chasing after Freddy so hard that you didn't have much time for family responsibility!"

"Not then, yet. Oh, I had my eye on him and made sure he knew I was around, but he didn't know yet that I was going to marry him. That came a few years later, and then he thought it was *his* idea!"

The sisters dissolved in laughter again.

"That's our Bernie, sweet and unobtrusive, but quietly insistent enough to get her way—even with unwary men! Poor Fred didn't have a chance." Evvy's eyes shone with love and mirth.

"Well, if Fred were still with us, you could just ask if him if he minded. I think I kept him happy to his dying day—so happy he didn't have time to think whether he could have done better! And if he could have, I wasn't going to be the one to tell him."

"You are right, Bernie! I think you did keep him happy," her mother agreed, still chuckling.

"Well anyway, I did miss you, Jessie and Evvy. I know you had several jobs before joining the navy, but after that, you didn't even get home on weekends. I had to find ways to have fun on my own—and we did even without you!"

"Ahh-hh! We weren't able to give you all the material things we would have liked to, but we sure did have some fun on the way," Rina added.

"I once mentioned in a Bible Class that we didn't have much of this world's goods when we were growing up but I never remember feeling poor," Marlene injected. "Our Pastor said, 'Broke is the state of your pocket book but poor is a state of mind!' I really credit you and Daddy for not passing on to us the anxiety you must have felt many times."

"You had the advantage of being one of the younger ones, Marlene." Jessie turned apologetically to her mother. "You didn't complain, and I did feel secure in your love, but I was aware of how hard you worked and how many things we did without. I guess that is why I saved so hard to make the down-payment on a washing machine for you when Lenora was born just after we moved back to Malden into Uncle Albert's house. I thought doing the washing by hand for eight people was hard enough without adding a ninth and all the diapers that come with a baby."

"That was so sweet of you, Jessie. You were only twelve, and it took you quite a while to save that money. I was really touched that you would spend it on that washing machine."

"I guess it was because I was only twelve that I didn't think about all the payments I saddled you with before it was fully paid—what a gift, when you could already barely make ends meet!"

Rina smirked sheepishly. "You're partially right. I did wonder how we were going to manage to pay it off, but in the end it was a blessing. I started doing Reverend Grigg's washing in order to make the payments, but once the last one was made, I had a way of making some extra money. Then several others heard about me doing washing and ironing for him and asked if I would do it for them, so I had a nice little income from your down-payment! It really helped out when Daddy got sick after Marlene was born. We would have had to have more help from welfare if it hadn't been for that. I know now that there is no shame going on welfare under difficult circumstances, but at the time I wanted to do everything I could to avoid that."

"I wonder if the stigma is mostly in our minds when we have to have help," Evvy mused.

"To be honest, I would still rather that people didn't know about that part of our family life. There are so many better parts we can talk about; I'd rather not go there," Jessie admitted, her eyes reflecting pain and humiliation.

Marlene put an arm around Jessie's shoulder. "Oh Jessie! Ours wasn't the only family to face difficulties. Just look what became of us. We're all doing well and have made a contribution to this world. Maybe it has made us more understanding of those who don't have everything handed to them on a golden platter. That understanding alone is worth a lot—at least if we want to be of some earthly good to our fellow humanity. If we are free to admit it to others in the same kind of straits, it will be an encouragement to them to live through their present circumstances. It may even make them feel better about accepting a hand to get them through."

"I suppose you are right, but I always felt some of those Malden folks looked down on us," Jessie confessed, then suddenly smiled. "I guess that is one thing that time can cure. Already many of the people who remember those times are gone, and if I outlive a few more, no one will remember."

"No one but you, Jessie," her mother gently suggested. "Maybe it is you who needs to come to peace about that. I am sorry you had to live with the fall-out of our financial difficulties, but I agree with Marlene. You all turned out pretty good and I love and feel a motherly pride in each one of you."

"I know, Mama, and you are probably right in your observation." She turned to her sisters. "Almost a hundred years old and she's still giving me good advice!"

"That's our Mama!" They chimed as one and then laughed again at being of the same mind.

"And being the worrier and responsible one is our Jessie!" Evvy exclaimed. "She told me once that when I fell and broke my arm on the ice, she thought it was her fault for not taking better care of me! Good grief! I wasn't very old and she was only two years older than me. But she was always looking after me—and the rest of you too! The rest of us shouldn't have had to worry—she did enough for all of us."

"I think we were all more like Daddy in that way than we'd like to admit," Marlene quietly added. "I suspect that was the source of many of his stomach pains. I know I've done my share of worrying."

"You are probably right," Jessie admitted. "Maybe we worry about different things, but quite a few of us do worry a lot. It's good that Mama balanced us out in that way. You always told us, Mama, that if we couldn't do anything about it, then we should just let the Lord take care of it. Usually that helped, but sometimes I used to think that we shouldn't abdicate our responsibility so easily."

"You didn't hear it right, Jessie. I said if there was *nothing* we can do about it, we should turn it over to the Lord. If there is something you can do, then do it. If there is nothing to do but worry, that's just like spinning your wheels or revving your engine in neutral—it's not going to get you anywhere, and there is a lot of wear and tear on yourself to no avail. If you turn it over to the Lord and he sees that there is something you could be doing, you will be in the necessary frame of mind for him to easily nudge you to do it. If you are all tensed up in a knot of worry, you aren't apt to feel that nudge." Rina took a deep breath and looked at each of her daughters with amusement sparkling in her eyes. "There! You have my sermon for the day."

"Maybe that is as good a place as any for Bernie and I to leave. We have an hour's drive or more to get home, which will give us good time to digest the sermon, Mama. We'll see you again on Saturday."

"So are Evvy and Lenora staying here?"

"I'm staying here, Mama, and Lenora is staying for supper. Krista is coming for her and staying for supper, so you will get to see her as well. She might even have her kiddies along. Maybe you should have a rest after Jessie and Bernie leave so you will be up to more company."

"I hate to miss any of your visit by sleeping, but you may be right," Rina conceded. "I guess if you are going to be here for a week I won't be able to stay awake for the whole time!"

Jessie and Bernie came to give their mother a hug and kiss before they left, and Marlene went to see them off. Evvy tucked the lap robe around Rina's knees and kissed her mother. "You just settle down for a nap. Marlene, Lenora and I will stay outside for a bit, then settle in the kitchen so you can have a breather before supper."

"I guess I'd better, but don't stay away too long. I want to see Lenora, too, before she has to leave."

"We'll give you an hour and then we'll come back in here. Sleep well, Mama."

Chapter 20 🍁

EVVY SHUT THE DOOR as she left the living room, and Rina closed her eyes. Although her eyes were shut, her mind didn't turn off so easily. The warmth of having her four oldest daughters around her still enveloped her. The majority of their living together had been in Malden. Lenora was born just after their move from Stafford. Even though it had been fumigated and thoroughly cleaned, the doctor wouldn't allow her to be born in that house because of the tuberculosis that had so recently been there. So she went to Marta's house in Stafford to have the baby. It didn't take Lenora long to find her place in the family. Although Rina was always conscious of the change in dynamics each time a new one was added to the family, some seemed to fit in more easily than others.

We put in a big garden on that lot—more garden than grass. It was enough to help out with a big portion of food for the family and some to share with the neighbours. Sometimes, if cash was short, we even sold some to the hotel or grocery store. The kids didn't really enjoy hoeing and picking, but they learned a lot about what it takes to feed a family.

Let me see . . . Lenora was just about three when Dad Litz got cancer and had to go to Toronto for treatments. He insisted that I go with him for that. By that time, we had established a good relationship. It still pleases me that he trusted me to provide support. Fanny was in such a state of self-pity and anguish that she would have been more of a drain than assistance for him. He told me things over the weeks we were there that increased my understanding of him and made it easier when the time came to look after Fanny—not that it was easy, but it made the time a little more tolerable. Dad only lasted a few more months even with the treatment.

The next crisis was much more alarming. How well she remembered that night.

"WHO IS THAT CALLING?" David poked Rina's shoulder.

"Oh dear, it must be Doris again. This is the third time I've been up with her."

"Is she feeling worse?"

Rina got out of bed and reached for her robe. "Yes. She's had this stomach-ache for three days now. Tonight the pain seems sharper. The last time I was up she had a fever, I think, and she was sick to her stomach but seemed a bit better after that. Maybe we'd better call the doctor and let him have a look."

When Rina got to the girls' room, Doris was lying at the end of the bed. "Mama'" she whispered, "My stomach feels big and hard—I can hardly touch it, it hurts so much. I could hardly speak loud enough to call you, and it hurts too much to cry even if I'd like to."

Rina laid her hand on Doris' forehead. Alarm shot through her with the force of a sledge hammer. Willing herself to speak calmly, she took a deep breath and told Doris, "Stay right where you are and lay still. I am going to call the doctor, then I will be right back."

Quickly she returned to their bedroom and whispered to David.

"David, I'm afraid it is Doris's appendix. I'm going to call Dr. Percy, but I just hope we caught it in time. Remember when we lived in Dubbin and Laura McDonald died of a ruptured appendix? Now that I think of it, Doris's symptoms are much like that. Oh, I should have thought of that before!"

David sat up. "Rina—no time for might-have-beens. Go call Dr. Percy. I'll get dressed and if we have to take Doris to hospital, we'll be ready to go."

Rina hurried down the steps and with trembling hands cranked the telephone to get the operator. *Hurry, hurry!*

"Operator."

"Please give me Dr. Percy—and hurry!"

She felt her impatience and alarm growing as the telephone rang, once, twice, three times. On the fourth ring she heard the click, then, "Dr. Percy here."

"Dr. Percy, this is Rina Litz. Doris has had a stomach-ache for a few days now. Tonight, she had a sharper pain. About two and a half hours ago, she had a bit of fever and was sick to her stomach. She seemed to feel a bit better after that, but just now she woke up again. Her stomach is quite bloated. She can't bear any weight on it and says it even hurts too much to cry. Her forehead is quite hot to the touch. I think you had better come to see her."

"Mrs. Litz, I think you have given me enough symptoms that I believe I know what is wrong. Get her ready to go to the hospital, but move her very carefully. I'll be right over and I'll take her to Stafford. I am quite sure she has appendicitis, and it may have already ruptured. If it has, she will be a very sick little girl. Perhaps you will want to go along with her. Little girls like to have their mothers with them."

"I'll be ready to go along."

"And I will be right over. Good bye."

Rina replaced the receiver on the hook and leaned against the wall for a moment. She took a deep breath. "Lord, forgive me for being so busy I didn't recognize the symptoms. Please don't take her away, but grant Doris healing. I didn't do all I should have, but right now I can do no more than get us ready to go and trust in you to do your best for us." With that, she was going up the steps as fast as she could go.

"What did he say?" David questioned as he did up the last buttons on his shirt and put his suspenders over his shoulders.

Rina yanked off her robe and nightgown and started getting dressed. "He thinks it is appendicitis and that it may have ruptured. He is coming right over. Oh David, how could I be so insensitive?"

"Now Rina, you are a good mother, but a very busy one. You've been finishing up the garden and the fall work along with your laundry jobs. Children have their tummy aches and it's quite understandable. Don't go whipping yourself for this. Just get dressed and get Doris ready to go. I'll go down and let the doctor in. Maybe the best thing to do is just wrap her in a blanket and take her that way. No sense dressing her and then having to undress her when she gets to the hospital."

"Yes, that would be best. I'll wake Jessie and Evvy so they know what is going on. Dr. Percy said he would drive her over and I could go along. Are you going too, or are you going to stay here with the children?"

"I think Jessie and Evvy can look after the rest. You will go to be with Doris, but I think I need to go be with her mother!"

"That would be nice. Even if Jessie needs to miss a day of high school, it won't be that bad."

"I think I hear the doctor's car coming up the street now, so I'd better get down there."

Rina put the light on in Doris' room. Evvy pried her eyes open and squinted in the brightness. "What's going on?"

"Doris is quite sick, Evvy. The doctor's coming to see her, but he thinks he'll want to take her to the hospital in Stafford. Daddy and I are going along, so we'll need you and Jessie to take care of the rest of the family. I will go talk to Jessie about it because she'll need to get you all off to school and then stay home to look after Lenora. I don't know when we will be back. Do you think you can help Jessie?"

"Sure, Mama. Is Doris going to be all right?"

"What are they going to do to me at the hospital, Mama?" Doris whispered.

"They will need to operate to take out your appendix, Doris."

"What's that?"

"It's a little part in your abdomen that you don't really need to live a good life. Sometimes it gets infected and then it needs to come out. Dr. Percy will take good care of you and Daddy and I will be waiting until it is all over, then we'll be beside you when you wake up."

"Will I feel better then?"

"Well, not right away, but if all goes well, in a few weeks you will be feeling much better and you won't have those tummy aches again. Here comes Dr. Percy."

"So we have a sick little girl here!"

Doris nodded her head ever so slightly.

Dr. Percy took the cover off and rested his hand lightly on Doris' right side.

"Oww-ww!" she whispered.

"That really hurts, does it?"

"Yes, it does!" Doris's face registered all the pain she was unable to voice.

"Well then, missy, I think we'd better get you to the hospital. What would you say if I gave you and your mother a ride in my car?"

Doris just nodded.

"Is it alright if we just wrap her in this blanket, Doctor?"

"Excellent!"

"David, do you want to do that and carry her downstairs while I go tell Jessie she is in charge?"

The time spent sitting, pacing the floors, praying and worrying went on and on. It was several hours later when the doctor came to the waiting room. David and Rina could see by his face that it wasn't the best news. They stood to their feet, their hearts constricted with fear.

"Is she alright?" Rina asked before the doctor could say anything.

"Mr. and Mrs. Litz, sit down. The surgery went well, considering all things. Her appendix was ruptured. We did our best, but she will be very sick girl for a while. If you believe in prayer, now would be a good time to avail yourselves of this." Dr. Percy wiped his forehead.

"Mrs. Litz, if you could arrange to stay with Doris, I believe it would be to her advantage. Your presence would be comforting to her. The nurses will be here, of course, but if you could be on constant watch, it would be good. We will tell you what to watch for and small things you can do to help care for her. Do you think you could?"

Rina looked at David with questions in her eyes.

"Of course, Doctor, we will find a way. Jessie can stay home and look after Lenora and keep house until you come home, Rina."

"I hate to take her out of school, but it's of utmost importance that Doris gets the care she needs. I think Jessie will understand."

"It will be a while until Doris wakes up, so perhaps you had better get a bit of rest while you have the chance. Can you find a place to go, or should we set up a bed for you right now? We will set one up in her room when she gets out of recovery."

"I can go to Marta's place for an hour or so."

"If you are back in two hours that will be soon enough—she will be sleeping for a while and then the nurses will look after her for a while longer before she is brought to her room."

For the first week, most of the time it was touch and go. We didn't know if she was going to make it. I felt so guilty! The nights were the worst because, although I had a bed in the room, I couldn't sleep well. In the dead of night, I kept wondering how I would ever live with the guilt if Doris would die. Every time she groaned I was sure it was going to be her last. I would strain to hear her breath and think she must have quit, so I would get up to check. The fifth night after the surgery there was a crisis. Her fever shot up, she became delirious and I called the nurse in a panic. She called the doctor and he came in, took her temperature, gave her a shot and examined her incision.

"Mrs. Litz, I am going to ask you to please leave the room while the nurses and I attend to Doris. We'll call you when we are finished."

"Can't I stay just so she knows her mother is here?"

"Mrs. Litz, since we gave her that last shot she is barely conscious, so she will be all right and I think it would be best if you leave for a few moments."

The nurse came, put a hand under her elbow and urged her toward the door. "You can go to the little waiting room just down the hall. We'll call you as soon as we can."

Her heart tightened in terror and her legs felt so weak she wondered if she could make it to the waiting room. Everything in her wanted to go back to make sure Doris would be all right—or at least to be there if the worst happened. She leaned against the wall partway down the hall. Sobs rose up in her chest.

"I have to get out of here!"

She hurried on down the hall, yanking a handkerchief from her pocket. When she reached the waiting room, she sought a chair around the corner in the most private part of the room and sank down, elbows on her knees. She covered her face with her handkerchief and let go as the sobs ripped up her chest like a series of small blades, tearing her deepest emotions to shreds and straining her throat with a distending pain that moved upward until it was spit out in hot tears. Her handkerchief was soon soaked and still she cried. Finally, her outburst subsided. With a huge sigh, she straightened and leaned her back against the chair. Tears continued to trickle down her cheeks, but she felt almost too drained to care.

"Oh Lord, I can't take this, I can't stand to see my little girl in such pain. I can't stand the thought that she may die. I can't stand not being able to make it better for her. Lord, I can't!"

"If you can't—let me."

It was almost like a whisper inside her head.

"But Lord, it was me that didn't pay enough attention when she had a stomach-ache. I should be doing something to make up for it."

"But I thought you said you can't."

"I did!"

"Then let me."

Rina sat with her eyes shut and let the conversation play over in her head. Letting go would also mean forgiving herself. She hadn't meant to disregard the symptoms. There really was nothing more she could do.

"All right, Lord. I acknowledge that I can't do any more. I confess that it is out of my hands and that yours are ever so much more capable then mine. And I admit that you know best. So Lord, scared as I am, I am going to give Doris to you. Do your best for her, and I will try to put my full trust in you. Forgive me if and when I waver, but Lord, I am putting her in your hands right now."

Tears ran down her face again, but this time they were tears of surrender and relief. She balled up her handkerchief and wiped them as best she could. With surrender, tiredness washed over her body, but there was a measure of peace within her.

She didn't know how much later it was when the nurse came down the hall.

"Mrs. Litz?—oh there you are."

"How is she?" Rina asked in a subdued voice, almost afraid of the answer.

"The doctor took out a few stitches and irrigated the wound. He has inserted a tube to drain the infection and we will continue to irrigate it. We hope that will encourage healing. Are you all right, Mrs. Litz? You have had a constant watch since the surgery."

"I think I will be all right. Tonight gave me a hard time, but I know now that there is only so much I can do. Although I would like to make my little girl all better, I am going to have to trust the final healing to the Lord."

"I don't think you could trust her to better hands, Mrs. Litz. Do you want to go back to her now?"

That seemed to be the turning point for Doris. She was still in the hospital for another ten days, but slowly she improved. All that time, Jessie did a valiant job of looking after the family. She never did return to high school. After Doris was fully improved, she kept helping Rina with her work until Maggie McLean, a young woman who had just started as a general practitioner in Stafford, asked if Jessie could work for her a few days a week. Bit by bit, her time increased until Jessie took a room in the McLean's home and assisted her with the house and office work as needed.

I always felt sorry that she had to end her formal education because we needed her help, but she did get an education working for Dr. McLean. Then she went on to help her husband in the newspaper business and became a successful woman in her own right. I'm so proud of her and

I hope she knows it. A high school diploma or even a college degree couldn't have made her more successful.

It was only two years later that Murray, Rae, Doris and Lenora all got their tonsils out at the same time. That was a busy time too, but everything proceeded according to schedule. They were quiet because their throats hurt (which was a nice change) but they weren't so sick that we needed to worry about them. I just kept the ginger ale and the Jell-O available, and in a week or so they were pretty well back to normal. They also had fewer sore throats the next winter.

That was her last conscious thought.

Chapter 21 🍂

"MAMA—DO YOU WANT TO WAKE UP?"

"Oh, Evvy! Was I sleeping?"

"Well, I would say so. I came in a while ago and you were out to the world. Your head was back, your mouth was open and you were gently snoring—yes, I would say you were sleeping," she laughed. "I hated to wake you up, so I gave you fifteen more minutes."

"I didn't sleep the whole time. I couldn't help thinking about our years in Malden; we had our best years there while you were growing up, but they weren't exactly trouble free. Lenora was just three when Grandpa Litz got cancer and died, then Doris was in hospital with her ruptured appendix."

"I remember that! Jessie was so conscientious! She wanted to make sure we all behaved just as well as if you were there, but I'm afraid we didn't always cooperate. I think part of it was that we were all scared for Doris. It seemed you only got back from being with Grandpa and then you were gone again. After all, Grandpa died after you were at the hospital with him, so we wondered if we ever would see Doris again."

"Yes, I suppose that would have crossed your minds. Sometimes I think I wasn't good enough about explaining what was going on and making sure you understood. There was so much to do I guess I was apt to tell the older ones and expect them to pass the message on." Rina turned the tassel on her lap robe. "The thing is, hindsight is so much clearer, but we can't go back and do things over."

"Oh Mama, we all make mistakes, no matter how good our parenting—and we are all thankful for you, so don't worry about that now."

The door from the kitchen swung open as Marlene and Lenora entered the room.

"So you're awake, are you, Mama?"

"She sure is! I was just going to ask Mama about the night you made your debut, Marlene! Did you know you had the neighbours listening at their open windows for your first cry?"

"Yes, Mama has told me they were rooting for her with every outcry of hers until they heard a baby's wail and the whole neighbourhood could finally relax!" Marlene laughed, "Good thing it was warm for February, otherwise I could have been the cause of an outbreak of pneumonia!"

"You can be glad you were a cutie! I had to look after you a lot that year when Dad couldn't work. Jessie was already working for Dr. McLean, so when Mama had to go over to Uncle Albert's to iron, Bernie and I had to look after you and the rest of the little ones."

"That wasn't a fun year for any of us, girls. I was doing laundry for everyone who would pay me to do it. With the iron press set up in Uncle Albert's shed across the river on the other side of town because it was the only place I could find room for it that I didn't have to pay rent—washing clothes at home, hanging it up on the lines until they were almost dry, then running to the other side of town to do the ironing kept me from gaining weight that year. I hated leaving the responsibility of the house to you, but with your dad off of work, someone had to bring home the bacon, as they say." Rina patted Evvy's leg. "Besides, you went to work in Toronto partway through that year, and then Bernie and Murray had to take over."

"But I sent some of my earnings home."

"Yes, dear, you did, and so did Jessie. We had to do everything we could to make ends meet. It helped a lot when I worked at the hotel when they had banquets on at night, because they always let me bring home the turkey carcasses or bones from the roasts.

Those leftovers kept the wolf away from the door more than once! It's surprising what you can make with almost nothing! Of course, we had that big garden too."

"Oh Mama!" Lenora's quiet voice quivered with sympathy. "That must have been hard. You still had eight mouths to feed, and just having had a baby . . . I don't know how you did it."

"You just do what you have to do one day at a time, and if that sometimes gets too much to handle, it has be whittled down to one hour or one minute at a time."

The doorbell chimed, interrupting their conversation. Lenora jumped to her feet. "That must be Krista and the kids. I'll go and let them in."

As soon as the back door opened, Jay and Zander's voices exclaimed their delight in seeing their Gram, and then running feet brought them closer.

"Hello Nana!" Jay came to give Rina a kiss.

"Hi Nana!" Three-year old Zander tried to climb up on her lap.

"Careful there, Zander," his mother cautioned. "You are getting almost too big for Nana to hold."

"But I want to show her my new twuck!"

"Here! I'll pull this chair right up beside Nana's, then you will be real close and you can show it to her."

Zander danced from one foot to the other until the chair was situated and then, with all the effort of his three year-old prowess, climbed up on it, leaning on the arm of Rina's recliner. With Nana's grey head and his curly blond bent together over the truck, Zander explained all its features.

SUPPER OVER, Lenora, Krista and the boys took their leave and Marlene, Evvy and Rina settled down for a while to just enjoy each other.

"I'm still hardly able to believe you are really here, Evvy! What a nice surprise!"

"It's good to see you again too. It makes me nostalgic for those months you came out to be with us. We had a great time showing you two around the Island. Daddy, in particular, loved to spend quiet hours slowly exploring places of interest. He was awestruck by the massive old growth Douglas Firs in Cathedral Grove. He could spend quite some time examining the flora and fauna wherever we went. I remember one trip with him that took two hours to travel five miles. He did so appreciate the beauty of God's creation."

"Yes, he did. For so much of his life he worked so hard to make a living for all of us he hardly had time to notice those things, yet I was always impressed at the things he did note, even in the busy times. Once he retired, he could let that part of him come alive. He appreciated nature and beauty wherever he was, but he did especially enjoy the island."

"I used to tell him that all we have is water, rocks and mountains; it's the way they are put together that makes them so interesting!"

"Now that's an understatement if I ever heard one." Marlene shook her head in mock disgust. "Perhaps you are basically right, but I think the blue skies, the amazing cloud formations and the trees have a little to do with it too."

"Granted! It perhaps isn't as simple as I said, but it is in the arrangement of those things wherein the beauty lies."

"One thing I really liked about where you live is how close you are to the ocean. I loved to walk on the shore."

"You liked what you got there too! When I was finished work, we would go out to Nanoose Bay and pick up oysters, then you would make oyster stew for lunch the next day—and that happened often."

"Mmm-mm! That makes my mouth water. I don't think I've had oyster stew since, and I do so like it—of course some of the delight was in picking them off the seashore yourself."

"I'm not sure if even picking them up myself would make me like oyster stew—but everyone has their own likes and dislikes."

Ignoring Marlene's comment, Evvy continued her reminiscing. "When we were growing up we hardly knew Daddy. He was away from home so much. He'd be gone in the morning when we woke up and if he did get home at night, we hardly saw anything of him. He didn't even go to church that much with us, did he?"

"No, he didn't. That is one place where we didn't quite see eye-to-eye. I was brought up to go to church unless you were really sick. Although I knew your Daddy worked hard all week, I thought he should go to church anyway and rest in the afternoon. He thought he deserved a morning when he didn't have to get up."

"But Mama, after you came to live with James and me, I was so surprised at the time he spent reading the Bible. It seemed every time he sat down, he had the Bible in his lap."

"I noticed that when he was out on the island with us as well. I, too, was surprised, because he didn't seem interested in church for most of his life. We children learned the importance of church from you, Mama."

"After he died, we looked through his Bible, and by the notes in the margins and the verses he underlined, there was no doubt that he had a personal relationship with the Lord."

"Could I have the Bible some time? I would really value being able to see those notes and verses with my own eyes."

"You can look at it while you are here, but I like using it myself. It helps me feel close to both my husband and my Lord."

"Of course, Mama! I wouldn't want to take it away from you if you are using it." Evvy patted her mother's arm. "You know, the year after Daddy died when you came out over Christmas was the first time I spent Christmas with some of my family since I left home. That was really special. I really got to know you then."

"You had six months of me that time. I was just going to come for six weeks, but you used your persuasive powers on me!"

"You really didn't mind, did you?"

"No, I really didn't. I enjoyed being with your family and getting to know them better. Even more than that, though, I still missed your dad, and it helped me in the transition to him being gone, which was hard enough as it was. You don't live with a man and love him through all life throws at you and then just forget him when he dies. For a long time if feels as though part of you has been amputated. Nothing feels right. That time with you helped a lot, although I had to face the emptiness of our room and bed when I got back here to Marlene and James' home."

"Do you realize that I am only seven years away from the age you were when Daddy died? I can hardly believe that. I know it will happen to one of us, but I dread the thought of being left behind if Peter would die."

"The price you pay for having a good marriage is missing your spouse intensely when they are gone, Evvy—but I wouldn't trade that for a marriage where you are left with only regrets, if-onlys and might-have-beens! It would be even worse to be glad that your spouse is gone."

Evvy and Marlene both nodded their heads. "I guess that puts things in their proper perspective," Marlene commented.

"You and Peter are always so busy doing things with and for people. Look at you—nearing eighty and still going to the workshop to read and do Bible studies. Maybe you should slow down and just enjoy each other."

"Who's that pot that's calling the kettle black?" Marlene's eyes shone with glee. "That wouldn't be the woman who, among other things, volunteered at Missions Services, served on their Women's Auxiliary and went to their meetings, took in people who needed a home, went rushing to the homes of grandkids in the middle of the night to stay with older children when a new baby was about to be born, helped with Boy Scouts of Canada, was Good Cheer person for the church and Miss Sunshine for the campers and served tea at the nursing home, pushing elderly people around in their wheelchairs when she herself was 89 to 93 or 4, would it?"

Both Rina and Evvy laughed with increasing gusto as the list went on.

"Oh, that couldn't be the same person!" Evvy wiped away the tears.

Rina raised her hand, calling a halt to the shenanigans. "All right, all right—point taken! I guess there's no use preaching when your life contradicts what you say." She chuckled. "But you may as well wear out as rust out. I guess it didn't hurt me if I'm still around at ninety-nine. Life is more fun that way. So go ahead, Evvy—and Marlene is already gearing up for the same kind of old-age—just enjoy yourselves whatever you do."

"Thanks for your permission—I think I will!"

"All that laughing tired me out. If I am to enjoy the rest of your visit, I had better get my rest. I think I will head to bed."

"All right, Mama, I will help you get settled." Marlene rose to help Rina out of her chair. Evvy rose too.

"It might be a good idea for us all to retire soon. Would you join me in having a cup of tea if I make it, Marlene?"

"Sure, that would be great. We'll ask James to join us if he can tear himself away from his book."

IN HER ROOM, Rina began undressing while Marlene turned the covers back on the bed.

"Evelyn's coming is one of the nicest surprises I've had in a while! Having five of you girls together this afternoon was a real treat! When you get to the stage of life I am in, those treats are rare. Believe me, I am aware of that and all the more thankful because of it."

"I am glad you are enjoying it. I had some questions as to whether the surprise would be too much for you, but Evvy wanted it that way. At least we got you a little prepared by telling you that Jessie and Bernie were coming."

"Talking about our life in Malden brought back a lot of memories. That year after your birth was an especially hard year, but time brings its own perspective."

Rina sat on the edge of her bed and kicked off her shoes. Marlene bent down to remove her mother's socks.

"I was too young to remember any of that, of course, but hearing you talk about it makes me ache for you. Caring for all those children would be enough challenge for most people, but then trying to make enough money to keep us going must have been overwhelming."

Rina sighed as she lay down on the bed.

"I think what was even harder was to see Daddy get depressed because he couldn't provide for his family. He hated seeing me work so hard, but there wasn't anything he could do about it."

Pulling the covers up over her mother, Marlene bent over to give her a kiss. "You just forget about all of that now and have a good night's sleep so you are ready for tomorrow. We don't want to wear you out before Saturday's family picnic. That will be a big day for you. We thought about having it at the park, but we decided to have it right here so you can come in and rest if you want."

"I'm looking forward to having the whole gang here. I thought that wouldn't happen until November and then Evvy, Peter and Bobby probably wouldn't be here. Thanks for all you do to make me happy, Marlene."

"Making you happy makes me happy too. I think all your kids would say that." Marlene set Rina's shoes under the dresser and moved to the door. "Goodnight, Mama!"

The door closed behind Marlene. Rina sighed again with a deep satisfaction.

Much as I sometimes wondered why the good Lord kept sending us kids when we could hardly provide for them, I sure love every one of them and it is so nice at this stage of the game to have them around. When they were youngsters it felt like a huge responsibility; now they are the best of friends and the tables have turned—they are the caregivers. I wish David could have experienced more of that. Oh, he did have a few years, and I guess after his stroke he thought he needed more caregiving than he preferred. I guess I just miss him when the children are around me. A very big part of the family is absent when he isn't here.

Maybe being sick isn't easy for any adult, but it's especially so for most men. That year after Marlene was born was too long for even the most uncomplaining man to endure. It started when Rae came home from school with the chicken pox. A few weeks later, Murray, Doris and Lenora got them. We thought that would be it, because the older ones already had them and the baby might be protected from them because she was so young, but then David came down with them and he got really sick. He couldn't seem to get back on his feet and the doctor finally diagnosed him with viral pneumonia and prescribed a lot of rest and as much sunshine as he could get. They might have better treatment for it now, but it took a long time for recovery then, and sitting around doing nothing wasn't easy for David.

IT WAS BAKING DAY. They were just about out of bread and now she found there wasn't enough flour for making a whole batch. She would send Doris and Rae down to the store with the wagon. They could manage to get it for her. Rina went to the dresser drawer to get money.

"Oh dear! By the time I pay for a bag of flour there won't be much left—and no prospects of replenishing the pot with more than I can get doing Rev. Grigg's and the Perkins's wash. That's not enough to keep us going. I have to find a way to bring in more money!" she mumbled to herself.

With her mind churning to find an answer, she moved to the back door. Shutting it behind her so she wouldn't disturb David, she called to Doris and Rae.

"I want you to take the wagon down to the grocery store and get a bag of bread flour. Here is enough money to pay for it. You can have a penny each to spend on what you want, but bring the rest back home." She tucked the bill into Rae's pant pocket. "Be very careful and come home as soon as you can. I need to get the bread started if we are to have any by supper time."

"Lord, please show me what to do. David has missed three pay-cheques now and there won't be any more coming for quite some time. I'm trying hard to skimp and save, but there are some things it's hard to do without—like milk and flour for bread. Please help me think how to make a bit more money. I'm turning to you because I just don't know where else to go. With ten mouths to feed, and me still getting over my last pregnancy, I feel over-whelmed. Lord, hear my cry!"

Barely back in the house, she heard a knock at the front door. *Oh dear! I hope that doesn't wake David.* She hurried to open the door. Bessie Trent, a neighbour from the edge of town, stood waiting.

"Good morning, Bessie! Come on in."

"Oh, I really don't have much time. I just came to ask a favour. Do you think Murray could learn to milk a cow? Let me explain. Abe just got a job that is going to have him out of town from Monday morning to Friday night. We like our fresh milk and our cow is milking really well right now, but I have almost more than I can do as it is. If Murray could milk her twice a day, in payment, you could have all the milk we don't need. It might be a help to you and it sure would be to us."

Rina's heart filled with praise. She couldn't have asked for a quicker answer to her prayer.

"I don't think Murray has ever milked a cow, but if Abe teaches him how to do it, I think he could learn and it definitely would be a help to us, with David sick. Thank you for thinking of us."

"Why don't you send Murray over tonight about five o'clock and he can have his first try at it. I know it takes a while to get the hang of it, but by the time Abe starts his job in two weeks, Murray will be doing all right. I must get back. I left Shirley in charge of the little ones and I don't want to leave her alone too long. Thanks so much. This will really help us out."

"Thank you, Bessie! It will certainly be a great help to us too!"

Rina closed the door and lifted her hands. "Thank you, Lord! I didn't expect an answer that soon, but thank you for assuring me that you will see us through."

The telephone jangled, interrupting her prayer.

"Hello?"

"Hello, Mrs. Litz?"

"Yes."

"It's Art Reddinger calling from the Hinton House Hotel. I understand that you do laundry for some folks?"

"Yes, I do."

"Is there any chance that you would be interested in doing the linens from the hotel? We have access to a press for ironing that we could provide. You would have to find a place to set it up, though."

"How often would it need to be done?"

"We have enough linen so that twice a week should usually be enough, but occasionally, if we have extra guests it may require a third day."

"Mr. Reddinger, I am very interested in the job. I will have to see if I can find a place to set up the press since I don't have room for it here. Could you give me a few days to see what I can arrange?"

"Certainly! We would like to know by the middle of next week—especially if you can't do it, because we need to find someone else."

"Granted! I will try to let you know by the end of this week."

"That would be great. I'll look forward to hearing from you. I hear you do good work, so I hope we can work something out."

"Thank you, Mr. Reddinger."

"You're welcome. Good-bye."

Rina replaced the receiver on the hook. Her heart filled with thanksgiving even as her mind reeled in disbelief. "Wow, Lord! You sure look after your children! Thank you, thank you, thank you!"

She opened the cupboard door to get out her bread-making supplies. A knock on the back door startled her. *Now who?* she wondered.

Her cousin Edith stood at the door, a tea-towel covering the pail in her hand.

"Hello! Come on in."

"How are you doing, Rina? We heard David was sick—and with the baby still so young, it must be hard."

"Yes, it is, but we are managing. I am feeling quite well, and Marlene is such a good baby, which helps. Of course, the older ones are a big help too. Jessie is in Stafford most of the time helping Dr. McLean, but the rest pitch in to do all they can."

"Ken and I just picked up our beef from the beef ring. It was our turn to get the heart and we don't really care for it, so I wondered if you could use it? Do you like it?'

"Yes, and yes!" Rina chuckled. "That would be great. It is a little while since we've had beef, so it will be a real treat. In fact, you're the third answer to prayer I have received in the last twenty minutes! Just about that long ago, I asked God to show me how to make ends meet and to assure me that he would provide a way. I was still shaking my head in disbelief from the first two when you came to the door with a third. Thanks so much!"

"Well, I was, of course, unaware of that prayer, but I'm glad I could help. I put a bit more than the heart in the pail—it's not the best cut, but I thought you could use it for stewing beef and maybe put it up in jars for when you need it."

"Oh Edith, thank you! I might normally say you shouldn't have, but this morning it seems so much an answer to my prayer that it would seem like rejecting what God provided. Thank you for being a part of that answer." Rina reached to give Edith a hug.

"I should really offer to stay and help you put up the stewing beef, but we have the rest in the car waiting for our attention, so I'd better get out there or Ken will wonder where I am."

"Don't worry. If God provided the meat through you, I will manage to get it done. Thanks again, Edith. Even your thoughtfulness is a real gift."

When the door closed behind Edith, Rina let the tears flow. Three different offers for help in three different ways was cause enough for gratefulness, but that they should come three in a row within minutes of asking for God's assurance was almost overwhelming. She felt unworthy of such a miracle, and yet, she rejoiced in the comfort and confidence in God's care that she felt.

She heard Marlene awaken. *I may as well feed her now while I am waiting for the flour.* As she settled on the rocking chair to nurse the baby, David came to the bedroom door.

"Who all was here this morning? There seemed to be an awful lot of coming and going."

"Sit down, David. I need to tell you about it. We sometimes wonder why things happen to us, and I know you have wondered why this and why now. I still don't know the answers to those questions, but after this morning, it doesn't matter so much."

As she told David about her morning, he listened with growing amazement.

"That is almost unbelievable. It would be even if it all happened in one day, but twenty minutes?" He shook his head. "Normally I would feel guilty or humiliated that we need so much help, but having it come right after you prayed . . . I can only be thankful. I don't like having you work so hard and I hate you taking on even more, but in light of how it happened, I guess I need to accept it." He shifted his weight on the chair and rested his chin on his hand. "I still wish I could be working for what we need, but it feels good to know God cares enough to let us know in such an obvious way."

"Why don't you just say a prayer of thanks for both of us right now, David?"

"You know I'm not much for praying out loud, Rina."

"I know, David, but I would like if you tried this once."

"All right."

David closed his eyes, so, as Marlene nuzzled her, Rina closed hers too.

"Father, unworthy as we feel, we truly have experienced your goodness this morning. Thank you for Rina's faith, her faithfulness and her spunk. Thank you for hearing and answering her prayer. There is no doubt in our minds that you care. Thank you, too, for those people who felt your nudges to help you answer that prayer. And Lord, if it's not too much to ask for, please send me healing so I can once again support my family. In Jesus' name, amen."

"Amen," echoed Rina. "Thank you, David, that was lovely. There sure is nothing wrong with your prayers even if you think you're not good at it."

"I think I will go out and sit in the sun for a bit. Maybe I'll even catch a few winks while I am doing it."

"I sent Rae and Doris for some bread flour. They should be back soon, and then I will get a batch of bread on the way and get busy on the meat. I think I'll put the heart in the oven for supper. If you feel like it, maybe you could think about where I could set up the press."

"I wondered about Uncle Albert's shed, but that's so far away. It would mean a lot of running back and forth."

"Yes, but I could take the laundry on the wagon. He probably would let me have the space without having to pay for it—that would be a big bonus."

Rina smiled when she saw David go to get his fiddle before he went out the door. Soon she heard him playing out in the back yard. She surmised that the morning's happenings had more effect on his spirit than he had been able to show. The strains of "Now thank we all our God" reached her ears. Thankfulness bubbled up in her own heart in response.

When the music stopped, she waited until the baby was finished feeding and then peeked out the back door. The violin was propped up against the porch railing, David was laying back on the lawn chair peacefully sleeping. Love for her husband and thankfulness to God mingled to warm her heart. She turned to put the baby in her bassinet and went back to the kitchen to begin looking after the beef.

By the end of the week, Rina had Uncle Albert's permission to use his shed and had met with Mr. Reddinger to negotiate payment and the rest of the details. Actually, there wasn't much need for negotiation because he offered her more than she would have thought to ask. The prospects of having that steady income made her glad, but thinking of the extra work made her wonder how she was going to manage everything. She would need to depend on the older children to do their part. She regretted making them work so hard, but for the time being, it was necessary.

Chapter 22 🍃

THE NEXT WEEK, THE PRESS WAS SET UP. She bought another copper boiler to heat water on the stove and extra wash baskets to transport the clothes across town. She asked Herbert to come and put up a few more clothes lines and he offered to make some racks for the wagon so her loads would stay on. He came later that day and delighted her with his ingenuity. Not only would they keep the baskets steady, he made them in such a way that they enlarged the capacity of the wagon.

The following Tuesday morning, she started the fire when she was up for the baby's night feeding so the boiler she had filled before going to bed could begin to heat up. She had picked up the laundry from the hotel earlier in the afternoon. When she rose at 4:30, she put the first batch through and hung them out in the dark while the next batch was washing. By six thirty, when Marlene awoke, she had even Rev. Grigg's things, the diapers and most of the family wash done. She fed the baby and made lunches for the school children before calling Evvy and Bernie to take over with breakfast and getting the younger ones ready for school.

After breakfast, she made sure there was something to keep Lenora amused. She folded the slightly damp linens into the wash baskets, loaded them into the wagon, fed the baby and settled her in for her morning nap.

"You'll be all right now if I leave for Uncle Albert's?" she asked David, who was resting on the couch.

"Sure I will be. When will you be back?"

"Just as soon as I can be. I will have to be back by two or soon after to feed Marlene. There are sandwiches up in the cupboard for you and Lenora, and if Marlene gets fussy before I get back, give her some water from the bottle that's up there too. It will take me a while just to get over there, but I'll hurry as fast as I can. It will take a bit of testing out to see what works, but I will go back and finish later if I can't get done before two."

By the end of the day, Rina felt as though she could go to sleep standing on her feet, but she felt deeply satisfied with all she had accomplished.

Two days a week—sometimes three—that was the routine Rina followed, week after week. Murray's work provided them with milk, which was used for drinking and baking, and there was often enough for puddings besides. Bessie even sent some extras along now and then. Shirley's hand-me-down clothes fitted Doris perfectly, and their cherry tree yielded bountifully enough that several baskets supplemented the Litz's meals and helped fill some jars. One of the other neighbours had a farm out in the country with an orchard and they often offered them fruit for the picking. They weren't living high, but their needs were met.

When the gardening began there was more than enough to fill the days she didn't have laundry to do, especially when the picking started—then there was canning to do besides. She figured it was probably from working so hard and the little sleep she got that she couldn't nurse Marlene as long as she had the others. She had to supplement her feedings with a bottle. In a way, that eased the situation on laundry days because David could give the baby a bottle if Rina wasn't quite finished with the pressing by two. Usually, by the end of the day, Rina was so tired she ached. David was still tired and lethargic. He was also depressed and withdrawn.

Rina looked at the clock as she hung up the mop—eleven o'clock! She took the baby from the crib and sat to nurse her, almost falling asleep. Once she had settled Marlene in the crib again, she took a deep breath and rubbed her eyes. Wearily, she dragged one foot after the other to the bedroom, undressed and sank into bed, utterly exhausted. David reached for her. "David, darling, please just hold me for a bit and let me catch my breath. I am dog-tired tonight."

"I'm sorry, honey-bun!" David's voice sounded hurt and apologetic. He withdrew his arm.

"David, please! I want your arms around me. I just need to have a chance to be held long enough to let go of my weariness." She moved closer to David and snuggled up to him.

Can't you understand that, unlike you, I haven't been in bed the last two hours after having had most of the afternoon resting and a morning of sitting in the sun? I was up before dawn to do twelve loads of laundry, picked four bushels of tomatoes and processed half of them while the laundry was drying, took two big laundry baskets of linens across town to iron them, delivered them on the way back, finished the tomatoes, stopping to nurse the baby—then, since you came to bed, folded the diapers, washed the kitchen floor and fed the baby again before coming to bed myself.

"I know you're working way too hard. I'm not very much use to you, I know, but I do still love you! I just wanted to let you know."

"I know, David," Rina sighed.

I need you too, and I know you need to show your love in the ways you can. I'd rather just go to sleep tonight, but I don't want to make you feel even more isolated from what is normal.

"Can you rub my back a bit? Ahh-hh that feels so good!"

Rina fought off the urge to just relax into a welcome sleep. She reached up to stroke her fingers through David's hair. "Darling, I do need you too! It's just that it's hard to let go of the hustle-bustle of the day in a hurry and give my whole mind and being to love-making. But when I am able to do that, it gives me strength to go on. That togetherness is the foundation that gives a lot of meaning to life. I love you, David."

"Ah-hh Rina, you are a real trouper, and I am looking forward to the day when I can get back to being there for you like you are for me. Sometimes I feel so useless, and I am afraid you feel that way too."

"David! I know you didn't ask for this—it's not your fault! I think maybe I've told you before, but I married you for better or for worse!"

"Yes, Rina, but it seems we hit more 'for worse' patches than 'for better' ones! To add to the humiliation, it seems it's always me making it worse for you and it's you that has to keep working to make it better."

"David Litz! Until now, I didn't have to go looking for work to keep the family, I didn't have an accident that threatened my life, and I didn't have chicken pox and complications and viral pneumonia. I'd say those worse things were worst for you. I just try to support you through them and do what I can to make it a little better. Looking for ways to support the family was your way of trying to make it better for me. The Lord gave me a healthy body and it's a blessing if I can use it to help see you and the family through some worse times—but David, allow me to share my tiredness, when I feel it, without making you feel guilty. At those times I just need your love and understanding and your arms around me. Can you do that?"

"I'll try. You know me well enough by now that you know it's easier for me to worry and feel guilty when I can't do all I'd like to than to accept that inability and just be thankful for my wonderful wife."

"I know, darling! Maybe God knew you needed to learn that lesson and this is the perfect time to practice letting go of doing and just learn to be."

"I might get lazy if I do that!"

"David Litz, lazy?" Rina snorted. "That will be the day!" She kissed him. "Come, my love!"

How often that scene was repeated in the next months— and frequently it was times when I was dead tired—but David did learn something through it. Eventually, he was much more able to just express his thanks and give me his love and support. He also found little ways to make things easier for me—even if it was just giving the children some guidance in helping with the work. I learned something too—how much small things can mean and that I needed to tell him what would be helpful instead of expecting him to know! It changed the weight of my load just to feel thankfulness for those minor things David did to make it easier. Even the change in his attitude, though it didn't allow him to do any heavy work, lightened the load. I still was glad, though, when David finally was well enough to return to his job almost a full year from the time he got sick!

RINA HEARD THE CAR turn in from the street and met David at the back door after his first day back to work. They reached for each other in an embrace.

"So how did the day go?"

"Very well! I am glad that I started doing odd jobs around the house in the last month or two. I think that got my muscles used to the idea they were going to be back to work! I'm tired, but it's a healthy tired, and Mr. Farquarson started me off with a lighter day. I'm telling you, he is one good boss!"

"Yes, he is, but I'm thinking more, right now, about the one good husband I have! How nice to have you well enough to be going off to work and to be welcoming you home at the end of the day!"

"It feels wonderful to me too, honey-bun!" David nuzzled her neck and started a slow dance, holding her close.

"Wow! Enough energy left to dance!" she hummed a bit of a tune. "Why don't you come have a cookie and a glass of milk to keep you going until supper is ready? I just finished baking before the children came home from school, but there are some left! They have gone out to play, so you can have some peace and quiet for a bit."

"Sounds good to me." He sat on a chair at the table. "I might just rest on the couch until supper's ready."

Rina set the milk and cookies in front of him. "That would be good, darling."

"I'll try not to make it a habit, but for the first while, I might have to have a rest. I know there are a lot of things I need to do around here, and I want to finally carry my weight again."

"Don't rush it, darling. Be thankful for what you have now and the rest will come in good time."

A MONTH HAD PASSED and David was into a routine again. When he came home early enough, he would do some odd jobs around the house or in the garden. Rina was still doing laundry for the hotel and her other clients, so her days were full. At the end of the first month of work, David came home just as Rina came up the walk from taking some linens back to the hotel. She looked tired.

"Rina, my love, come and sit down." He opened the door for her and followed her into the kitchen. Taking her hand, he led her to a chair and sat down beside her. He brushed the damp tendrils of hair from her forehead. "Can't you let go of some of your jobs now? I got my second paycheque tonight. I think we can manage."

"Yes, we probably could, but I thought if I could keep the hotel laundry for two or three months more and put that part in the bank, we would have a bit of a nest-egg, should we have something unforeseen pop up again. After that, I could just do Rev. Grigg's and a few of the older folks'."

"I hope we don't need it, but I see your point. I just hate seeing you work so hard!"

"I will do it just until the garden starts yielding, then quit. That way, I can give the hotel advance notice."

"Yes, then you'll quit just in time to work just as hard at something else!" David joshed. "It wouldn't hurt you to have a bit of a breather."

"Last year I did both, plus Marlene was just a baby and you were sick, so it will seem a lot lighter this year. It would be nice to have those reserve funds just for peace of mind."

"Okay, love; just know I won't object if you want to quit sooner."

What a difference that made—doing it because I wanted to save for a rainy day rather than being under pressure to do all I could just so we could eat and have the most basic things for life! It was such a pleasure having David able to be looking out for me instead of the other way around.

I guess that is life! Sometimes we are on the giving end of things and sometimes on the receiving end—and at both ends it makes a lot of difference whether it is a pressing necessity to give or receive or just a desire to do it. That is another place where such a little detail can make such a big difference in our attitude. Ah-hh the human heart is so inconsistent and fickle! The same work can either drain you of energy or energize you. Receiving is accompanied with either the heaviness of embarrassment and humiliation or with joy and true thankfulness. It all depends on the circumstances and even more on the attitude.

Rina turned over on her left side and sighed.

No matter how old we are, we still learn—it just takes some people longer than others.

SATURDAY ARRIVED before they knew it. James and Marlene borrowed tables and chairs from the community centre and had them set up on the lawn. The garage was cleaned out for tables to hold the food. Three barbeques were heated and ready to go by the time people started to arrive. There was a whole contingent coming from the north. Jessie, all three of her children and eight of her ten grandchildren, and Bernie, all four of her children and all ten of her grandchildren were able to come. And of course, some great-great-grands would be coming with that bunch too. Bernie had the most great-grandchildren—ten of them! Rina knew they would be missing the western folks, some of Doris's and Rae's children as well as Carolyn and her children, and of course they would be missing Murray, Rae's Hazel, and Bernie's Fred.

It didn't seem right to Rina that she should outlive one of her own children, two of her in-laws and even one of her grandchildren, but that's the way it was. Marlene thought there could be 132 coming. What a crowd!

I'll be missing you especially today, David. I wish you were here with me to enjoy having that much of the family around. But I'm sure looking forward to it. James even went to get a new reclining cushioned lawn chair so that I can be comfortable. They really baby me—and I have the audacity to just enjoy it! She grinned mischievously. But they are making me wait inside until people come so I can last longer.

James came in the back door. "Everything's set and ready to go. People have started to arrive, so is the guest of honour ready to make her appearance?"

"Guest of honour? I thought Evvy was the guest of honour!"

"Oh, she will be honoured too, but as long as you are the matriarch of the clan, you will always have the most honoured position, ma'am." James bowed low. "Now, could I have the pleasure of accompanying you outside? Your Cadillac is at your service and I am standing by."

"I was just thinking about how good you all are to me, James—so it shall be my pleasure to be escorted by such a kind and handsome man!" With James' assistance she rose to her feet. "I would do a deep curtsey in response to your bow, but I might land on the floor and then you would have to pick me up!"

"Then just let's skip it. Your beloved family awaits you and we wouldn't want any tomfoolery to delay that." He opened the door so she could go out on the veranda.

Chapter 23 🍁

SHE WAS BARELY OUT THE DOOR when Jessie's daughter Leanne noticed her and ran to the steps to help her down. "Good to see you, Gram!"

"Good to see you too, Leanne. Get me down the steps and then I will give you a proper hug!"

Leanne carefully gave her a hug. "Come on over to your chair, Gram. We've got it all ready for you with an afghan to cover you if you need extra warmth."

"Did your kids come too?"

"The boys came with us, but Gail and Ken are still on their way. They should be here shortly."

One by one, the family all came to greet their Gram—from the oldest to the youngest. As each car full arrived, her heart just seemed to expand with love. The older ones she recognized easily, but some of the younger grandchildren she hadn't seen as often or as recently, so she had to resort to asking so she could call them by name. She still sent a birthday card to each of them, but it was getting harder and harder to keep them all straight—especially when there were a few by the same name not too far apart in age.

It was surprising how she could definitely see the Litz in many of their faces—or was it Kurtz? Some did look suspiciously like she did when she was younger. Some of her daughters were beginning to look more like their mother too! Surprising how the twenty years between seventy eight and ninety-nine didn't seem like as much of a spread as they did between newborn and twenty-one year-old! By now, her eldest daughters and herself were all old women! *Guess I'd better not tell them that, though. They might not appreciate being told even if they know it.*

Jessie came toward her with her granddaughter Jenny in tow. Behind them walked a handsome young man Rina assumed to be Jenny's new husband. They had been married last winter when she was too sick to attend the wedding.

"Mama, I want you to meet Jenny's husband, Tom Rupp. Tom, this is Jenny's great-grandmother, Rina Litz."

"So glad to meet you, Grandma! I have heard so much about you. Sorry you weren't able to be at our wedding."

"It's good to meet you, Tom. I, too, was sorry not to be there, but I was quite sick last winter just at the wrong time to be able to celebrate with you."

"I hoped you might be able to meet my own Great-grandmother Hirsch there. She was able to be at the wedding but she has suffered some ill health since then. She is still hanging in there, but she is in a nursing home now."

"Did you say her name was Hirsch?" *Surely not! It couldn't be, could it?*

"Yes, Susannah Hirsch."

"What was your grandfather's name?"

"Thomas. I was named after him. Why? Did you know them?"

"No, not really. But I'm curious. I guess you wouldn't know what his father's name would have been."

"I guess I had better know what his name was! It has been handed down to his offspring with some pride. He was the owner of a textile mill in Bolton and a member of parliament for that area for some years. Gerhardt Hirsch was his name."

"Well, I'll be!" Rina exclaimed. "I think I need to tell you a story. Get a chair, you two, and sit down. This may take a little while."

The young couple's eyes and faces were full of curiosity, but they did her bidding.

"Okay, Gram, what is the scoop?"

"As a young girl, my mother, Ellie Kessler, was engaged to your Great-great-grandpa Gerhardt. They had planned to get married and already had dreams of moving to Bolton. Ellie's sister, Regina, died in childbirth, though, leaving two young daughters. Ellie's parents asked—well they really insisted—that she break her engagement and marry her sister's husband, John Kurtz, so that the girls would stay in the family. That was a very hard and heart-wrenching thing that they requested. She couldn't think how to refuse and they really gave her no alternative, so she did what was asked of her."

"Oh Grandma! That was a terrible thing for them to do!" Jenny frowned in horror.

"I can't imagine anyone doing that. What kind of a marriage did Ellie and John have?"

"Ellie was a pretty determined woman. She struggled much, especially the first while, but she was also wise. She knew unless she gave it every effort to learn to love John, she would have a life of regret and bitterness. She told me that they did learn to love each other more deeply than they thought possible in the early days of their marriage."

"So then they had you?" Tom asked.

"Oh, no! They had one son, but when he was just eight, John was killed in a farm accident, leaving Mama with her two nieces, now her daughters, and a son. After a few years, she married my father, who was John's double cousin, and then I was born. She always said that it was such a different experience because with John they needed to get over their first loves before they could learn to love each other, whereas she and my father, Jake, already loved each other when they got married"

"What a story!" Tom shook his head, trying to absorb the facts. He laughed. "Wouldn't Gerhard and Ellie laugh to know their great-great-grandchildren married each other?"

"Yes, I daresay they would! I find it rather satisfying to know, and I wish you a long and happy marriage! I hope you will be able to not only find an ever deepening love for each other, but some gratification in knowing you are fulfilling a love your ancestors had to leave unfulfilled." Rina laughed. "Please forget what I just said, I'm sorry! Don't let that put pressure on you! Just concentrate on building your own relationship for the joy you can find in each other and forgive the ramblings of an old woman."

"Don't apologize, Gram. I think knowing this story makes our love all the more special." Jennie reached out to take Rina's hand.

"I echo those sentiments. May I call you Gram too?" Tom asked.

"Sure can! You're a part of the family now!"

"Everyone ready to eat?" James called out. "Gather round! Would you like to pray, Maw?"

"Help me stand up, then."

"You can stay seated, Maw. We'll gather around you." He raised a hand. "Quiet everyone! Gram's going to pray."

When all was quiet, Rina began. "Kind heavenly Father, we're almost overwhelmed at the lavishness of your grace and goodness." Her voice broke momentarily. "You have given us so much and we as a family together celebrate your kindness today. Thank you for each one who is here today and for those who are not able to be here. We think, too, of those who have gone on before us." Again, Rina needed to pause as she ached for those not present. "So Lord, for the food before us, the family around us and most of all for the faith within us, we give you our thanks. Bless our time together, and may we one day be gathered around your throne, not one of us missing. In Jesus' name we pray, Amen."

"Thanks, Maw! We appreciate your prayers." James laid his hand on her arm, emphasizing his words. He raised his hand then and announced, "Now, everyone can come to the barbeque for your choice of meat and then line up on each side of the tables in the garage for the rest of the food. The drinks are on the side-wall. If you need anything, just ask." He grinned, "If we can help we will; if we can't, you'll have to do without." James chuckled at his own joke.

HOT DOGS AND HAMBURGERS and all the salads and relishes everyone had contributed were enjoyed. When the desserts and ice cream fully sated their appetites and everything was cleared up, the adults gathered around in a large circle to chat while the children went to enjoy games.

Rina just sat back in her recliner and listened, revelling in having so many of her family gathered together.

Bernie was questioning Rae.

"I was fixing the eaves trough," he protested.

"The way I remember it, you were going to fly off the porch roof. That's what you told me you were doing," Lenora corrected him.

"Aw, that is just what I said because I didn't want you to think I would fall over some mundane thing."

"Well, you split your head open and had to have stitches."

"Seems to me you did that on a regular basis, Rae." Doris interjected. "You did it again when you fell off the dam in Malden."

"Yeah—I think for a while there it was open more than it was closed. I guess that is when my brains fell out! So you have to make allowances for me."

"I don't know about that," chipped in Lenora, "but I remember Dad saying that you were your own worst enemy and that if trouble was anywhere near, you would be the one to find it."

"Oh, but I tried to avoid it! That is why I always drove so fast. I wanted to get to where I was going before I had an accident!"

"Is that why you got run over by the Jeep that time you and Murray were going up Winery Hill?"

"Well, no, not that time!" He had the grace to look a little sheepish. "I thought I could get up the hill faster myself, so I jumped out, but it was muddy and I slipped in underneath the wheel."

"So maybe Mom was wrong that time when she was riding with you in your new car and you were going so fast some of the rest of us were scared but she just said that you wouldn't want to kill yourself, so you wouldn't kill her," Marlene suggested.

Rae just shrugged his shoulders. "Maybe being my own worst enemy would apply to the time I wrecked Dad's watch by accident and I was afraid to own up to it, so I threw it over in the neighbours' garden. When Dad couldn't find his watch I was quiet. I succeeded until the next spring when the neighbour worked his garden, found the watch and recognized it. He brought it over to Dad, who just sort of looked around, saw me and assumed it was me—I wouldn't know why!" He grinned.

His siblings roared in laughter. Rina heard comments between the laughter like:

"You would wonder!"

"He knew trouble when he saw it!"

"You probably had that overly innocent look that just spelled guilt!"

"Well, I don't know, but I was taken to the wood shed and got the belt for it even if almost a year had passed. I guess he had a sense of justice that wouldn't let him pass it off." He shook his head as though he couldn't understand why. "There was more than one time I wished I would have taken his advice, but too often it was after the fact. Take that time I had saved up enough money to buy a car; there was a house for sale up a few streets from ours, and he suggested I buy the house, then use the rent to buy a car. I didn't think I could wait long enough for that, so I went ahead and bought the car. About three months later I shmucked it up so good I couldn't drive it. It was then I wished I would have taken his advice. At least I would still have had the house and the means of saving up for another car! I guess hindsight is better than foresight."

Quite a speech for Rae! Even though he is lots of fun and has that dry sense of humour, he is usually the quiet one. A few words from him, said in his inimitable way, has more effect than a long speech from one of the others. He does have the same sense of humour that his daddy had, though.

"I guess Daddy always liked hanging onto his money and thought you should too! Remember the story about him when he was just a little tyke? He still had his long hair and the curls that were Grandma Litz' pride and joy. She gave him a nickel and sent him to get a loaf of bread. He decided to go across the frozen river, but he went through the ice. Someone saw him and pulled him out by his curls, so they probably saved him that day."

"Yes, but he still had the nickel in his hand! He hadn't let go! I guess that set the trend for his life—hang on to every penny as long as you can."

Oh you kids! When you have hardly any money, you have to hold on to the pennies. You don't know how much your dad would have liked to be more generous, but he had to hang on to the pennies so you would have the bare necessities of life.

"I still have a few of Daddy's curls in the house. They're in a frame with a few of mine. I keep forgetting which are his and which are mine." Marlene leaned forward in her chair. "Mama knows, though. I guess I should mark them while I still have her around."

"I still have a few as well." Evelyn added. "I took a few with me when I went to Halifax. One time, we pinned a few of them amongst your curls, Marlene, and we couldn't have told which were yours and which were Daddy's, so no wonder you can't tell the difference now."

"As I got older, though, they were there only because of the Saturday night ritual of bath and then having our hair curled into long ringlets while Daddy listened to Foster Hewett broadcasting the hockey game. My hair was so thick it would take two rows of ringlets to get all the hair curled. One night someone went to pass a stool over my head to someone else and smacked my head. I let out a holler. Daddy got quite upset and said I had enough pain just getting all that hair curled without getting hit in the head. He didn't understand the need for all that primping."

"That reminds me of the time Bobby and I were visiting in Ontario and Mama and Daddy decided to take us on a little trip up north. Dad was in an extra gay mood. You know that Mama always felt that Peter's folks were higher on the social ladder than we were. Well, that night we got one room in a motel. Bobby and I were on one side of the curtain—Mom and Dad on other side. He said something—I don't remember what, but Mama reminded him that Bobby and I were Strongs now and the Strongs would be more sophisticated. He said, 'Well, maybe the Strongs are far more sophisticated, but I am extra *stupisticated*!' as though that was indeed superior, then he howled with laughter at his own wit!"

"Sounds like him," Elaine commented. "After he was out to visit you, Evvy, he told me about how your roads had so many twists and turns and were always going uphill or down, then he said, in fact, you had bought a quart of cream in town and by the time you got home it was butter!" Everyone laughed. Evvy brushed her hair back from her face.

"That couldn't have been the day that it took about two hours to drive five miles because he wanted to stop to see every bit of flora and fauna along the way. That day, the cream had every chance of turning *sour* before he got home! He sure loved nature as well as his jokes and his family."

"He was a good father-in-law, and I loved him dearly. But he was always bringing me food to fatten me up. He seemed to know what was most tempting to me. Well, look at me now! I don't think even he would call me skinny anymore."

"Oh Elaine, you may not be as thin as you first were when you got married, but I still wouldn't call you overweight. You maybe have just joined the rest of us in being a normal weight!" Bernie rushed to assure her. "You know he worried about everything and everyone. He probably worried that you wouldn't have enough reserves to keep you going if you got sick or something. He worried about me hitchhiking around the summer I picked peaches over near Queenston. Looking back, I can understand. I probably would have worried a bit if my children or grandchildren hitchhiked around too, but it was fun and we lived in a safer world then—or at least it seemed that way."

Jessie wiped the remains of an ice-cream cone off her little great-grandson's face. "Daddy may have been a worrier, but when he got his fiddle under his chin, his cares vanished. He could really get that thing going—especially when Uncle Bill and Cousin Lester were around. The three of them could set anyone to dancing—and if you couldn't dance you'd want to tap your toes and clap just for the joy of it."

"I remember that too," Sharon added. "Some of the things you have been talking about happened before I remember or even before I was born, but I never hear *Blackbird*, or *O dem Golden Slippers* without thinking of him."

Marlene reached out to give one of the children a hand with their ice-cream. "I know that you, Evvy, taught yourself to play the organ, but I guess Cousin Lester got all the family talents in fiddling—he went on to win some old-time fiddlers competitions—something none of us ever did."

"We had other talents, though," Rae informed them with dignity. "If Murray were here he would tell you that we could keep people agog! One of his favourite ways was when it was just getting dark and we were out driving; we would come up to a stop light and he would dash out of the car, run up to the headlight and light a match. When he got it close to the headlight, I would pull the light switch so the lights would come on. People coming to the corner from the other directions would look amazed—it looked as though he had to light them that way!"

"That sounds like something Murray would do. You never knew what he was up to. He would make it look so genuine he almost convinced you that you were the crazy one for doubting it!" There was nostalgia in Elaine's voice as she laughed.

"Granddaddy was like that too," Sally piped up. "I remember once when they were living here with Mom and Dad, Grandma took the dog out for a walk. Gramps locked the door behind her. When she came back, Gram tried the door, then knocked. Gramps just looked at her through the window and waved as though that's what Gram wanted—and he kept doing it as though he had no idea she wanted to come in."

Sally's shoulders began to quiver and then she abandoned her story to the laughter that shook her entire body. As Elaine watched she began to join Sally in laughter. One by one the others joined until no one knew whether they were laughing at the story or at the mass hilarity that had infected them all. Finally, they began to wipe their tears and asked Sally to finish her story. "In the end, I was the one who let Gram in. Then you should have seen the two of them. Gram grabbed a pillow and threw it at Gramps. The pillows flew back and forth for a while until finally Gramps stood up and held onto her arms to keep her from picking the pillow up again. Remember that, Gram?"

"Yeah," drawled Rina with an amused and embarrassed grin.

"Shall I go on?" Sally asked.

"I don't know what you are going to say, but you may as well."

"Gramps hugged you and pulled you down on the sofa and you started acting like young teenagers in love!" Sally's voice dripped with mock distaste.

"So you young'uns think you are the only ones that know how to be in love?"

"We-e-ell!"

"Well what, young lady?"

"Actually that scene gives me a lot of encouragement, Gram. I think if the two of you could still be in love after all of those years, maybe there is hope for me too!"

Good! I know Sally has had some rough spots in her marriage, so I'm glad if David and I could provide some inspiration. This isn't the place to do it, but maybe I should tell her sometime that the love she observed came about partly because of the rough times David and I had too. Love grows stronger through those times when there doesn't seem to be too much reason to keep loving but you remember your vows and your commitment and love anyway. When you get to the other side of the rough spot you discover that not only do you still love each other, but your love has grown deeper to a more comfortable level—and that's exciting too!

She realized that her contemplation had caused her to miss some of the conversation. Elaine was talking about the time Murray and she had taken David and her on a camping trip to Bayfield.

"We caught several fish there and had a wonderful fish-fry several times, but Dad decided we could do some fishing on the way home too. We went on back roads and wherever he saw a river where he thought the fishing would be good, we would stop and get out all our fishing gear. He was always the first to get his hook in the river. We would barely have gotten ours wet when he would decide there were no fish there, so we'd pack up and move on. We must have stopped at least a dozen times or more. By the time we got close to London, he was so hungry for fish we ended up going to Port Stanley and buying fish to take home so we could satisfy his yen."

"Even if he wasn't fishing, Daddy liked to drive on the back roads. He thought you could see more there—and he probably did see more, because he sometimes was looking at the trees and fields and scenery more than the road!" Lenora cleared her throat and shook her head from side to side. "Mm-mm! I think he sometimes dusted the weeds on each side of the road in turns if there was no other vehicle in sight."

"And if you had the nerve to ask where we were going on one of those side-trips of his," Doris added, "he would say, 'We'll find out when we get there!' We usually did come to a familiar road, but I don't think even he always knew where we were."

"I still think the funniest story about Daddy was when we lived on King Street in London." Marlene's snicker and the amusement in her eyes indicated what was to come. "We had the ice box that had a pan underneath to catch the water as it melted—you young kids wouldn't know anything about it. It was a forerunner to a fridge and a real valuable innovation for the housewife—anyway, Daddy had quite a barrel chest on him and, because he had a small waist, he found it hard to keep his pants up, so he wore suspenders. Often in the evenings when it was warm, he would pull his suspenders off his shoulders while he took his shirt off, and just let the suspenders hang while he relaxed. One night, Dad decided the pan needed emptying—but forgot he had dropped his suspenders. He carefully pulled out the pan of ice cold water and started across the floor to empty it in the sink. The water started to splash back and forth as he moved across the kitchen. Yep you guessed it—some of it hit Dad's chest. He let out a whoop of surprise and sucked his stomach in. Down went the pants, leaving him standing in the middle of the kitchen in all his glory. What a sight!"

The titters around the circle broke into a loud chortle and then into helpless laughter as those who remembered relived it again. Even those who hadn't been there at the time, fed by Marlene's vivid description, were well able to picture it in their minds. The younger children left their games and came running.

"What's so funny?" they asked.

"Ask Aunt Marlene; no one else could tell it quite the same."

Aunt Marlene obliged and retold the story, adding some actions. By the end of the story, the children were laughing along with the adults, who found the new version even more hilarious.

That time, as in many, David's sense of humour kicked in right along with everyone else's. Although he set the tray down and made a quick grab for his pants, he then stood laughing at himself with the rest of the family. How often he was reminded in the subsequent years, whenever he dropped his suspenders, "You'd better steer clear of the ice water, Daddy!" Whenever he carried a bucket of water, he would be cautioned, "Keep your suspenders on!" It became an oft-repeated family joke.

"That accident was funny, unlike some." Jessie reminded them. "Evvy broke her arm, Rae kept splitting his head open and getting run over and the like, but I remember the time when we were living in Stafford and Doris tipped her high chair over by pushing against the table. She fell against the stove and burned her face. Poor little thing! She screamed for a long time and it took quite a while until she healed. That was her favourite side to sleep on and she couldn't lie that way for quite a while. Another time when she was older, the handle came off the tea kettle and her leg got scalded. She's almost as accident prone as you are, Rae."

"Except that I got burns instead of stitches like Rae."

In a large family there will always be some accidents—some because there are just too many directions for one mother to watch. I never did get over hurting when my children hurt and wishing I could protect them from injury, whether that was physical or emotional. At the vantage point of present age, I wish I would have expressed that to them more often. I had what I now know was the wrong idea—that if I sympathized with them too much it would keep them from finding ways to work through their hard times. Perhaps just sharing some similar difficulty or predicament that I experienced would have given them hope that they could grow through their own. Even today, I hurt for Rae and Elaine because they have lost their life partners, and I see the heaviness of what some of the grandchildren are going through even though they try to hide it from me or make light of it. Thank the Lord I can still bring it to him and let him take care of it.

Chapter 24 ✿

AFTER A LONG AFTERNOON of reminiscence and sharing, one by one, people began to leave. Those with younger children left first, she supposed, to get them back to their own homes and routines. *Little ones can only take so much time away.*

Eventually there were only the ones from nearby and then, after snacking on leftovers, even they left. It was beginning to get cool in spite of the thick cover they had brought out for her. She shivered.

"Marlene, I think I had better go inside. I'm starting to get cool even with this nice afghan you brought me."

"Oh, I'm sorry, Mama! I guess I've been rushing around cleaning up and didn't think about you just sitting there. We don't want you getting cold or coming down with pneumonia again."

"Oh, I'm not that cold, I just think now is the time to go in. Just get my walker for me."

"Here you go! Evvy, do you want to go in with Mama while I finish here?"

Inside, Rina said she thought she would just head to bed. "It's been a long, satisfying day. I may not go to sleep right away, but I will have a lot of good things to think about." She sat on the chair beside the bed, kicked off her shoes and began to undress. "What a wonderful feeling to have so many of your family around you. It would have been nice if your children and grandchildren could have been here too."

"They would have enjoyed it, Mama—not only your blood relatives, but all your Centre Children. Those you sent cards to after you got to know them feel as though you are their grandma too. You were so faithful in keeping in touch with them."

Rina pulled the nightgown over her head and looked Evvy in the eyes. "It was no trial to me. I like writing letters and they endeared themselves to me when I was out there. It was one thing I could do from here to add a little happiness to their lives. If you just turn the covers back, I can get in now."

Evvy helped her mother move from the chair to her bed.

Rina sank down on her pillow. "Ah-hh! That feels good! I guess I am more tired than I thought. Do you mind pulling the covers up? Sometimes my arm just won't cooperate."

"Sure will! Can I give you a good-night kiss?"

"I hope so!" she puckered up. "You could give me a lot of those before you would over-extend your quota." Her eyes shone with love.

"Good night, dear Mama." Evvy tucked the blankets around her. "Sweet dreams!"

"Oh, I'm sure they will be."

Evvy turned out the light and shut the door.

RINA SIGHED, releasing the weariness she felt. The day had been deeply satisfying, but her head was spinning with all the memories that had been aroused and all the activity of the day.

> *It's always amazing how everyone remembers the same incident from a different perspective—and when there are ten kids to remember it in ten different ways it can sometimes get quite amusing. Of course, I remember those same episodes in quite a different way myself.*

She had heard the two oldest girls discuss their leaving home. They seemed to think they were fully grown by then. To her, they were too young to be leaving home. Oh, Jessie had gone just to Stafford first, and since she had lived there often, it wasn't so bad. But when Evvy decided to go to Toronto to work for a while, she experienced some real fear for her. She went with a friend—but Jane was no older than Evvy and perhaps even more adventuresome, so it wasn't a great comfort to a mother. She herself was very pregnant just then, so that may have heightened her anxiety.

Carolyn was born in March of 1941, a few months after Evvy left for Toronto. Rina went to the hospital to have her. That was a new experience. She'd had all the others either in her home, her mother's or Marta's. She had more waiting on in the hospital than she'd had for years! It was rather nice.

Evvy's friend Jane got homesick about three months after she left, so she came home. Evvy stuck it out for another three, but she missed her friends in Malden and came home too. She found work in a restaurant. Then, in the fall of '42, she decided she wanted to join the Navy. She announced to her mother her desire to do as several of her friends had done.

Inside, Rina had felt her heart sink. She wasn't sure she was ready to let her daughter go, much less have her choose something that might put her in danger. However, she hid her hesitation. All she said was, "Well, if your friends are all joining up and that's what you want to do, I believe we have done a good enough job of bringing you up that we can trust you wherever you go."

She told me later that she appreciated the trust we placed in her even more when she heard other girls telling how their parents argued and tried to discourage them when they spoke of enlisting. She said her mama's little speech was pretty effective.

In February, Jessie left to join the Navy too. She was given the same message. They were both good girls and they deserved the trust we put in them. They grew up to be responsible people and both of them have gone on to make their lives worthwhile.

IN DECEMBER, Rina went back to the Stafford Hospital when Sandra was born. She chuckled as she remembered the nurse who had taken her to her room after being admitted.

"So, Mrs. Litz," Miss Horst asked solicitously as they walked down the hall, "Is this your first baby?"

"My *tenth*." Rina curtly replied.

"Your what?"

"This is only the second time I've been in hospital for the birth of a child, but it will be number ten."

"Your husband was married before?" Miss Horst still did not fully comprehend.

"Oh no! I gave birth to them all, but the rest were born at home."

It still took Miss Horst a moment to take in the truth, but when she did she almost ran Rina the rest of the way to her room.

"Let's get you settled," she commented nervously. "It probably won't take you long to deliver if this really is your tenth."

"Oh, I think I can count, Miss Horst—and it *is* number ten."

She had determined to stay there for ten days just to make the most of the chance for a long rest and to enjoy the new baby and have her all to herself, but Evvy got a leave and decided to surprise them by coming home five days after Sandra arrived. There was no way was Rina going to be in hospital the whole time her daughter was home. She had some persuading to do with the doctor, but she came home to spend the Christmas season with the whole family. Rae had moved to London to live with David's brother that fall so he could go to high school there. That left only seven children at home. She missed those three, but it did relieve the congestion in the house a bit. For Christmas, though, the whole family was home, including the new baby, so although it was crowded, they managed to find room for everyone.

From the time she was very young, Carolyn was troubled with high fevers. Rina remembered the first time she had convulsions along with the fever. That had really scared her. She sent Bernie to get Mrs. Frazer, who lived next door. When she stopped convulsing, they put her in a tub of cool water to bring her fever down.

I knew to do that myself, but the convulsion scared me so much I couldn't think what to do. That was the first time. After that, I got that little tub out as soon as her fever went up. Even then, she had other episodes. Finally. the doctor said her tonsils were so bad they had to come out. He decided that we may as well do Marlene at the same time. In those days they took tonsils out routinely. They don't do that anymore.

We had the surgeries done and brought the girls home, then about an hour after we got home, Marlene started haemorrhaging. We raced her in to Doc's office, but he sent her back to hospital and they kept her overnight. I hardly knew where I should be. Carolyn was so young and Sandra was just a baby, yet Marlene really needed me. I'm glad that is all behind me.

We had eleven good years in Malden. Eleven years without a move. That was some kind of a record for the Litz family up to that time. Then David got the itch again.

"RINA!" she heard David call as the door slammed behind him. She had just carried some empty jars to the cellar.

"I'm in the cellar, but I will be right up."

She climbed up the steps as fast as she could. She wondered about the excitement she heard in David's voice. He didn't usually call for her as soon as he got in the door.

"What is it, love?"

"How did you know that it is anything at all?"

"Oh, I know you well enough that I can tell when there is extra excitement in your voice. I know you have something to tell me."

"Well, I do have something to run by you."

"Out with it! I don't do well with suspense."

"On my route today, I stopped at a restaurant and there was a man there from London. He works for an asphalt company. He said they really need help at the plant and they are offering a really good wage. It's almost double what I make now." David reached for her and pulled her into his arms. "I haven't asked this of you for quite a while now, but would you consider moving to London and letting me give it a try? It feels like more of a challenge than driving a delivery van. I've kept at it because it is a steady income, and although I do get to meet a lot of people, it does sometimes feel boring. I have always liked construction work and a place where I can figure out how to do things better or more efficiently. There isn't much place for creativity in this job."

Rina grinned. It sounded as though David thought as long as he was talking there would be no chance for her to refuse him the opportunity. The thought of moving again really didn't appeal to her at all—especially with a one year-old and a three-year old in tow. It had been such a relief to be able to stay in one place this long and she hated to bring their hiatus to an end. But how could she refuse when he sounded so excited about it? He had stayed at this job a long time, and he was right. He certainly was capable of much more.

"So—what do you think?"

"Well, David, there are a few things I'd like to know. First of all, where are we going to live?"

"I wanted to talk it over with you first, but if you say yes, I will speak to my brother and see if he knows any place we could rent."

"And if you give it a try and you don't like it?"

"By what I heard, I think I will, but if I don't, I guess we could come back to Malden."

"So do we just rent out this house until we know for sure? We've been making payments to Uncle Albert and, with the children leaving one by one, it gets more suitable for us all the time. I like living in Malden and I had visions of us living on and retiring here."

"We can rent it out for the time being, and then if it goes well, we can sell it, finish paying Uncle Albert and use what is left to put a down payment on something in London."

"We've done things in our lives at greater risk. So if you really want to, go ahead and at least find out from your brother what is available."

"Oh Rina, thank you. You really are a brick—a loyal and faithful wife! I can always count on you." He gave her another squeeze. "I was hesitant to even ask it of you because I know how much I've put you through, but lately I've felt so trapped and uncreative. I hate feeling so pathetically humdrum doing the same thing over and over, day after day."

Rina could hear the eager excitement in his voice and regretted the feeling of anxiety that nagged at her. How could she deny or even wish to reject something that felt so good to him? She would just have to shush those apprehensions when they arose.

David called his brother that evening and acquired the promise that he would look out for a place. David called the asphalt plant and told them he was interested in the job on the mixer. They did an interview over the phone and he was hired. They said he could sign the papers when he came. He asked to be able to give his boss three week's notice, then he would start the following week.

You would have thought he had been handed a reprieve from slavery! He was so excited. Rina's apprehension increased, for now the job was accepted but they still didn't have a place to live. Nor was there one when the time came for David to begin work. His brother offered him a room so David could begin the job, and Rina stayed behind until he could find something. Rina's heart sank. Living apart again! It wasn't the way she wanted it.

When school was about to begin in September, she wanted the children to begin in London where they would be going. Finally, David came home one weekend with news.

"I don't know how you'll like this, but Bill and I have prepared a place for us to live."

"Where is it, and why don't you think I will like it?"

"We-ell . . ." David looked at her, looked away, then returned to look her in the eyes. "It is rather makeshift. We found an old semi trailer and moved it into Bill's back yard. We've built in bunk beds enough for all the kids except Rae and Murray, who can share the room Rae has been using. It won't take much heat because it's so small, so we put in a small stove. There is room at the one end for our bed, and if you put a curtain in between, it will give us a bit of privacy. In the kitchen end is the stove and place for a table. We've built steps up to the back and a smaller door to get in and out. It will be a tight squeeze, but I hope it's just temporary, and the kids can get into their schools for September."

As often when David was trying to justify his actions even more in his own mind than to her, he was talking in one blue streak, trying to get all the facts and explanations clear to make it as palatable as possible.

Rina's mind went back to Dubbin. Would they still be in the trailer this winter, and would it be as cold there as it had been so long ago? What else could she do? She didn't like living apart from David, and he was thoroughly enjoying his job.

With a heavy heart, she forced a smile to her face. "All right, David, we can give it a try. With two little ones needing crawl and play space, it won't be the most appropriate living space, but at least we'll be together."

Bernie was committed to her job until November, so arrangements were made for her to stay in Malden until then. They found the Austins, a young couple who needed a place to rent for two years. They were ready to move into their house.

When the neighbours found out we were actually leaving, they held a farewell party for us. They took up a collection and we were given a nice sum of money. The younger girls were each given a doll. Marlene and Lenora each received a woollen kerchief. Marlene was so upset that Carolyn and Sandra had nice dolls and all she had was a scratchy kerchief! I'm sure the neighbours thought they were making Marlene feel good by giving her a more grown-up gift, but she would have dearly loved a doll. That farewell party felt more like a wake to me. I wasn't ready to leave Malden and our life there. It hadn't been trouble-free by any stretch of the imagination, but we were surrounded with good neighbours and friends of long-standing that made even the tough times tolerable. I didn't know anyone in our neighbourhood in London except for Bill and Amelia and, by then, I knew what the trailer looked like and it didn't help my misgivings a bit!

We ended up living there longer than anyone foresaw!

Chapter 25

EVVY LET THEM KNOW, the November before the move to London, that she was getting married in Victoria to a young man who was also stationed there with the air force. When Rina inquired about who he was and if Evvy was sure he was the one, she was gratified to learn he came from a good family with more background and prestige than their own. Evvy had not only asked herself the right questions, but had prayed about it and been assured that her choice was a good one. Rina and David were sad they couldn't be present, but were glad that Rina's brother, George, who lived in Vancouver, would have the honour of giving the bride away.

Not to be left behind, Jessie, who had stayed in touch via letters with a man from Malden, came home on a leave; they announced their engagement and the next time home in May, they got married. Because they hadn't been able to be present for Evelyn's wedding, David thought they shouldn't be at Jessie's either. They only had a small wedding anyway.

The girls hadn't been living at home for some time, but it still felt different, knowing they were gone for good.

The winter passed and, although they survived, when summer came it became stifling hot in the trailer. David purchased a tent and they spent most of the summer on the beach in Port Stanley. That was no picnic for Rina either. She did most of their washing in the lake, but Sandra was still in diapers, and cooking on the beach wasn't what she would call fun either.

When fall came, they were stuffed back in the trailer for another winter. Near the end of the school year, Rina was called into Bill's house for a telephone call. Mulling the message over in her mind, she knew what she was going to present to David that evening.

"David, the Austins called this morning to say they were moving out at the end of June."

"I love my job, Rina. Can we put the house up for sale?"

"I've been thinking all day. You know we can't stay in the trailer for the summer months. How would it be if I go back to Malden for the summer with the kids? I really don't want to come back to the trailer for another winter. I've had enough of that. I would like if you would make a concentrated effort to find something else before September. If you do, then we could put the house up for sale—but please, not until we have a better place to live."

We had a wonderful summer among friends again, even though it was more like camping out in the house with just the bare necessities. David did find us a different place to live.

THE LAST WEEK of August David took them to see where they would be living. He took them to a street just off Hamilton and stopped in front of a business building. Rina got out of the car and looked around to see the house.

"So where are we going?"

"Come around to the back."

She and the children all followed him up the little alley at the side of the building. Out back there were boxes and various pieces of paraphernalia laying around. David opened the back door. There was a fairly large landing with four or five stairs going up straight ahead, but he led them to the right and down six steps where he opened another door. There, straight ahead of them was a semblance of a kitchen: a few cupboards, a sink, an electric stove and an icebox. The rest of the space was one large room. Three small windows along the left side and one at the back just around the corner from the stairs were all that gave natural light. The rest, when David pressed the switch, was lit up by bare bulbs hanging from cords.

"We're not going to live here, are we?" Lenora asked. Her eyes were wide with fear and her voice trembled. "I'd be scared to live here!"

We're leaving the trailer for this? Rina wanted to ask in despair, but remained quiet.

"Oh Daddy!" Doris admonished. "Couldn't you find something better than this?"

"No, young lady, I couldn't. We'll keep looking, but for now, this is it. We can hang some blankets and sheets to separate the spaces and I will put in better lights, but we can make this do for a while, can't we?" he finished up with a pleading voice, his eyes fixed on Rina.

"I think we had better find renters for the Malden house for now." Her tone was measured and noticeably tense.

"Does that mean you'll accept this, or that you want the option to escape back to Malden if you can't stand it?"

"If I have to, I'll accept this for now, but I pray it will be temporary."

David looked a little crestfallen. "I will try to find something better, but can't this do for now?"

"David," Rina laid a hand on his arm and with her other hand on the side of his face looked directly into his eyes with as much love and understanding as she could muster. "You need to realize that you are at work through the winter from sun-up until sunset. The older children are in school during the day, but the little ones and I are here all day, every day. It is mostly a cement floor and will be cold in the winter—not nice or even healthy for them to sit or play on. Even if I do everything I can to cheer it up, it can't be very bright and pleasant. Better lighting will help, but it'll be hard to keep clean."

"Okay honey-bun, I hear you! You're right! You do spend a lot more time at home than anyone else and you've been cooped up in a trailer for two winters. Sorry I couldn't find anything better, sweetheart."

That night, David continued their conversation.

"It seems to be hard to find places to rent. Every time I find something I think is suitable, when they find out we have eight children, all of a sudden it becomes unavailable. What would you say if we looked for something in this area to buy? If we sell the house in Malden and pay off the mortgage, we should have enough for a down payment at least. We'll try to save as much as we can between now and then as well. And at the asphalt plant, if you don't take any sick days, the boss gives a quite nice bonus at Christmas. That could go into the house fund too."

"That sounds good to me. If you are sure you like your work and you want to stay there, then I am willing to put up with the basement apartment until we can find a place."

They settled into their new quarters. Rina found some inexpensive print with big yellow flowers that she sewed together to make a separation between the living and sleeping areas and curtains for the windows. She bought a new oilcloth for the table with bright yellow flowers as well. It did cheer up the place. She frequented auction sales and rummage sales to pick up anything else that could bring some cheer to the dank, dark basement. At one auction, she found an area rug that looked reasonably clean. That was better for Sandra and Carolyn to sit on to play. David found a light fixture with multiple bulbs that brightened the living area.

Lenora, Marlene and Carolyn shared a double bed, Doris and Bernie another and they had a crib for Sandra in one of the sleeping areas while Murray and Rae shared a bed in another and David and Rina had an area of their own. You could hardly call it privacy, but at least there was separation.

Marlene hated school. She was afraid of the teacher. Rina was inclined to agree that there was some reason for her fear. One of the children in her class was epileptic. When the teacher saw her starting a seizure, he would throw a blackboard eraser at her to try to bring her out of it. Rina couldn't imagine that would be the best treatment, but she did understand that it scared Marlene.

In addition to not liking school, the children hated coming home to what they had dubbed *The Hell Hole*. Murray started working at the plant with David, and Bernie and Doris found work at restaurants.

In early spring, David came home jubilant. "Hey girls, you take over here. I've got something to show your mother. We'll be gone about an hour."

"Where are you going? What are you going to show her?" the girls wondered.

"She'll tell you when she gets home. Come on, Rina!"

"Okay, okay! I'm coming." She had questions in her eyes. "You're not even going to give me a hint?"

"No, I want to see your face when you find out."

They got into the car and went up Rectory Street and turned onto King. David stopped in front of a big square brick house. "Look at that," he said, pointing at the house.

"Yes?"

"How would you like to live here?"

"In this house?"

"Yes. Come, let's have a look inside. I've got the key."

They entered by the front door. A large staircase wound up to the right. A closet door was underneath the second part of the stairs and there were doors to both the right and left and a hallway to the left of the stairs.

"Wow! Where do we go first?"

"Let's go to the left here. This is a living/dining room and there is another door out of the dining room part that leads back to the hall, here. Now turn to your left, here in the back part . . ."

"Oh-hh! What a nice large kitchen—big enough for a table that could hold our whole family and a few guests! Nice cupboards and sink too!"

"There are stairs back here that lead to the back part of the upstairs, but let's go and look at the other half of the front part first and then go up the front stairs."

They went back into the hallway. To the left, behind the stairs, was a small room, then at the front another larger room. David showed her into that room.

"I thought this could be our room. It would be away from the children, giving us real privacy—something of which we get precious little right now. Come, let us go upstairs."

At the top of the hall was a sizeable bathroom. One of the bedrooms was quite large and the other two, though smaller, were still of generous size. Another door led to the back part of the house, where there were two more bedrooms and a spacious hall with a large window and a door that led to a balcony above the back porch.

Rina kept exclaiming at all the rooms and the beauty of the hardwood floors.

"This is beautiful, David, but it must be beyond our means—isn't it?"

"I don't think so, Rina. It belonged to the mother of one of my coworkers. She is in the hospital and not expected to live. Even if she did, she won't be able to come back here. She wants Jim to sell it, and she said she wants it to go to a family who will really appreciate it. I think we qualify—and so does Jim. I told him what I thought we could manage as a down payment on the $5000 price he wants for it and how much a month we can handle. He says that is all right, so, my love, if it meets your approval, it's yours!"

"Oh David!" she reached for him, tears welling up in her eyes. "I never dreamed of living in something so beautiful!"

Love and delight sparkled in his eyes. "You don't know how long I've waited and how often I longed to give you something that would please you the way I see this does."

"Oh, it most certainly does. The last two years have been difficult because we left behind such a good life in Malden—I sometimes wished for more space, but I liked it there. But the last two years will make me appreciate this lovely, lovely place all the more. It feels like a mansion. I can hardly wait to show the children."

When they got home, the children wanted to know what the big secret was. Rina just told them that Daddy wanted to show her a house that they maybe could buy. They waited until the deal was closed, then they took the whole family over. When they stopped in front and pointed to it, the children had the same reaction Rina had.

"This house? For us?"

When they got inside, even the older ones almost ran through the rooms yelling, "Woo-eee!"

"Look at this!"

"Another room here!"

"Wow!"

"Mama and Daddy, are you really serious? We're really going to live here?"

"Yes, darlings, we're really going to live here! Isn't that great? Isn't God good? And your daddy too! He really found us a good place this time—and it's going to be ours."

We were hardly into the house when David's sister asked if her son and his new wife could park their trailer in our backyard for the summer.

Even though the house was big and better than anyone could have imagined, they soon began missing the old-fashioned two-holer facilities of some of their former places, for the young couple had to use their washroom facilities too. A few months later, they were persuaded to take in three more boarders: a young war widow with her five year-old daughter, whom they allowed to have the big bedroom upstairs, and another young woman who had no place to go.

With fifteen people using one bathroom, and eleven of them women, the boys soon said that the only way they could get in the bathroom was to shove a live mouse under the door!

Even at the worst, though, we had a lot more space than in the trailer, and it was brighter and more cheery than either the trailer or The Hell Hole. I don't think I woke up one morning in that house without saying, "Thank you, Lord!"

That October, Evvy and Peter presented us with our first granddaughter and Jessie and Will weren't far behind, because their son came in February of '47. It seemed unbelievable, because our own Sandra was just three.

Rina grinned.

My children didn't take long taking over where I left off! And once started, the floodgates for change were open!

The very next year, Bernie married her Freddy and moved back up north of Malden. Murray and Elaine were married the following year. We had a year off, then Doris and Cliff and Rae and Hazel both got married the next year and Lenora and Hal the next. By the year after that, we had ten grandchildren.

Oh, how fast things are transformed!

Rina's body was tired, but her mind continued to whirl on. It was quiet in the rest of the house. The digital alarm clock now read eleven o'clock and she didn't think sleep was anywhere near. But the next thing she knew, she heard noises outside her door, and when she opened her eyes it was already morning.

Chapter 26

BREAKFAST WAS ANOTHER TIME of catching up and reminiscing, but it had to be cut short in order to get to church.

"Are you up to going along, Mama?"

"Much as I'd like to, especially with Evvy here, I think I might be pushing it, since I'm still rather tired from yesterday. I think I will just stay here and rest."

"One of us can stay with you."

"No, no! You will only be gone less than two hours. I'll just settle down on my recliner and I'll be all right until you get back. I'll probably sleep most of the time."

While they were doing dishes, she heard Marlene tell Evvy about the family's move to the store on Hamilton. Rina smiled. *It sounds as though my sanity is in question regarding that long ago decision.* Dishes done, Marlene, James and Evvy left for church. She settled back with a satisfied sigh. She thought of the girls' conversation about the store. Their father had some questions back then too.

DAVID LOOKED AT HER as though she had gone off the deep end.

"You are really serious?"

"David, Sandra is eleven, Carolyn thirteen and Marlene will soon be out on her own. It leaves me home alone all day and I feel useless. The store would give me something to do and people to meet."

"You want to sell this house?"

"No, I'm not ready to do that. I love this house. I thought we could rent it out. We could even make two apartments out of it— one upstairs and one down. We could maybe make a bit of money for our retirement that way. There is an apartment above the store big enough for the three girls and us. Can we at least have a look at it?"

"Darling, if that is what you want, I'll go along with it."

They went to look at the store on Hamilton road she had seen for sale when she had walked past on her way back from the grocery store earlier that day. They looked and bought—all within one week. The storeowner was kind in helping Rina learn the ropes of running the small general store. Stocks were low and the shelves looked a little empty. Rina's ingenuity kicked into high gear. While they waited for the date of possession, Rina saved every cereal and food box that she could. These were carefully taped shut to look new and put on the top shelves to make it look as though they had lots of stock on hand.

It looked good, anyway. In today's self-help stores, it wouldn't have worked, but in those days, it was the store-keeper who got most things off the shelves and I knew which were full and which weren't. It gave us time to stock the shelves as we could afford it.

They had barely moved into the upstairs apartment when David's mother took a stroke and needed constant care. No one else in the family seemed to be able or willing to take her in.

"Girls, you are going to have to move into one room so we have room for Grandma Litz."

"Oh Mom, do we have to?"

"It isn't like you haven't slept in the same room together before, and it's a lot better than we had in some places."

"No, Mom, we didn't mean sleeping in the same room." Marlene lowered her eyes.

"Do we have to have Grandma live here?" Sandra and Carolyn asked together.

"Now girls! Grandma can't manage on her own right now. She needs someone to help look after her and it seems we're the only ones who can."

"Can or will? Why do we always have to be the ones who will?" Sandra asked.

"She is always complaining and seems so angry. If she wants something, she wants it right away. It doesn't matter what anyone else wants," Carolyn added.

"I know Grandma isn't the easiest person live with," David admitted, "but we will do the right thing and give her the best care we can for as long as we can manage."

The girls did move into the same room, leaving one available for Fanny. Had it happened a month sooner, they would never have bought the store, but now they were committed to it. Neither the years nor the stroke had altered Fanny's disposition. Constant nagging and criticism became the norm and Rina was the brunt of most of it. David, of course, could do nothing wrong—except, perhaps, defend Rina. Even his inability to spend much time with her was readily excused. She complained to him and the girls about Rina, though.

"You need to tell your wife she should have some respect for your mother, David. She told me I would have to wait if she had a customer. Imagine, making her husband's mother wait when she is in real need."

"Mother, Rina does have a store to look after! If you really need her, she will come."

"I called and called her today and she didn't come for a long time."

"Mother, if you called only when you really need something, she would come right away. But you keep calling her for any little thing, even when you know she has a customer."

"Da-*avid*! Shame on you! This is your mother. Have you forgotten?"

"I haven't forgotten, Mother!"

Rina tried to find a way to satisfy her. She gave her a bell to call with if she needed something. She explained that if a customer was present it might take a while, but she would come. She also had a bell installed on the door of the store so she could hear if someone arrived while she was upstairs. Some days she felt as though all she did was run up and down the stairs in answer to one bell or the other.

The moment the girls came home from school, Fanny had them running for all kinds of real or imagined needs—all the while complaining about how their mother had neglected her all day.

"I'm so sorry, Rina, love." David, with his hands on her shoulders held her at arms length and looked her straight in the eyes with real apology, then drew her close to him. "It seems unfair that after years of enduring rejection and antagonism from my mother that you should be the one who is saddled with looking after her in her dying days. It grates on my sense of justice to put you through this. If I was home taking the most of the weight, that would be different. She is my mother. You already cared for your own mother when she was dying. You shouldn't have to do it for mine too—especially when she has no appreciation for what you do."

"David, darling, don't feel so guilty about it. Granted, it is often very tiring, and I guess everyone likes to be appreciated, but sometimes I wonder if some of her ill-will comes from knowing she hasn't been nice to me and now she has to be subjected to accepting my help whether she wants to or not. It probably doesn't help, either, to know that none of the rest of the family would do it. Maybe there is a part of me that reaps satisfaction from "heaping coals of fire" on her like the Good Book says when we return good for evil." Rina tipped her head back to meet David's eyes. "Maybe that isn't very nice of me. Deep down, though, I do wish I could prove to her that I would like to be on better terms with her—to love and be loved." She paused. "Maybe that is too much to ask. I would settle for just being accepted. After all, it is her son who is the love of my life."

"I'm sure it galls her that you are willing to care for her after all the years of her putting you down and fighting you every step of the way, but it doesn't make it any easier on you. I'm sorry."

"Don't fret about it, David. I wouldn't want to live with the knowledge that she made me bitter enough that I wouldn't care for her when she needed it." Rina reached up to give him a kiss. "We don't know how long it will be, but we will take one day at a time. I will try to care for her as best I can. I may also need to be firm with her when she is being unreasonable, but I will be kind about it."

There were times in the next year and a half that I may have been a bit short with her. She started again, demanding David's attention just after we went to bed. One night I went instead of David. She got very angry when I refused to call David. He'd had a hard day. Oh, he would have got up and answered her call, but I thought it was worth a try to see if we could break the habit and I asked him to please give it a chance.

For several nights, when she called David, I went instead. The third night she ranted and raved but, bless David, he didn't come. After that she was better. Oh, she did try again a few times, but when I kept coming, she must have realized we meant business.

Even so, it became a heavy responsibility, and the girls got mighty tired of the constant demands. In the end, she took a massive stroke through the night and when we got up in the morning, she was gone.

JAMES ROBERTS lived just down the street from the store and became more and more of a regular customer—especially when Marlene was taking a shift to look after the customers. It didn't take long for Rina to realize it wasn't the products they carried that held such fascination for James, nor was he there because he was a loyal customer. By March of 1956, she knew another daughter was about to leave the nest.

They announced their wedding date for May 19. It was to be only a small wedding. David stuck to his guns and made his usual announcement when one of their children were being married.

"Marlene and James, I wish you the best, but you know that your mother and I can't be at the wedding . . .

"Because you couldn't be at Evvy's wedding," chimed Marlene, Carolyn and Sandra together.

David blinked twice, shook his head, and then grinned. "It almost sounds as though you've all heard that before!"

"Only six times, Daddy! I told James that you wouldn't come. He didn't want to believe it." she playfully punched James' arm. "See! I was right." she turned to her father. "I'd like to have you there, Daddy, but I figured after not going to seven of your children's weddings, I couldn't expect you to be at ours. What are you going to do to keep your mind off what is happening?"

"Now, now!" David objected, "It's not that I have to keep my mind off anything, it's just that—"

"It wouldn't be fair to Evvy!" the girls chorused in unison.

"Oh dear, I think my family knows me too well! The decision still stands, though"

MAY 19 CAME and David announced that he needed to go to work for a while in the morning. The wedding party departed for the church soon after noon. David still wasn't home, so it fell to Rina to give Marlene their best wishes and blessing.

She held out her arms for Marlene and drew her into her embrace. "Marlene, we have done our best to prepare you for life and James is a good man. Don't forget that God will help you through all that you face if you ask him, and remember, just because you are no longer at home it doesn't mean that we won't be praying for you. We'll be here if you need us."

"No, Mama, I won't forget that!"

"Then God be with you and bless you and James as you begin a new home and a new family." She carefully kissed Marlene's forehead, so as not to mess up her makeup.

As the door closed, she continued to watch until the car pulled away, then stood staring into space, remembering her own wedding day and all the special days of her children's she had missed. She would have liked to be there, but she honoured David's wishes. The phone interrupted her reverie.

"Hello?"

"Is this Mrs. Litz?"

"Yes, it is."

"You had better get to the hospital. There was an accident at the plant. David has been taken by ambulance, although we don't think he has been seriously injured. His coat got caught in a conveyer belt. It's a miracle that he was able to keep from getting pulled right in, but he probably has some lacerations and burns as well as muscle strain from tugging and pulling to free himself."

"Oh dear! The rest of the family is at a family wedding, but I will take a taxi and be right there."

Rina hung up the phone and immediately took it off the hook again to call a taxi. She raced to change her dress, grab a sweater and her purse, run down the steps and lock the door behind her. She sat on the steps, her legs too weak to hold her. Twenty-five years ago, she wasn't sure what she was going to find when she got to the hospital. This time it sounded as though it wasn't life-threatening, but just thinking what the news could have been had he not been able to free himself made her shudder!

"My dear David! You shouldn't have been so stubborn and unreasonable! If you would have been at the wedding, you wouldn't be in the hospital now!" She put her hands over her eyes and pressed them against her forehead to try to erase the thoughts that rushed through her head.

"At least our children are mostly grown and gone, but David, I want to have you around for a while yet! It would be nice to enjoy some years of retirement, but we're not quite there yet. Come on, taxi, come!"

As if in answer to her command, the taxi appeared around the corner and came to a stop in front of the store. She was at the curb by the time it came to a stop.

"To Victoria Hospital as fast as you can safely make it, please."

Directed to David's room at the hospital, she hurried down the hall, wondering what she would find. At the door, she paused to see which of the six beds he occupied. Seeing his name, she approached the bed.

"How's the father of the bride?" she asked, stroking his arm.

David opened his eyes. It was obvious he had been given a sedative; it took him a while to answer. "The father of the bride would have been better off at the wedding, thank you," he commented wryly with a grimace. "Oh, it even hurts to talk."

"David Litz, you sure know how to keep a loving wife on edge! The best I can do is be thankful that you're still with me!"

"You're not the only one! For what seemed like an eternity, I thought this was going to be lights out for me. Those big conveyer belts don't like to let anything stand in their way!" He winced again. "It took everything I had to hang on until my coat finally tore off. Then my shirt got cut and I was afraid it was going to get caught" A little sob tore his throat. "Honey-bun, I thought I'd seen you for the last time. All I could think was 'What a "gift" for Marlene—to lose her dad on her wedding day.'"

"I don't think we'll tell her and James about it until they return from their honeymoon. By then, I'm sure she'll think it is a gift to still have you. Just what all did the accident do to you?"

"I've got some lacerations and burns on my side and ribs from where my skin touched the belt a few times when it almost got me. The muscles in my arms and chest and even my legs are hurting because of the effort I had to put in to stay away from getting completely caught in it. Doc says I will be quite sore for a while. He figures it will be several weeks before I get back to work."

Rina bent over the bed to give him a kiss.

"You just concentrate on getting better. Unlike the time in Stafford, we have some money set aside and I have the store, so we can manage quite well until you heal. The most important thing is that you are still with us."

"How did you get here?"

"By taxi. My first thought was to call Rae, since he lives closest, but the whole family is at the wedding."

"I guess that is where we should be!"

"Does that mean you would change your policy for the last two?" Hope rang in her voice.

"Now, Rina, that . . ."

"Wouldn't be fair!"

"Well, it wouldn't. How would the rest feel if we would suddenly go to the weddings of our last two children when we haven't gone to any of theirs?"

Rina's eyebrows rose perceptively as she contemplated her reply.

"They just might think you have finally come to your senses, and rejoice that their younger siblings get to benefit from your sudden insight!"

David had the grace to look nearly discomfited with his obstinate views, even with his eyelids almost closed in his drug-induced lethargy.

"David, you'd better just let yourself sleep. I'm going to see if I can meet with the doctor to get his opinion of your condition, then I'll come back to see if you're asleep. If you are, I will go on home. I'll be back tomorrow."

When she returned, David was in a deep sleep. Not wishing to disturb him, she blew him a kiss and called the taxi to go home. As she waited, she wondered if this would throw David into another depression.

Perhaps it will be different this time. He is much more happy and fulfilled in his job now and the children are grown and most of them off on their own. We are the owners of a lovely home and I am happy with my work at the store—there is no need for him to feel inadequate or under pressure. I know depression is usually not rational, but I hope that he is feeling good enough about himself and his accomplishments that he doesn't sink into that illogical thinking.

Chapter 27

WHEN SHE THOUGHT THE WEDDING would be over, she called Rae and Hazel, who were living in the King Street house.

"How did the wedding go?" she asked.

"Very well!" Rae's kind and gentle voice always brought delight to her.

"Marlene and James are off on their honeymoon?"

"Yes, they were looking quite happy when they left."

"Daddy had a bit of excitement today."

"More exciting than being at his daughter's wedding?"

"I think he would rather have had that excitement!" Rina said sarcastically.

"Uh-oh! What now?"

"He got himself caught in a conveyer belt at work."

"Oh Mama! Is he all right?—He can't be all right, but I take it he is still alive?"

"Yes. His clothes were torn off, but he managed to keep from letting his body be drawn in."

Rina went on to explain his wounds and how the doctor said it would take some time to recover and for the muscles to heal.

"Do you want me to take you to the hospital tomorrow?"

"I would like that."

Arrangements were made, and for the next few days before David came home, their children took turns taking their mother to visit.

During his recuperation, Rina was so pleased that his tendency to depression did not materialize. It was less than three weeks when he persuaded the doctor and his boss that he was ready to return.

David's job gave him challenges that gratified his need for testing out his skills. As always, he was finding better and more efficient ways to do things. For once, he was getting the recognition and appreciation he deserved. Several raises gave him further incentive. When he came up with a new mix for asphalt that was superior to what had been used, the company gave him quite a promotion.

FIVE YEARS LATER, when the company expanded and made plans to establish a business in Newfoundland, David was asked to be in charge of installing the equipment there. By that time, Carolyn, too, was married. They were stationed near James and Marlene in Halifax.

"What do you think, Rina? Should I take the job?"

"You know I hate living apart! How long would it take?"

"Probably two or three months."

"That seems like a long time to be apart."

"If we sold the store, you could come along."

"We might not be able to do that soon enough, and there is Sandra to think about."

"If I do accept, I will make it a stipulation that I get to visit my daughters before returning to Ontario."

"That would be nice—but it makes me want to go along too! What would I do in Newfoundland while you were working, though?" She ran her fingers through her hair as though that might help clarify the situation. "How soon do you need to tell them whether you will go or not?"

"I think they are pretty much expecting me to go. I'm not sure how they would take it if I said 'No' to the request."

"You mean your job would be in jeopardy."

"Maybe not my job, but my chances of advancement."

"Well then, David, there is nothing to consider. You will go."

"Are you sure, Rina, honey-bun?

"Of course we'll manage! Just get ready for a lot of reading—I will be writing you a lot of letters." Her arms went around him. He reciprocated and drew her close.

"I don't know how many letters you will get, but I will phone home at least every week." He lifted her chin and kissed her lips. "Rina, I know you don't like us being apart—neither do I, but thanks for being so supportive. I do think it will give me a raise, if nothing else, but I expect it will give me a promotion and some recognition within the company. You have always risen to the challenges with which I have presented you. I love you!"

EVERY OTHER DAY, Rina posted a letter to Newfoundland. Those letters included an account of not only her days and the news of family and community but the longings of her heart for David's nearness. Every Saturday night around seven o'clock, Rina waited for the telephone to ring. Her longing for him, always tangible in her "Hello," was especially poignant one night at the end of the seventh week.

"Ah-hh, my honey-bun! I love to hear that anticipation in your 'Hello.' I just wish I was there to hold you in my arms."

"I could go along with that—for sure! How is the work going? How soon do you think you will be finished?"

"Rina, darling, I've just about had it, whether the work is done or not. The workers out here are unionized and I'm just not used to it. They only want to do so much in a day and if someone other than the person assigned to a certain part of the job chips in to help, there is a great uproar because they are taking someone else's job. I can't help with anything for the same reason. I'm not used to that kind of supervision; I like to work along with my men. Here I'm not allowed to lift a finger to help. Because of that there is just one hold-up after another and it is taking a lot longer than it should. I'm losing patience!"

"It must be drawing to a close, darling, so try to hang in there."

"I'm training one of the more responsible men to take over. The minute I think he can do it, I am asking the company if I can leave it with him and come home."

"That makes it hard for me to encourage you to do anything else. I can hardly wait to have you here again. You'll still go to see the girls, won't you?"

"Oh yes! I'll hold them to their agreement. Keep those letters coming, though! I read them over until the next one arrives. Sometimes I get two a day, but that is because one of them has been delayed. I look forward to every one of them."

They chatted on for a bit and reluctantly ended their call.

"Keep me posted as to when you're leaving."

"I will! Goodnight, my love. Sweet dreams!"

It was only a week later that David informed her he would be leaving for Halifax the following Tuesday. He would call her from there. He ended his call with, "Ten more days and I'll have you in my arms! Take care, darling!"

THE SOUND of James, Marlene and Evvy coming through the back door brought Rina back to the present.

They could have waited a few minutes until I relived meeting David at the airport after all that time away. Was it good to see him! I couldn't keep the tears of joy from my eyes. What was even better was to see that he had a few of his own!

Evvy and Marlene peeked around the door.

"Hi girls! How was church?"

"Church was fine! Did you sleep away the morning?"

"Oh I did better than that! I relived a few years of the past! It seems the older you get, the more you do that! Good that I had an interesting life or I might get bored!" she smirked.

THE DAYS PASSED too quickly until the day Evvy had to return to her home. When she said goodbye, both she and her mother realized it could very well be the last time. Rina was aware that at one time it would have bothered her, but at this stage of the game she just felt grateful for this one more time that she could be with her second daughter. She was so proud of how she'd turned out and how much she had accomplished in life. Some could have been dismayed at having a mentally handicapped son, but both Evvy and Peter counted it as a blessing and privilege to have been entrusted with this special child. Bobby was now suffering from some early onset dementia, but he'd had a good life. She was so glad she'd had the opportunity for those six months to be in their home.

When your children get married and move away from home, even if you see them frequently, both of you change over the years. With Evvy, we saw each other so infrequently it took a little time to fully appreciate all the growth that had taken place. I am sure she saw changes in me too. At least, I would hope so.

NOW SUMMER WAS ALMOST PAST. James and Marlene were talking about going away for a few weeks.

"What would feel best to you, Mama? Sally usually has you stay with her, but this close to school starting isn't the best for her. Would you like to have us find someone to stay here with you?"

"Why don't we try the respite care at the nursing home next to the Senior's Centre? That way I can still go there and I can see how the rest of the world lives!"

"Are you sure you want to do that, Mama?"

"You and James deserve some time away. Even if I was up to camping and could go away with you, I think it would be good for just the two of you to go. A lot of people my age are in the nursing home all the time. I'll be all right for a few weeks."

"If you're sure, I'll make arrangements, but only if you really want to do it."

"Go ahead, Marlene."

Marlene went to her office. A few minutes later, she came out again. "It's all settled. We'll take you in on Monday and get you settled, then James and I will leave Tuesday. But Mama, when you are there, you make sure you wait for the nurses to take you from one place to another. It will be unfamiliar territory and we don't want any falls. I will tell them about your diet so you don't get your sugars out of whack, and you can go to the Centre two days a week."

"Don't worry so much, dear girl! I'll be all right. You just go and enjoy yourself. Even if something unexpected happens, don't feel guilty about leaving me for a bit."

"What do you mean by that, Mama?" Alarm tinged her question.

"I didn't mean anything by it, but at my age you never know, and I know you well enough that if I took a stroke or something, you would be apt to blame yourself for not being here. I don't want you to do that."

"All right, all right—just behave yourself!"

"Are you trying to take the fun out of life?" Rina joked.

Marlene rolled her eyes and gave up in despair.

RINA SAT writing a note to her granddaughter. She paused momentarily, her pen suspended over the page as she wondered how many letters she had written in her lifetime. If she had copies of all of them, they would make a thick volume of memoirs. It would not only tell a tale of her life—the everyday happenings, the crises, the times of celebration—but it would also reflect her philosophy, little bits of admonishment and gentle suggestions for facing difficulties and, she hoped, a whole lot of encouragement. She smiled as she continued. Acting on her thoughts, she included a bit of encouragement to her granddaughter. Mealtime was coming close. She finished off her letter.

I know Marlene told me not to try to walk by myself, but the nurses are so busy. I can surely make it to the washroom and get washed up for lunch.

It took a bit of rocking back and forth to get up and out of her chair, but finally she stood, holding firmly to her walker. With utmost care, she manoeuvred the walker past the washroom door so she could open it wide. She backed up until she could reach the sink. Grasping the sink, she turned the tap and wet her hands. With her right hand she reached for the soap dispenser. She hardly had time to panic as her wet left hand slid along the smooth surface of the porcelain and she felt herself falling. There was nothing she could do to stop the fall. She ended with her head and shoulder jammed between the toilet and the wall. She tried to reach the cord that would activate the call bell, but it was just out of reach.

"Well now, Rina Litz! Now you've done it! You were a bad girl once too many times. You should have listened to your daughter," Rina scolded herself out loud.

"Nurse!" she called. "Nurse!"

She watched as a pool of blood spurted from her nose. *I always did have bad nose bleeds, but I guess just about anyone would if they bashed their beak on a hard toilet! You might as well settle down until a nurse gets here.* She felt herself getting faint, but willed herself to stay alert.

Come on, nurse, just come this way! Stay with it, Rina! It's your own fault that you ended up here; the least you can do is stay awake and let them know how it happened.

In spite of her effort, she started to feel confused. She didn't know how long she lay there, wedged between the toilet and the wall, but finally help arrived. There was a great kerfuffle as they apologized and exclaimed their horror that such a thing could happen. More staff came to help gently lift her up and get her in her bed.

She hated the thought of her family finding out. Marlene and James deserved their time away. She didn't want them to have to rush home; neither did she want to inconvenience any of the rest of her family. But of course, the nursing home would need to let them know. They brought her something to eat, but she wasn't all that hungry. Her cheek hurt where she had hit something and she had cut her lip with a tooth.

"That is enough! I don't need any more. Could you get me a straw, Sue, so I can sip a bit of water?"

"Sure, Rina, right here! Try it on the right side of your mouth; it doesn't look quite so bad there. So sorry this had to happen."

"Ah! It was me who was the bad girl. I just thought I would save you girls a bit of work and be ready for lunch when you came. Now I've made it worse."

"Don't blame yourself, Rina. We had a bit of a ruckus down the hall, or we would have found you sooner. You are our responsibility, so don't go blaming yourself. We'll take better care of you now— even if it is too late to save you from falling."

"Will you do me a favour, Sue? Get me a mirror. I'd like to see for myself just how bad the damages are."

"Oh Rina! Maybe you would be just as happy if you didn't see."

"Is it that bad?"

"You took quite a bump."

"And I'm old and my skin is thin. That goes with age. I think I probably have faced worse things in my life."

"Why don't you wait until your family comes?"

"Oh, all right, I'll let you off the hook."

When Nurse Sue left, Rina reached for her bedside table.

"Now, if I can get this contraption to work I'll see for myself and no one will have to know I saw it."

Finally, she lifted the mirror. What she saw wasn't a pretty sight. "You old coot! Your face looks like something that just came out of the meat grinder and got splattered all over the floor! Oh well! I wasn't entering any beauty contest today any way!" She sighed. "I might have known. As bruised as my arm is, my face was sure to be worse because it took the brunt of the fall. I just wish my family wouldn't need to find out, but I guess that is wishing for too much. "

She closed the top of her table and pushed it away again so no one would know she had seen herself. She lay back on her pillow and closed her eyes.

She woke hearing someone saying "Mama!" She opened her eyes to see Doris, Rae, Elaine and Marlene's daughter Sally standing around her bed.

"So you came to see the beauty queen, did you?"

"Your sense of humour wasn't injured in the fall, I gather," Rae commented in his dry wit.

"You have to protect what is most necessary! Beauty is only skin deep, you know." Rina smiled as broadly as her swollen lip allowed. "Sorry to give you all such a scare. I hope you haven't spoiled James and Marlene's vacation by letting them know!"

"We thought we'd come to see for ourselves how you are faring before we do." Doris carefully smoothed Rina's hair back from her forehead. "Looks like you did quite a number on yourself."

"Yes! I should have waited for the nurse as I was told to. They are all so busy and almost run off their feet. I thought surely I could make it to the washroom by myself to get washed up for lunch. I was leaning on the sink while I reached for soap, but my wet hand slipped and down I went." She looked at Rae. "You make sure they don't call James and Marlene. There's nothing they can do now. Let them have their little holiday!"

Rae reached for her good hand. "You seem to be more chipper than you look, if I may say so," he grinned. "Perhaps they won't need to be told. They'll be home in three or four days anyway."

"Good boy! I could always count on you to help if it was at all possible!"

"You came to my rescue often enough too, Mama! The Lord only knows how often that was."

"Sally, you won't tell them if they call, will you?" It was more of a statement than a question.

"I can't promise that, Grandma. I may tell them you had a fall, but as long as you are in good spirits I will assure them you are all right and they can finish their holiday. I brought a bouquet from Mom's flowerbed for you. I'll set it here on your bedside table."

"Thanks, dearie! Flowers always cheer me up."

"I brought the latest addition of the *Esprit* magazine for my favourite mother-in-law." Elaine handed it to her, eyes full of love. "I don't know if you can see to read it with one eye almost swollen shut. I know your kids used to say you could see them getting into mischief with your head turned the other way, so maybe it won't seem that big a challenge after that. There are a few nice little poems in it this time and a good article on being content. If you can't read it, perhaps I can do it for you. I'll be back to visit you tomorrow."

They all sat around and visited for a short while. It was hard to keep track of the conversation when she was flat on her back, so at times she dozed off.

Sally stood up. "I think we've been here long enough, Grandma. We should let you get your rest so you can recuperate."

The rest rose from their seats. "At least one of your family will be in each day to see you," Doris reassured her. "If you want to see more or less of us, all you need to do is ask."

"I'm always glad to see my family, but I do feel rather sore from my bruises, so I may need a bit more rest for a few days."

"So, regular but short visits may be just what you need?"

"Sounds good to me." Rina smiled up at her. "Of course, if you don't mind if I go off to sleep mid-sentence or if you want to watch me snore, you can stay as long as you want!"

Through the night, every time Rina moved it seemed that she hurt all over. In between she wandered between memories, dreams and reality. When she awoke, she felt confused by the faint light and unfamiliar sounds. She called out for Marlene, but she didn't come. When she finally fell into a deep sleep, it seemed to be no time at all until a nurse roused her to get her ready for breakfast. It took her a moment or two before she could get it together.

"Who are you? Where is Marlene?"

"Rina, you are in the nursing home, remember?

"In the nursing home?"

"Your daughter and her husband went away for a little vacation, remember? You came in for respite care while they are gone."

"Oh yes! What is the matter with me? I forgot."

"The fall you took yesterday probably put you off a bit. Don't worry!"

"That's what makes me hurt every time I move."

She suffered through getting washed up and with some difficulty she got into her chair. They were going to take her to the dining room with her walker, but it was just too much. They brought a wheel chair. She was more tired than hungry, and by the time she got back to her room all she wanted was to get into her bed and sleep again. The nurse helped her stand.

"Oh! That really hurts!"

"Let's just take it easy. Sit on the bed and I'll help you swing your legs in."

Rina winced and let out a groan. "Creaking and complaining like my joints have done for a while is one thing, but this is something else."

"Do you want something for pain? I can get the R.N. to bring you something."

"It probably would help me sleep better. I didn't get much last night."

"You should have asked for something."

"To tell you the truth, I couldn't figure out where I was. I did call Marlene, but of course she didn't hear me." Rina grinned. "I guess she was too far away."

"I'll go get the R.N."

With the pain medication administered, Rina tried to relax. While it was taking effect she thought of David being here in the same nursing home. She was on the other side of the issue then. She had rebelled at the necessity of putting David in the nursing home, but his stroke was too severe for them to care for him at home. She certainly couldn't manage it, for it was even too much for Marlene and James to handle.

It was probably harder on me than on David. He seemed resigned to it, but I wanted so much to be the one to care for him. I came almost every day and fed him when I was here. Now I'm the one needing help. I hope I can be as sweet about it as he was, but I hope it isn't as long as he had to be here. If I can't go back home, I'd rather not live too long.

The medication was taking over and she felt drowsier by the moment as the pain subsided to a more tolerable level. Faintly she heard the activity in the hall, but she soon drifted into a restful sleep.

"Mom Litz—how are you doing?"

The sound came to her through a deep fog. She tried to open her eyes.

"Did you want to wake up and see some of your family?"

Rina's eyes opened. She stared without comprehension.

"It's me, Elaine, and David."

"Elaine?"

"Murray's Elaine and our son, Dave."

Recognitions dawned. "Oh, Elaine! Where's Murray?"

"Mom," Elaine paused. Pain and uncertainty clouded her eyes. "Murray's gone, Mom. Remember, he died of a heart attack eleven years ago? But I have Dave with me today."

Rina blinked her eyes, the puzzled look indicating the wheels turning in her brain. Finally she conceded, "I should have known that. I'm sorry.'

"That's all right, Mom. Things are a little mixed up right now."

"Are you still in a lot of pain, Gram?" asked Dave, giving Rina a gentle kiss on the good side of her face.

"I was this morning, but they gave me a pain pill after breakfast and I guess I've been sleeping since. What time is it?"

"It's two o'clock. They told us they let you sleep, but if you want some soup or a sandwich they'll bring it for you."

"I hardly know. I just woke up and I dread the thought of moving, but a cup of tea and a biscuit would probably be nice. Marlene would say I need it to keep my blood sugars in line."

"Yes, of course! Dave, would you go and ask them to bring it right away?"

Rina had her cup of tea, sitting on the easy chair beside her bed. Elaine read from her *Esprit* magazine and Dave fluffed her pillows and helped her back into bed before they left.

The next three days, just as promised, at least one of her family appeared some time during the day. Increasingly, her memory slipped—as did her ability to keep up with what was happening. She often called them by the wrong name or found it difficult to identify her visitors. Her sharp wit and ready replies weren't forthcoming. Occasionally, she would surprise them with an observation or unexpected comment. On one issue she was always clear, and about that matter each of them were asked the same question.

"When is it that James and Marlene will be back?"

"They will be back on Saturday, Mama."

"Don't tell them about me until they get home," she would always caution them.

WHEN MARLENE and James arrived home and were told the whole situation, they immediately came to visit her. Marlene was visibly shaken, although she tried to cover it up when she saw her mother recognized her coming through the door.

"Marlene! You're back!"

"Yes, we are, and it looks like none too soon! I'm so sorry, Mama!"

"Now Marlene! I was a bad girl. I did what you told me not to do. It wasn't anyone's fault but my own. I want you to know that. I also want you to know I didn't want them to tell you until you came home. You deserved a holiday."

"They didn't tell me how badly you were hurt. They should have, but they didn't!"

"Did you have a good time?"

"Yes, we did, but now I wish we wouldn't have gone."

"I was afraid you would feel guilty. Marlene, I can't live forever. I'm glad you're back. I've been waiting for you to come back. I wanted to tell you not to feel guilty. Promise?" Rina reached for Marlene's hand and implored her with her one good eye.

"Oh Mama! You do ask some hard things of me."

"Marlene?" There was urgency in Rina's voice but it also rang as something between a command and a reprimand.

"I'll try, Mama. But I hate to see you so badly bruised. It must have really hurt."

"Oh, I think I've been hurt worse," she assured her. "James, if she forgets, you remind her what a good daughter she's been and that she has nothing to feel guilty about. Will you?"

"Yes, Maw, I will. I know how she beats herself up about things. I will be glad to remind her."

"Good, James! You've been so good to me too!"

"It's been our pleasure, Maw."

Rina visibly relaxed and appeared to be at peace. Marlene asked the nurses if Rina's evening meal could be brought to her room so she could help her and have a bit of privacy in the meantime.

"Have they been giving you good meals, Mama?

"Yes, they have—oh they aren't like your meals, but for an institution I think they are good." She took another spoonful of soup.

"The last few days I can't tell you for sure. They have been a bit of a blur. I think the pain medication has made me sleepy and forgetful."

She pushed her tray back. "That's enough! It's hard to eat when your mouth is sore."

"You should have a bit of your fruit yet, Mama."

"Marlene, I'm really tired. I've been waiting so long to have this talk with you, but now I need to rest again. You said you didn't even unpack everything. Go home and do that—you can come again tomorrow."

Marlene looked askance at James and shrugged her shoulders. "That sounds as though we're being dismissed!"

Rina grinned feebly. "You are! But you can come and give me a kiss. I love you."

"All right, then!" Marlene gave her head an exasperated shake but came and did as her mother bid her. "We'll probably go to church in the morning, but we will see you right after lunch."

"Bye, Maw!" James, too, gave her kiss on the good cheek and they left with a last wave.

"There, that's done!" Rina sighed. She felt as though she had made a gigantic effort to complete this final task. Now she felt utterly drained. She sank down in the bed and closed her eyes.

She was barely aware of the nurses coming and going and doing their assigned task throughout the evening and during the night. She was not aware of the daylight when it came. It felt as though she was slowly sliding down a gentle slope into—into a warm, misty, haze . . . ah-hh, there were Mama and Papa, dimly visible through a pinkish cloud. She tried to get nearer, but they seemed to stay at the same distance. Did she hear Murray's voice? She couldn't be sure.

Now they were moving her. She felt herself being lifted. She was floating down a hall. Her eyes finally opened. The brightness was almost too much. They passed people—other nurses, other residents, some in wheelchairs—and finally they were in another room. Settled in another bed, she closed her eyes as they tucked the sheet and blanket around her.

"Your family is coming," someone said.

What do they mean? Mama and Papa and I think Murray were here just a minute ago. Maybe David and the kids are coming too. Is it going to be another reunion? We had one not long ago when Evvy was here, but reunions were always nice—never too many.

"Yes, she fell when she was washing her hands. Her hands slipped on the basin and she was wedged between the toilet and the wall for a while before the nurses came."

Who is here? Is it Jessie or is that Doris?

"Poor Gran! No wonder she has such bad bruises!"

Some of the grandkids must be here too.

"I guess she had quite a nosebleed too—but she's always been susceptible to those."

Ahh-hh! Marlene! She's a good girl! Well of course, she's my girl. I've got a lot of good girls!

"No wonder it bled this time! It looks as though she really hit her face hard."

Nosebleeds! I've had those since I was a little girl. One of the last times, Marlene sent me to the hospital by ambulance. They laughed at me because when they said they were going to use a bit of coke to stop it, I asked how Coca Cola was going to help a nosebleed. They meant cocaine—but I didn't know they used cocaine for things like that. Is that what is making me sleepy now? I would like to tell them but I can't seem to make things work.

She gave up and drifted off again. She dreamed about the King Street house when she and David moved back there after they sold the store, but it seemed there were rooms she hadn't remembered were there. They could make more apartments there for people who needed a place to stay. When she tried to go back to tell David, she couldn't find him, she just kept finding more and more rooms. She wondered if she ever would get out.

She'd been alone a long, long time. Why didn't David come back? Where had he been staying so long? Why didn't he want to live with her? They had been so good together. If she could just find him or even talk to him on the telephone, surely he would come back. Surely she could persuade him that they were better off together.

She became aware that a nurse was taking her pulse.

"Can I phone David?" she managed to ask.

"Maybe later," the nurse replied. Even in her semi-awake state, she could hear the condescension in her voice as though she was placating a child. All she wanted to do was talk to her husband. With sudden clarity it hit her.

David isn't coming back. He died. That's why he isn't here with me. He would be if he could.

"Just wait, David. I'll come to you."

"When peace like a river attendeth my way
When sorrows like sea billows roll,
Whatever my lot, thou hast taught me to say,
It is well, it is well with my soul.
It is well, it is well, It is well, It is well with my soul."

Someone must have put music on. Nothing like the old hymns to bring peace to one's soul.

She drifted off to sleep again.

"IT LOOKS as though she is sleeping peacefully, anyway."

"I know she's going on one hundred, but I still find it hard to believe we may not have her very long anymore."

Ah-hh! The girls must be here again—and they think I'm on my way out. Well, maybe they're right. It's all right by me. Reaching one hundred doesn't seem so important any more. She couldn't even think why it once was a goal she had set for herself.

"Should we try to wake her, or let her sleep on?"

"I think it would be all right to at least let her know we are here."

"Mama, we came to see you today. Jessie, Bernie, Doris and me—Marlene—are here in the room now. Rae, Elaine, Lenora and Sandra are out in the waiting room and will come in when we leave. We're taking turns to stay with you. Can you see me, Mama?"

"Look, she's opening her eyes—at least her good one!"

What a feat!

"I think she knows we are here."

Of course I know you're here, I just can't seem to tell you.

"We love you, Mama."

I know, and I love you too!

"See that look in her eyes? And there's a tear there too."

Marlene wiped the tear with a tissue. "You've been a good mama to us all! We hate to think of life without you, but if you are ready, we want to let you go." Jessie and Doris stood beside Marlene.

Bernie came to the other side of the bed. "We'll always love you whether you're here or not." She kissed her hand. "Maybe we should let the others come in."

There was some commotion while they left and the others came in. Rina struggled to keep her eyes open as they each came to the bedside.

Rae—you were always so kind and helpful to everyone. Elaine, Murray loved you and you became such a good part of our family. Lenora, you were our transition child; you heralded a time of stability in our family, you're so special. Sandra—my baby! You, too, were special.

She could think all these things and more, but she could not put it all into words. Even keeping her eyes open was almost more than she could do. She relaxed and felt warmth in knowing her family was there. She was aware of the girls coming back again and let the buzz of her children's voices become a lullaby to soothe her.

Her family's voices faded into the background as before her rose a pathway bordered by the most beautiful flowers she had ever seen. The sky shone luminous, a most resplendent cerulean blue. She gasped in incredulous amazement and delight.

"What is the matter, Mama? Do you need something?"

Rina's forehead wrinkled in bewilderment. Whose voice was that? It seemed out of place—intruding on, on, on—now where was she? What had she been doing when she was interrupted?

"Do you want a sip of water, Mama?"

It was Jessie. No, it must be Marlene. Rina shook her head to let whoever it was know that she didn't need a drink. That wasn't what she wanted now.

She tried to open her eyes, but the left one wouldn't cooperate. She wanted to see who it was who was near her. Maybe it was David. He always wanted to take care of her. He had tried so hard. How often he told her he had hoped to provide a better life for her and his family. It didn't really matter.

She should tell him, but she didn't know if she had the strength to do it. Tiredness seeped through every part of her body. Putting forth every effort she could muster, she whispered, "It . . . doesn't . . . matter . . . darling! It . . . doesn't . . . matter . . . now. I'm coming home."

Through the haze she heard them speaking again, but she didn't hear David's voice. Had he heard what she said?

"She's trying to say something."

"Did she say it doesn't matter?"

"I think she said something about coming home."

"Poor Mama!"

Someone began to stroke her hand. Maybe it was David. Maybe he was going to take her home. Her heart gave a little pulsation of delight. How good to have him close again. It seemed like so long.

Ah-hh! There was that path again! Against the lucent azure a bright light appeared—a voice called. She recognized that voice—it was the voice of her Master! She squeezed the hand that held hers. With joy she turned her face in the direction of the long-awaited summons reverberating through the cosmos—the call of her name inviting her to come home. Without hesitation she ran and skipped with gladness and utter abandonment—toward the light and home.

Also by Ruth Smith Meyer

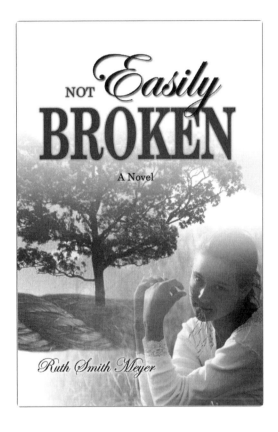

ISBN-13: 9781897373101
Word Alive Press. 2007

Not Easily Broken is the heart-wrenching story of Ellie, Rina's mother, facing incredible demands and devastating loss. The reader will be amazed at the courage and strength that emerges as Ellie proves that a life entwined with God is indeed not easily broken.